Alice MacDonald Greer Mystery Series

Ghost Justice is a work of fiction. All incidents, dialogue and characters, with the exception of some well-known public figures, are products of the author's imagination and not to be construed as real. Where real-life historical or public figures appear, the situations, incidents and dialogues concerning those persons are used fictitiously and are not intended to depict actual events or to change the entirely fictional nature of the work. Any legal issues and analyses are fictional and not intended or to be taken as legal analysis or advice. Coffee County and Coffee Creek exist solely in the author's imagination, where they are located somewhere in the Texas Hill Country between Dripping Springs and Fredericksburg.

Published by Stuart's Creek Press, LLC
Dripping Springs, Texas
Book Design: Bill Carson Design.
Library of Congress Control Number: 2025916489
ISBN 978-1-7327229-4-1

For Carol and Virgil

Chapter One

Not My Problem

Early Monday morning, Alice slipped through the old iron gate that kept the three burros out of her yard and presented a carrot to each eager muzzle. Still jet-lagged from yesterday's flight home from Scotland, she latched the gate and drove down her long gravel drive onto Old Hays Road.

But as she made the next sharp turn onto the two-lane blacktop locals called "the creek road," she braked hard. Across the intersection, a green banner tied to a fence proclaimed: "SAY NO TO CONCERT VENUE!"

Huh. That must have gone up last week, while she was overseas visiting Gran, her dead husband's mother, to talk about her upcoming wedding. Pretty bold for the generally laid-back town of Coffee Creek, but Alice approved. Big concert venues belonged in Austin, with its crowds of students. Out in the Hill Country, locals still gathered in traditional beer halls to dance and listen to music. Alice cringed at the idea of a giant venue landing like a bomb on Coffee County, with its clear creeks and narrow winding roads, its ranches and wineries.

However? Not my practice area, not my problem, she thought.

The creek road followed the blue-green waters of Coffee Creek to the small town of the same name. Nearing town, she glanced uphill at the historic ranch house where her law client Ellie Windom had lived—and died. Her murderer had tried to murder Alice as well. Ellie's fences sported another green banner. Maybe Ellie's sons put that up, Alice thought.

Live Oak Street, its venerable live oaks shading the sidewalks, glowed in morning sun when she parked at her office, an old stone bungalow two blocks from the Coffee County Courthouse. The sign outside announced: "Alice MacDonald Greer, Attorney." Alice still felt a twinge of surprise at that declaration of independence. She'd moved her law practice from a large Austin firm to Coffee Creek—a move that felt like trying to pole-vault for the first time—after the disappearance and presumed death of Jordie, her husband and her two children's father.

Her office was quiet, save for the refrigerator humming in the kitchen. No sign yet of Silla—the red-headed barrel racer who ran Alice's practice with the same energy and precision she brought to the rodeo ring. Silla was a lifesaver. A real one: a few months ago, she'd saved Alice's life.

Alice made coffee and carried a cup to her office. She peered at Silla's sticky note on her desk: New appointment, at nine: "phone calls." No client name. What the heck was that? At ten, routine appointment for clients signing their wills. Then at two, an intake meeting with a new client, James Surratt.

At seven-thirty Silla arrived, red ponytail bobbing, clutching a fragrant grease-stained bag. "Biscuits, Alice! Camellia Diner." The Camellia, across from the courthouse, provided Silla with a rich source of local news and gossip.

Alice followed Silla and the biscuits to the kitchen, refilled her coffee cup, now with Silla's note stuck to the side, and joined her at the small wooden table. "How was the trip?" Silla asked.

"Good. Gran's an amazing woman. And thanks to you for running the office all week. Silla, who put up the green banners about the concert venue?"

"Whoo-ee! That hit the local news last week after Friends of Coffee Creek publicized the date for the public meeting," Silla said. "Which is tomorrow! Finally dawned on folks that California investors propose concerts for five thousand people on thirty acres on the south side of Old Hays Road, maybe half a mile from the intersection with the creek road. Now the neighbors are having conniptions." She put a plate of biscuits on the table, then brought butter and honey from the refrigerator.

"What'll they do about parking? And more traffic barreling down Old Hays Road?"

Silla looked up from buttering her biscuit. "Residents already call it Old Hays Deathtrap—all those curves."

"Five thousand people!" Alice shook her head. "What will the developers do with sewage from five thousand people? There's no sewer system out there!"

"Oh, that's the fun part," Silla said. "They applied for a land application permit. Gonna store the sewage effluent in huge holding tanks."

Alice frowned. She recalled from an environmental class at UT Law that "land application" meant applying treated wastewater to surface soil, where theoretically it would sink harmlessly through layers of dirt. But she'd just driven down the creek road past the rocky slopes above Coffee Creek—broken limestone, skimpy soil. Not ideal for absorption. She also recalled that land application permits were not allowed to let disposed effluent enter streams.

"So, your new client this afternoon, James Surratt," Silla reminded her. "He's active with the Coffee County Master Naturalists. Teaches them to test stream water. He's coming alone; his wife's out of town, but he wants to get started updating his will. Also—you've got Rotary today at noon. And on Friday the mayor called. She didn't want to bug you last week, but she's got a question on the concert venue."

Alice waved Silla's sticky note. "What's this 'phone calls at 9:00'?"

"Late Friday three of our clients called asking you to represent them in protesting this venue permit. I told them you generally handle real estate and trusts and estate law, not environmental permit litigation. But I promised you'd give them some other names."

"Yikes. I'd better call them first thing." If they wanted to challenge the permit, their lawyers would want to submit comments before the public meeting.

Silla pointed at the plate of biscuits. "Don't you want one?"

Alice shook her head. "Not when I'm thinking about sewage treatment effluent from five thousand concert-goers."

"Or about getting into that wedding dress."

Alice grinned. "I don't think I'm going to wear my great-grandmother's dress, Silla. Won't match my boots."

Back in her office, she stopped at the bookshelf, which held a few family pictures: one of her children, John and Ann, with their dad and his mother, Gran, at Gran's farm on the Scottish coast; another of Alice's parents as UT students, beaming from a canoe on Lake Austin. Then Alice picked up a small gold frame with a faded black-and-white snapshot of her own great-grandparents, taken in 1914. With a demure smile and a long white Gibson Girl dress, her great-grandmother sat sidesaddle behind her beau, on the Indian motorcycle he'd ridden from Austin to north Texas to court her.

Alice remembered the moment she'd slipped into that same lacy white dress for her own wedding. She'd felt a deep connection to her great-grandmother, to family, to tradition. Miraculously the photo and the dress survived. She still treasured that lovely old dress, tissue-wrapped in a box. But wearing it now?

Her life had changed—radically. In a few weeks, the last weekend in

March, she'd say "I do" to Ben Kinsear. Both had lost their spouses. Their respective kids were nearly grown. She and Kinsear would embark on a new life. For this second wedding, she had a different dress in mind.

Okay, get busy. First, call some lawyers who could handle an environmental permit case for her waiting clients. She found a number for Nancy Greenberg, law school chum and experienced environmental lawyer. "No can do, Alice," said Nancy. "Sorry! I'm on maternity leave, or I'd jump on it. Sounds like it's going to be exceptionally nasty. And exceptionally expensive."

"Why exceptionally?"

"Look at the issues. First, aren't these folks already building a similar venue in Nevada?" Alice scribbled a note to self: check online info on that venue. Nancy continued: "So they'll claim the plan's already been approved in another state. Also, your protestors will need experts, including engineers, to address the risks of land application. They'll need a soils expert on the suitability of the proposed disposal area. They'll need a geologist to explain the subsoil and the site geology, maybe a hydrogeologist too, to testify which aquifers might be impacted. Your clients will need to show how they'd be personally affected. If they're upstream, what's the impact? Except noise and traffic?"

"Nancy, there's no public water out here north of town. Everyone depends on a well, or rainwater collection, or both."

"Good point," mused Nancy. "Peoples' water wells should all be shown on the permit application. But if they're old wells, the well logs may not be online, and the owners will need to get that information into the record to show potential personal impact. Again, experts and expense. Sorry, but good luck!"

Alice tried two more lawyers. The second, at her old Austin firm, said, "That application definitely sounds dodgy, but right now I'm on the other side of the issue—defending a decent land application permit in a contested case. Sorry—I'd better say no." The third said, "Land application? Not my area—I handle only traditional water discharge permits into streams. You might try Sandy Graves. She's recently won a couple of contested permit cases."

Alice had met Sandy Graves at a legal ed conference. She found her number and dialed. "Thanks, Alice! Sounds intriguing! I've had luck lately with experts from a new environmental engineering firm. If your folks are interested, tell them to call today so we can file comments!"

Hallelujah. Alice sank back in her chair, relieved. She picked up Silla's list of the clients who'd called, envisioning their homes—one lived south of Old Hays Road, downhill from the proposed venue; two more lived downstream along Coffee Creek where it bordered the creek road.

Alice called each one. The more she heard, the more she worried about the venue's potential impact. One client said, "Alice, I'm downgrade from the venue site. Meaning downhill from any drainage off the venue. I have only a well. I don't have a rainwater system, so I don't have a tank and can't get water delivered, like some people do. If the venue soil doesn't absorb all the effluent? If the storage tanks spill or leak? If my well gets contaminated? Then I'm screwed. How could I clean up the aquifer?"

Another said, "Alice, I'm right on the creek. My grandkids spend hours in there fishing, swimming. These concert people propose to store thousands of gallons of treated effluent in big tanks, then land-apply it. But what if something happens to the tanks? What if they leak and seep into the creek? What if the tank controls get hit by lightning? What if some employee just screws up with too much discharge?"

Alice recited contact info for Sandy Graves to each client, told them they needed to act right away, and suggested other neighbors might want to split legal costs and join them.

Silla stuck her face in Alice's door. "Conference room, Alice. The Craigs are here to sign their revised wills. Everything's ready—I've got our witnesses in the kitchen having coffee."

Alice tried to shift mental gears back to wills and tax law. She'd met the Craigs when she first arrived in Coffee Creek. Now in the conference room she greeted them as old friends. After she walked them through their requested revisions, the witnesses joined to watch the Craigs sign and to provide the supporting affidavit. All in good order, Alice thought, but as she hugged her clients goodbye, her mind kept returning to the image of two vast tanks holding sewage effluent atop the vulnerable geology of Coffee Creek.

At eleven thirty Silla popped into Alice's office. "Alice! Remember the mayor? She called again and wants you to stop by City Hall before lunch at Rotary. She said to alert you that the public meeting on the venue happens tomorrow night. Plus she wants your take on the venue investors."

"My take, huh?"

Silla grinned as Alice dutifully grabbed her jacket and headed out the front door. The City employed a couple of lawyers, but the mayor had recently steered some solid pieces of business Alice's way, including revision of various city contracts. "It's business development!" she called. Alice wasn't so sure.

HELEN CURRIE FOSTER

C h a p t e r   T w o

Listen, Do You Do Wills?

City Council met upstairs in the old limestone City Hall, next to the town park. Alice loved climbing up the wide stone staircase that led to the council chamber, where she nearly always spotted people she knew—citizens marching upstairs with purposeful faces, or descending, sometimes pleased as punch, sometimes ready to punch.

The council chamber was rapidly emptying. Mayor Betty Wilson was immediately visible, her white hair splendidly bouffant, à la Ann Richards, and her trademark purple cat-eye spectacles perched on her nose. She hurried toward Alice and grabbed her arm.

"Alice! I need you to meet Jerry Weathers. He's project manager on this concert venue deal. And I want you to talk to the baby engineer assigned to the project." The mayor gave Alice a sharp look over her purple glasses. "Lemme know your take. Jerry's the guy in the pink tie. Come on!"

Intrigued, Alice followed the mayor to the knot of men standing by the door. "Jerry!" commanded the mayor. "Come meet Alice MacDonald Greer. She's a lawyer. She helps us straighten out the City's contracts."

Weathers wore a navy windbreaker with a blue checked shirt and, yes, a pink tie. He looked about forty-eight, had a confident lift to his head, blue eyes, a small smile. Alice, always curious about men's shoes, took a quick peek. Whoa—leather sneakers. Yes, the expensive ones that some football player wore in the TV ads. Wolf & Shepherd? Weathers grabbed Alice's hand, held it, gave it a minimal shake but didn't let go. Still smiling, unblinking, he leaned forward, a bit too close for her comfort. "Great to meet you, Alice."

He was breathing on her. She found herself tugging her hand free and stood straight. "You're based in—Nevada, Mr. Weathers?" she asked. A half second later she realized why she'd pulled back. His lips were smiling, but his eyes weren't.

"No, Apex Partners are based in LA, but we travel nationwide. We intend to build the same great venue here that we're building outside Vegas. My Apex sidekick's Conrad O'Leary." He looked toward a man standing near the paneled wall and surveying the room. Muscled, unsmiling, tight-lipped, he nodded at Weathers but stayed put. "Conrad keeps our projects on schedule. Very efficient. The construction guys call him 'the enforcer,' but that's how we meet deadlines."

Not the warm fuzzy type, Alice thought. "Your engineers are licensed in Texas?"

"Oh—well, no. Of course we hire local folks for engineering. We're using a Dallas outfit, Worth Engineers."

Alice didn't consider Dallas "local." Three hours north up I-35....

Weathers turned, peering over his shoulder. "Charles, come on over here. Alice, meet Charles Boone. He'll be handling local issues. And he'll be at the public meeting tomorrow night. Charles, Alice does law work for the City."

A young man in chinos and blazer stepped forward. He was taller than Weathers, with short reddish-brown hair, hazel eyes, and an anxious smile. Alice extended her hand. His was damp, but he passed the handshake test. Just friendly and finished.

"You're working on this venue project, Charles?" Alice asked.

"Yes ma'am." Sounded like a Texan.

"Where'd you get your degree?"

"Um, Texas A&M. Civil engineering." Another shy smile. "I wish you'd call me Charlie."

She'd already spotted the small orange notebook sticking out of a front pocket in the young man's chinos. The classic orange notebook—a dead giveaway for engineers, according to Alice's engineer uncles.

Weathers interrupted. "Very high grades, we're glad to have him on board. He's already a Texas P.E., Professional Engineer, if you understand?" Alice understood perfectly well—great that Charles was already a P.E., but she mentally sent Weathers to the penalty box for arrogance. "Good to meet you, Alice, hate to leave, but we've got another meeting." Weathers smiled, walked away, and was buttonholed by the city road engineer.

Alice persisted. "Where're you from, Charlie?"

"Um, New Braunfels."

Right down the road. "Did you design the project?" Alice asked.

"No, our Dallas office coordinated with the engineers working on the Nevada project. My job here is to liaise with the engineer at the state agency, you know, answer technical questions about Apex's application. Mr. Weathers also told me this morning that I'd be the one fielding questions at the public meeting tomorrow night."

"Really." She was surprised.

"You're right, that's a lot of material to absorb. I've gone through our file—everything I've got at the—in our office."

"Where is your office?"

He blushed. "We rented space in the old Coffee Creek Hotel. I've got a room there too—a studio apartment. Good internet. Plus the coffee shop—great cinnamon rolls."

The old downtown hotel had been renovated for short-term rentals. Still, Alice didn't think it was much of a "local office."

He glanced at his watch. "I need to touch base with the state agency today. I'm checking over our application before the public meeting, including the construction drawings we already submitted and some new ones that differ, to be sure we comply with all requirements including impervious cover—you know, that we won't have more building and paving than the regulations allow. Or any other issue."

"You aren't the soils engineer, though, are you?"

"No ma'am. Another guy's in charge of that. But he won't be at the public meeting tomorrow. I—I'll be relying on his report."

Uh-oh, Alice thought. No fun, having to rely on a report you didn't write.

Charlie blinked several times. His cheeks turned pink. He hesitated, then leaned forward. "Listen, do you do wills for people?"

Alice was momentarily nonplussed. "You want to get yours done?"

"Yes, ma'am. Our civil engineering prof told us that all civil engineers need to get their wills done as soon as they start work, because construction sites can be dangerous. You're not just sitting at a drafting table, you're dealing with heavy equipment, hazardous waste, working at heights. And my dad's dead. I want to take care of my mom and my sister."

Alice felt an uninvited rush of maternal sympathy. Surely doing a simple will for a baby engineer wouldn't create a conflict with the City, would it? She needed to think about it. "Call my assistant, Silla, and see if you can come in this week. After the public meeting, right?" She handed him a card.

"I'll be easy," he said. "My mom will be the executor, and everything goes to her except for $5,000 to my little sister, Jeanie. She's a junior at Texas State. And she'll get my truck, if anything happens to me." He gave a small snort. "Feels weird to talk about this. Oh, and no debts—I've paid off my student loans."

"How'd you do that so soon?" Alice asked, interested.

"Worked two jobs all the way through A&M—night watchman in the music library and cleaning cars on weekends."

"Wow. Good for you. That's tough, managing two jobs plus civil engineering classes."

Charlie shrugged. "Had no choice. My dad always worried about being in debt. My mom thought it shortened his life. He died when I was a senior in high school. I'm helping with Jeanie's tuition now."

No wonder he's so uptight, so worried, Alice thought. "How'd you pick civil engineering?"

His worried face changed immediately. His face lit up. "Bridges! That's what I love best. Someday I hope to design a bridge. When I get my first vacation, I'm planning to go see a couple. There's a floating bridge in Seattle on seventy-seven concrete pontoons. And I want to see some old bridges—the Bunker Hill Bridge in Boston and a humpback covered bridge in Virginia. And someday when I get to Europe—"

"Yes?"

"The Greeks built a bridge called the Arkadiko, at least three thousand years ago. And there's a caravan bridge in Turkey, supposedly built 850 years BCE. I'm going to visit those."

"What about Japanese bridges?"

"I'd love to see them. Europe first, though. I've promised to take Jeanie there next year after she graduates."

Alice's heart hurt for this boy, who'd taken the world on his shoulders.

"Well," she said, "again, give Silla a call at my office."

"Charles," Weathers barked over his shoulder from the doorway. Charles said, "Thank you," and followed, turning back for a quick smile at Alice.

No leather sneakers on the kid. Just your basic steel-toed work boots—rather appealing. Alice gave him a smile in return.

Mayor Wilson grabbed Alice's arm again. "Can you find out about this engineering firm? And Apex Partners? Are they for real? Also—" the mayor sounded frazzled—"I need you to show up at the public meeting on this concert venue just in case. Bradley Ott in our legal department sent in the City's comments on the proposed permit—you know Bradley—but he's in the hospital with bacterial pneumonia."

Yikes, not much time to prepare. "Of course I will. Can you send me a copy of the City's comments? And Bradley's cell number?"

"I will. You can drive me to Rotary," announced the mayor. "And you know this'll all come down to how much impervious cover the developer can get. Every zoning case, every variance...bigger driveway, more roof, you name it."

Alice nodded. Impervious cover meant manmade surface coverage—paving, roofs, patios—that prevented rainwater from sinking into the soil. Governmental entities sought to limit excessive impervious cover, which could both release uncontrolled stormwater runoff, causing flooding, and prevent the ground from absorbing rainwater needed for water supply.

This week Rotary's lunch at the community hall was catered by Big John's Barbecue, one of Alice's favorites, offering a choice of pulled pork or chopped brisket or both, with potato salad, slaw, and banana pudding. Balancing their plates, Alice and the mayor headed for the table that included the county probate judge and Alice's favorite clients, the three guys who owned the Beer Barn, the town's beloved beer and dance hall. Everyone at the table was talking about the proposed concert venue.

"Worrying about our water supply is enough to make me skip lunch!" barked the mayor. Then she picked up a spoon and attacked her banana pudding. "But I need my strength."

****

When Alice walked back into the office, Silla said, "Remember James Surratt? Scheduled to meet you about his will this afternoon? He's asked to postpone until the day after tomorrow. Says he feels like crap and is saving his strength for the public meeting tomorrow night. Also, your newest fan called—Charlie Boone? He said you told him at City Hall that he could call to ask if he could visit about his will on Thursday or

Friday. I said yes because he sounds so nice."

Alice stood still, thinking. The City itself owned some surface water rights in Coffee Creek and used that water to supply its small water system serving the downtown area. The mayor had asked her to check out both Apex and the engineering firm—and now, to attend the public meeting on the proposed permit. Would a young engineer's will—a completely separate set of issues—raise an ethics issue, a conflicts problem?

"Silla, we might have to cancel. But call him back and tell him we'll check conflicts and later this week give him options for a date. I should have a better handle after the public meeting on what the City's position might be."

"Okay. Also, the mayor sent you a copy of the comments on the concert venue that Bradley Ott submitted. And his phone number. She said he's not on a ventilator so to feel free to call him!"

Back at her desk, Alice reviewed Bradley's comments on the terms of the proposed permit. Pretty solid job, she thought. She picked up her phone. "Bradley, how are you?"

A hoarse groan. "Don't ever get this crap, Alice. Thanks for picking up the ball here."

"I'll go to the public meeting, just to wave the flag. I'm glad you included a request for a contested case hearing, in case the City winds up litigating."

Bradley coughed. "Listen, Alice, Walter Bowie—you know, chief engineer at the water plant? Walter was a huge help. He's worried."

The chief engineer would likely have to testify if the City went forward with a contested case hearing. "I'll get in touch. Let me know of anything else. You get well, okay?"

Alice left a message for Walter Bowie. Then, with the mayor's instructions echoing in her head, Alice looked online at Apex Partners, LLC. Snazzy website; some glowing public relations blurbs about "innovative construction practices" and "close cooperation with engineering and other disciplines." No contact information on officers or key employees. Pictures of various building sites but no specific locations. And no mention of the Nevada project.

She found Silla. "Can you dig up some intel on Apex Partners, LLC, probably incorporated in California? And Worth Engineers' Dallas office?" Silla could wheedle astounding information from her computer.

Alice was glad to do more work for the City—it helped pay the bills. But wastewater permits? Not in her wheelhouse.

"Sure. Listen—your buddy M.A. called. She insists on making your wedding cake. Plus, our critical path issue: decide where the wedding will be. Beer Barn? M.A.'s guest house? Your place? Kinsear's place? Church? Until that's decided, we can't send invitations! And most important— what are you going to wear?"

"Yikes." A welter of wedding details whirled in her head. As to the cake, M.A. Ellison—a retired high school biology teacher, now running the local Tea Garden B&B—was unstoppable. And the wedding? To Alice's eternal gratitude, the moment Silla learned about the wedding, she'd insisted on handling all arrangements herself.

"No worries," Silla said, with that irresistible smile. "It'll be superb. But you've got to decide where."

"Kinsear's back in New York this week," Alice said. "The hedge fund guys at his old firm asked him to consult on some deal. He'll be back late Friday, and we can finalize location." Yikes, "finalize" sounded so...so final!

"Did Kinsear choose his best man yet?" asked Silla.

Alice broke into a smile. "Muddy Mackin." Muddy, an elderly rancher in far west Texas north of Big Bend, had hired Alice to protect manuscripts written by a missing songwriter who'd once worked at Muddy's ranch. Kinsear and Muddy had bonded in their search for the young man.

"Great," said Silla. "Can't wait to see Muddy again. And with me in charge of your wedding, what could possibly go wrong?"

Chapter Three

So Very Un-Merry?

Early Tuesday before dawn, Alice padded out onto her deck with her binoculars. She hadn't slept well. For hours coyotes had yowled far down the creek—yearning for what? Love and connection, like humans. Low in the east she found Venus, glowing bright, and Mars, faintly pinky-orange and higher up. Dimmer, poised between them, Saturn. Planets really do look different from stars, she thought. And how comforting that the long string of planets keeps trailing along with our planet, so we can be soothed by catching a glimpse of them at different times in different seasons.

Now, at dawn, she made coffee, grinding beans, patting the grounds into the small espresso maker, listening to it begin to hiss and burble, then heating and frothing the milk. Always that first sip, leaving a rim of froth on her lip, made sense of life.

What about this wedding? Was she ready? She'd lived through five Christmases after Jordie's helicopter disappeared over the North Sea, not knowing whether he was dead or—somewhere else. Only last year had his bones been found and identified. Now her son John was finishing a graduate degree in Edinburgh, and her irrepressible Ann would graduate from college in June. Except for the burros, Alice had lived alone for five years. What would it be like to have Kinsear around...much more of the time?

For life?

Was *Kinsear* ready? His wife, Betsy, had broken her neck, jumping her horse, a few years back. He'd been solo dad to daughters, Isabel and Carrie, since then.

Why am I dithering? she wondered. Since that fall day when he walked into the Fredericksburg beer garden, and she felt again the same rush of warmth she'd felt during their fling in law school, pre-Jordie, Kinsear had slowly re-inserted himself into her life. She remembered their breathless trip to Big Bend and their night at the casita at the Gage Hotel. She remembered climbing with him up to the rocky window in the Chisos Mountains, where you could look south far into Mexico. She'd watched him cooking in his ranch kitchen for a huge Thanksgiving family dinner, including Alice and her children. She'd seen him with his shotgun, holding off invaders at an old lady's ranch. And doggedly, carefully, wielding a shovel to help an archeologist dig up the body of a long-missing songwriter.

Hadn't he earned his spurs?

Hadn't she earned hers too? Alice never felt completely satisfied with herself. Did anyone? But surely it was time to move forward, to grab life by the short hairs, to let herself love this man as he—and she—deserved.

Sunrise turned the kitchen orange. Big Boy brayed loudly outside by the fence that kept all three burros out of her cosseted roses. No appointments today, as far as she remembered. Just that public meeting tonight. She tugged on leggings and a top and sandals, then packed chino pants and a shirt and jacket and her boots into the car and headed to the yoga studio three blocks down Live Oak from her office.

Alice and her best buddies from book group—Red, Miranda, and Jane Ann—met at early yoga every Tuesday. "Spring training," Miranda called it. The quartet arranged their mats on the back row so they could whisper. Miranda, tall and blond, managed Madrone Bank. Alice's best friend, Red Griffin, former law firm administrator, ran her own operation—Red's Rescue Ranch for abused horses. Jane Ann, a tall and imposing brunette, ran Coffee Creek Title Company. Alice knew that without their support, her new career in Coffee Creek would never have taken off.

When class finished, the four, stretched and sweaty, convened on the porch. "I'm going to the meeting on that concert venue permit," Red declared. "Are you?" The other three nodded.

"Have the venue investors closed on the property yet?" Alice asked Jane Ann. "You're doing the title work, right?"

Jane Ann shook her head. "Uh-uh. But we're swamped right now, so that's fine with me. The investors are using some brand-new outfit down in San Marcos. Word on the street is, there's a hiccup holding up the closing. I haven't heard what it is."

A hiccup?

The four women agreed to meet that night at Alice's office after the public meeting. Red promised bread and fruit. Alice promised cheese.

Silla was already at the office when, face glowing, feeling virtuous, Alice opened the front door.

"You've been out riding," Alice guessed, noting Silla's boots, jeans, and cowboy shirt. Silla now owned an interest in a local riding stable.

"Yes ma'am. Can't let that horse get bored. Or sulky. Hey, you had another call from that Boone boy. He's hoping Thursday will work, if you agree. Isn't he awfully young to worry about a will?"

"Probably afraid for his life. He's got to be worried about the meeting tonight. He's assigned to cover all the technical areas, and Silla, he's just a baby. Given the knowledgeable people likely to show up—like the master naturalists—he'll face tough questions. And a hostile crowd."

"Only one baby engineer's appearing for the applicant? Shouldn't the investors at least send their lawyer?" Silla shook her head. "Most of Coffee Creek's likely to show up, ready to make mincemeat of the poor boy."

Alice had spent enough time at public meetings to know how it felt to face an audience of disgruntled citizens. For lawyers and engineers, that came with the territory. Remembering Boone's anxious face, she guessed he was about the same age as her son John. How would she feel watching John make an unpopular presentation before a packed house of angry citizens? Her stomach would be in a knot.

"Remind me again, what time tonight?"

"Seven o'clock, in the high school gym."

No appointments for the rest of the day! Alice gleefully exited the office and ran back to her car. First stop: Goodson Kells to check on her wedding boots. Initially she'd envisioned ivory boots. Mr. Kells had talked her into "a color adjustment," as he called it, showing her some toffee-colored leather, so soft it felt like glove leather. He suggested a few stars in a soft coral. She peeked in his dusty show window in downtown Coffee Creek. Mr. Kells's daughter unlocked the door—locked because Mr. Kells admitted only customers at the top of his waiting list—and grinned at Alice. "They're nearly finished! Come see!"

The boots were so soft, so flexible, she worried a bit. "Don't fret," said Mr. Kells. "They'll stand up tall for you. How do you like the star color?"

She loved it.

Next stop—cheeses for tonight. Coffee Creek Cheese was usually closed on Tuesday, but Alice had called ahead. She drove back up the creek road, turned right on Old Hays Road, and then turned right again into the driveway of the small hilltop ranch called Goat Hill that Merilee Givens had transformed into a premium cheesemaking operation. Merilee ("Merry" to almost everyone) had begun making chèvre cheeses here six years earlier from her small herd of Nubian goats. Now her products sold briskly around Austin. Alice had met Merry when their daughters bonded at summer camp. Merry's daughter, Francine, was studying in San Antonio at the Culinary Institute of America and coming home most weekends to help make cheese.

Alice pulled into a parking lot bounded on the left by a high stone wall. In front of her stood the original ranch house, connected on the right by a portico to the stone building housing the cheese shop and creamery. Further to the right stood the old barn, its wood weathered to a soft gray. Alice opened the gate in the wire fence and walked down a gravel path, lined with early-blooming blue sage, to the shop. A slightly goaty ambiance greeted her as she opened the door—fresh, promising, and a bit raunchy. Inside, the sales room was empty, quiet.

Alice walked past the sales counter and knocked on a stout door bearing the sign "KNOCK FOR ENTRY." Locks clicked; the door swung open. Merry Givens, her dark curls partly covered by a white cap, was already walking away. Alice followed her into the spotless cheese room, with its stainless steel round tub for heating milk, and adjacent cheese tub. Long sharp knives, sparkling clean, lay on a chopping block. Alice remembered watching, fascinated, while Merry held a knife in each hand and sliced the mat of cheese into careful squares.

Merry seemed to be limping.

"When did you start locking this door?" asked Alice, curious.

"Maybe a month ago," Merry said, still with her back to Alice, adjusting a gauge on the milk tub. "Denny kept barging in without remembering how clean it's got to stay. So now I lock it," she went on. "Profit margins are too thin for sloppiness. I can't afford a bad batch of contaminated cheese. A clean cheese room helps maintain consistent quality. Customers like consistency."

Merry turned around to face Alice. Alice always enjoyed Merry's looks—her curly dark hair, her hazel eyes. Now she gasped at the huge purple bruise on Merry's left cheekbone and the purplish-green swelling that nearly closed her left eye. A line of stitches marked her forehead.

"What in the world, Merry? Were you in a wreck?"

"No. I had a weird accident yesterday, trying to get the new Jersey bull out of my trailer. Plus I already had a sprained ankle, so I wasn't at my best. The bull went nuts. Knocked me for a loop."

"A *bull?* What bull?"

"I bought a few Jerseys. I want to try my hand at some cow's milk cheddar."

"Good lord!" Alice felt horrified, not only at the bruising, but at the exhaustion on Merry's face. Who was helping her? "Surely you weren't trying to get a bull out of a trailer by yourself?"

"Well...somebody had to do it."

"What about Denny?" Two years ago Merry, a widow, had married a younger man, Denson Ward. Alice had heard whispers that their relationship had turned bumpy.

"He wasn't here. And the bull went wild. I've never known a Jersey to act like that bull did."

Alice listened, anxious not just at the bruising but at the lines around Merry's tired eyes, her downturned mouth. She looked bone-weary.

"You were here by yourself, and with a sprained ankle? How did that happen?"

"Another dumb accident. I was by myself, climbing down the old wooden ladder from the barn loft with a crate of cheese boxes, and one rung just slipped out. Fell right out of the ladder! That's never happened before. I landed funny on my ankle."

And again, she'd been alone.

"So...Denny's no longer helping with the cheese making?" Alice recalled Denny had been selling cars when he met Merry. He'd quit that in favor of selling insurance, saying he was done with standing in a car lot in the Texas heat. When insurance didn't pan out, Merry had tried to involve him in the cheese business, asking him to handle advertising and work the sales counter. "What's his new gig?"

"He's studying to get his Realtor's license." Merry gave Alice a strained smile. "Cross your fingers. Now let's find some cheeses for you."

As they stood by the big glass-fronted refrigerator full of cheeses, Alice asked if Merry would be at the public meeting on the concert venue.

Merry frowned. "I don't know anything about it, and I've got a big delivery to make tomorrow. And I don't particularly want to go out in public looking like this."

"Isn't the proposed site just down Old Hays Road from here? Didn't you get a letter from TCEQ—from the Texas Commission on Environmental Quality—about the permit application?" Alice knew nearby land-owners were entitled to notice.

Merry shook her head no. Odd that she got no letter, Alice thought. Merry looked distracted; Alice watched her hands shake as she wrapped up Alice's purchases.

Alice hugged her and departed, laden with cheeses, but even more worried about Merry. What was Denny up to when he wasn't helping Merry—which appeared to be most of the time? Alice couldn't believe he was studying that hard. She wondered about Francine's take on the situation but hesitated to go behind Merry's back. Maybe her daughter Ann could touch base with Francine. And why was Merry so—so very un-merry?

Chapter Four

Where Was He?

By seven o'clock that evening Alice and a thousand other Coffee Creek citizens were perched on the hard bleachers in the high school gym. She sat close to the front, with Red, Jane Ann, and Miranda. Three representatives from TCEQ sat at a long table in the middle of the gym floor, with a table microphone. A separate microphone was placed closer to the audience. A woman with a TCEQ nametag hovered over a table by the door, passing out information to the attendees. At seven o'clock sharp, one of the three agency employees at the center table stood and introduced himself as Will Oxford, a lawyer for TCEQ, and asked the other two employees to introduce themselves. Alice remembered Oxford from a workshop on surface water rights. Competent, cautious. He gave a brief overview of the permit application, then announced that the applicant's representative would now field questions from the audience. He looked expectantly toward the entrance door. Raised hands appeared all across the bleachers. Alice kept looking around for Charles Boone but couldn't spot him.

The audience began to buzz, peering forward, then looking toward the back of the gym. Where was the Apex representative? The woman from TCEQ stationed at the table by the door hurried across the gym floor and whispered to Will Oxford. He frowned, then spoke into the microphone: "The applicant's representative is not present at this time. Accordingly, we will proceed with questions from the audience. The agency will respond as appropriate. When you come forward to speak, please give your name and address."

A man in a cowboy vest and boots popped up and strode to the microphone. "Howard Barden. I live at 321 Dora Lane along Coffee Creek. I pump water from the creek for my horses. I don't want them drinking sewage effluent from the venue. How does this permit protect my horses?"

Next question, from a resident on the plateau south of the venue: "There are sinkholes and rock crevices all over this limestone we live on. And all under it too. What studies has the applicant made to ensure that no effluent will get through the little layer of dirt Apex says it's going to lay out there at the venue, and make its way down through the limestone right into our well water?"

Applause broke out. Will Oxford tried to quiet the crowd.

A woman approached the microphone from the far side of the gym:

"Mary Landon from 301 Dora Lane. Where does the applicant propose to get the dirt needed for the land application area? How much does the applicant propose to buy? Has the applicant field-tested the type and depth of the dirt the applicant proposes to use? If so, what were the results? If not, why not?"

One of the state representatives seated at the table said, "We've asked the applicant to submit all tests made so far. We do not see any such test results in the file."

The next speaker approached the microphone: "My name is James Surratt." That got Alice's attention. "I live south of the proposed venue, on Mexican Buckeye Road. Coffee Creek runs through our property, which our family's owned since Coffee Creek was founded." The crowd quieted. "My grandfather taught me to fish on that creek. My kids and grandkids spend hours with me on our land, exploring, learning to hunt and fish." He looked around at the crowd. "As many of you know, I've been testing Coffee Creek stream water for years. As the creek nears town, its water quality is often close to what the EPA calls 'pristine.' The Clean Water Act requires that agencies protect against degradation of water quality. Treated effluent may look clean but can still contain nutrients from human waste and can cause algae blooms when dumped into our streams. If our water quality deteriorates, what's the plan to protect the citizens who depend on that water? Also, these land application permits always state that the permit 'will not authorize a discharge of pollutants into the water in the state.' How will this applicant prevent the discharge of pollutants?"

Vigorous applause. Surratt continued. "I also have a well. My well water comes from the Trinity aquifer. Many of us out here in the Hill Country depend on our wells. Has the applicant conducted any dye tests or other tests to see whether effluent from this massive proposed land application will penetrate the aquifers we rely on? Or affect our wells? Or contaminate the creek? If the applicant hasn't conducted tests, how can the state conclude we won't suffer negative impacts? What research—if any—did you do? Where are the results?"

Again, strong applause. Pretty convincing, Alice thought.

The line of would-be speakers dwindled. When the last few had had their say—many of them indignantly pointing out that the missing applicant had provided no answers to their questions—Will Oxford reminded everyone present of the right to file objections to the proposed permit within the comment period. "Remember that affected persons can appeal the final permit."

"This permit should not be issued!" someone yelled. "Where's their lawyer? Where's their project manager? Somebody should've shown up to answer our questions. You ought to hold another public meeting!"

The crowd rumbled in agreement.

Yikes, Alice thought. Someone sure screwed up. She slipped down the aisle and buttonholed Will Oxford. His eyebrows lifted, and she reminded him they'd met before. "Where is Charles Boone? He was supposed to speak for the applicant."

He shook his head. "All I heard was that the applicant couldn't send a representative because of some accident."

"Accident?"

"That's all the info we got."

Alice frowned. "I came to this meeting to hear the applicant's answers to some big questions. As did everyone else!"

He shrugged. "You're right. Same here. Have to say, I'm really surprised."

As she turned to leave, a young woman pressed forward. Alice heard her say to one of the TCEQ reps, "I'm Charles Boone's sister. Do you know where he is? I'm trying to get hold of him. He wanted me to meet him here early." Anxiety in her voice....

"Sorry. No idea."

Alice turned, trying to remember. Was her name Jennifer? No. Jeanie. Curly reddish hair, like her brother's. "Jeanie, here's my card. Your brother called my office about an appointment. If you hear from him, could you let me know? And may I have your number?"

Jeanie reeled off a cell phone number. "But I wish my brother would answer his phone. His truck's not at his apartment, either. I'm gonna try again." She vanished into the departing crowd.

"Hey, Alice!" called Jane Ann. "The wine is calling!"

Where was Charles Boone?

*****

The book club gathered as planned in Alice's conference room. Jane Ann opened a sauvignon blanc, and Miranda uncorked a petit verdot. Atop the credenza Alice set out bottles of Topo Chico along with Merry's cheeses. Red supplied a baguette from Abby Jane's Bakeshop and a large bunch of grapes.

"Well, cheers, ladies," Jane Ann said, lifting a glass. "What a disaster, that hearing tonight. Alice, have you ever seen an applicant completely fail to show for a permit hearing like this?"

"Nope. Part of the purpose is to give the public a chance to ask questions of the applicant. The TCEQ guy said there'd been some 'accident' but didn't know what it was." She shook her head. "I'm worried about the young man I met Monday at City Hall—he'd told me he was supposed to handle the hearing for Apex. Then tonight at the hearing his sister said he wasn't answering his phone."

"Maybe the Apex guys just bailed," Red suggested. "Just decided to ignore the protesters."

"Maybe," Alice said. "They're from out of state...maybe they thought the public was irrelevant." But her mind was on Charles Boone. Had he called TCEQ as he'd planned? Had he finished absorbing all the permit details? Why hadn't he shown up?

"Mmm," said Miranda. "What was life like in Coffee Creek before Merry started making her fabulous cheeses? How's she doing, by the way? I haven't seen her in a while."

"Not too well since the Jersey bull bashed her in the face," Alice said. "She's decided to try making cheddar cheeses too."

"Jersey bull? Jerseys are placid! Are you sure it was a Jersey?" Red demanded. Red knew her cattle. She'd grown up on a ranch.

"She said Jersey, and she said it went nuts," Alice said. "It sounds like when she was trying to get the bull out of the trailer, the bull charged out and the gate bashed her cheekbone. She's got stitches on her forehead too. What bothers me is, Merry was all alone."

"What about what's-his-name, Denny? Although I hear he ditched the insurance business," commented Miranda. "He's on the flighty side, doesn't stick to anything for long."

"Seriously, I never heard of any Jersey acting like that," Red mused, spreading more cheese on a slice of baguette.

"I was surprised not to see Merry at the hearing," Jane Ann said. "With that proposed venue just up the road from her property, you'd think she'd be worried about the impact."

"She should be, because she pumps creek water for the goats into her stock tank," added Red.

Alice thought how depressed Merry had seemed. If land application effluent hit the creek, what would it do to Merry's goats? And Alice was still surprised Merry hadn't gotten notice of the venue application from TCEQ. And why she seemed not just depressed, but scared.

"Hey, are we going to discuss the book?" asked Red.

After critical arguments about the month's selection, followed by the usual hilarity while each member read her favorite or least-favorite paragraphs, the book group said its goodbyes. Alice started home. The moon was rising, sparkling on Coffee Creek as she made her way up the creek road. Was the moon shining on Charles Boone? Where was he?

Chapter Five

Dishonest From The Word Go!

Seven a.m. on Wednesday; Alice had just enough time to brush the burros before the vet showed up in late afternoon to give them their annual shots. She found the donkey brush and way-laid Big Boy. He stood motionless for her quick caress on his ears, then leaned gently against her as she began brushing his back. She found herself leaning back against him. As always she felt her own breath slow, felt calmness descend on her shoulders. A little burro therapy.

"If ever you manage to get in the house, Big Boy, I bet you'll want a bubble bath?"

Enormous brown eyes with their black lashes looked up, blinked once in affirmation, and closed again as she worked her way down his forelegs. "Maybe lavender bubbles?" she murmured, shifting to his hind legs. "Or Eau de Donkey?" He looked sleeker now. Queenie and Princess watched cautiously from a safe distance. "Your turn," she told them, slowly approaching Queenie, then gently brushing. But Princess cavorted away, flipping up her back legs. Brush rejection. The vet would have to deal with a dusty donkey.

Alice headed for town. As soon as she entered the office, Silla popped up from her desk. "Alice. Call Barbara Winthrop. Here's her number."

She frowned. "Who's that?"

"Henry Winthrop's daughter. He came to that talk you gave about getting wildlife management status on agricultural land. You walked people through the application, remember?"

Alice vaguely recalled a burly man, soft-spoken, shy. He'd thanked her after the meeting. "But he's not a client."

"No. He's got heart issues, and his daughter moved home to help him. His ranch sits at the corner of Old Hays Road and the creek road."

"What does he need?"

"Barbara attended the public meeting last night. When she told her dad about it this morning, he raised a question about covenants. According to Barbara, in 1973 his friend Larry Johnston owned 280 acres of the original Carothers Ranch, at the corner of Old Hays and the creek road. Johnston offered to sell Winthrop 200 acres at the corner but wanted to break the remaining eighty acres into two parcels with frontage on Old Hays Road, one of fifty and one of thirty acres.

Winthrop's memory is that he agreed to buy the 200 acres if his friend assured him he'd put covenants against commercial use on the two smaller parcels. Winthrop asks if he can still enforce those covenants. He doesn't keep his deed at the house but says it's in his bank lockbox. He also says Merry Givens lives next door, on the fifty-acre parcel. Barbara asked you to help, so I've drafted an engagement letter."

She handed Alice a draft. "Looks great," Alice said. "Send it on and ask Barbara to watch for it."

In ten minutes Silla sped into Alice's office with the signed letter. "You're hired."

Alice's mind was buzzing. "Is it possible," she said, "that the venue parcel is subject to these covenants? Is that what Henry Winthrop's wondering?"

Silla smiled her "I've got this" smile, waving two sheets of paper. "Here's the legal description of the venue—from the permit application. No street address, but it mentions thirty acres. And I pulled the deed for Henry Winthrop's 200 acres from the property records."

"Excellent," said Alice, taking the documents. She noted that Silla's mind was racing ahead, as usual. "Can you also find the original 280-acre deed to Winthrop's friend Johnston?"

By eight-fifteen Silla had found the requested deed. Alice, pen in hand, confirmed that Johnston's 280 acres were indeed purchased subject to some 1973-vintage covenants recorded in the Coffee County Property Records. But Johnston's deed did not describe those covenants. She went back to Silla's desk. "Now we need a copy of those 1973 covenants on the original ranch."

After Alice had shown Silla how to run titles at the Coffee County Courthouse, Silla had become a whiz on property records. As she began rapid-fire tapping on her keyboard, Alice watched, too antsy to return to her office.

The printer whirred. "Here," Silla announced.

The 1973 document listed what was allowed and what was prohibited on the property at the intersection of Old Hays Road and the creek road, which appeared to include all 280 acres deeded to Larry Johnston. Prohibited activities included commercial operations other than sale of the property's agricultural products.

"So how can the developer propose a concert venue on the property?" Alice demanded. She picked up the phone and called Jane Ann. "Listen to this." Alice recited the covenant restrictions. "I don't think the developers can put commercial activities on the venue property! How come nobody knows?"

"Ignorance abounds," said Jane Ann. "Some deeds just mention the book and page of the original document containing the covenants without giving details on the covenants. Maybe that's the case here." Her voice became judgmental. "When my firm sends title documents to a proposed buyer, we reference and describe every applicable recorded document, including references to covenants. We also offer to provide buyers copies of any document they ask for. But some buyers don't or won't pay attention. On a land purchase! Crazy."

"But maybe it's not carelessness?" Alice proposed. "Maybe some buyers just hope nobody will notice that they're doing something prohibited by their deed?"

"Yup," said Jane Ann. "That happens."

"Does this count as a 'hiccup'?" Alice wondered. "Is this why the investors haven't closed on the venue property?"

"I wouldn't be surprised."

Alice thanked Jane Ann and found Silla. "Let's make copies of all applicable covenant documents for the Winthrop property. I'll draft a transmittal letter saying it appears Winthrop has the right to enforce the no-commercial-use covenant, referencing the attached documents. Then I'll call to discuss. Of course, Henry Winthrop may not have the stomach for a legal fight."

"True."

"Still, just in case, we'll establish from the county appraisal records the current owners of the fifty-acre and thirty-acre parcels." Alice expected that included Merry Givens. "This legal description from the permit application says the venue parcel begins about six-tenths of a mile from the intersection of the creek road and Old Hays Road and extends about a quarter-mile further."

The two women hovered over Silla's computer, staring at the aerial map of properties along Old Hays Road.

"Here's Merry's property, fifty acres next door to the Winthrops."

Alice scanned the appraisal description, then clicked to the next property. Immediately east lay a thirty-acre parcel belonging to—

"Oh, for God's sake," said Silla, her voice dripping with disgust.

"What?" asked Alice.

"The thirty acres next to Merry? Taxed to Teena Ann Traynor!" snapped Silla. "Worst barrel-racer in this county! No, in the entire Hill Country! Maybe all of Texas!"

"What's so bad about Teena Ann Traynor?" Alice asked.

"She spurs her horses! She yanks their bits! Her horses have sore mouths! In fact, she got disqualified for whipping and abusing her horse at the Wimberley rodeo. And at the Rooftop Rodeo in Estes Park. She's vicious." Silla took a deep breath, face grim, mouth set. "I love to beat her. And so far I always have. I cannot abide anyone who hurts her horse."

Quite a character assessment of both women, Alice thought.

Silla punched keys on the computer. "Here's her website. Take a look at that face! Look at that smile! She's—she's dishonest from the word go!"

Alice peered over Silla's shoulder. Teena Ann's website featured a giant close-up of Teena Ann—chin down, hazel eyes wide, bouffant dark curls. She was smiling up at the camera with astoundingly white teeth.

"Store-bought eyelashes," Silla added. "So thick she can barely blink. Amazed she can even see where the barrels are in the rodeo ring. And look at this getup!" She clicked on another photo—Teena Ann aboard her horse, sporting a white hat with a gold band, a gold glitter cowgirl shirt unbuttoned to show ample cleavage, and jeans so tight they looked painted on. "For her it's all about the glitter and the money."

"Anything else you want me to know about Teena Ann?"

"For Teena Ann, rules are mere suggestions. She bats her eyes, tries to manipulate the judges. She's a spoiled brat, grew up with too much money. Just an arrogant twit," Silla concluded.

"We're sure she owns the proposed venue property?"

Silla pulled up the deed to Traynor from the property records. She and Alice stood side by side, comparing the legal description on Traynor's deed with the legal description in the permit application.

"Perfect match," Alice said.

"So there's our problem," Silla said. "Teena Ann Traynor! If you're thinking she won't put up a fight on the covenants, good luck. Her daddy's still got some big bucks. He'll likely bankroll her. She's bad news."

Alice nodded. Teena Ann didn't sound like a woman sensitive to the public good. "As if we needed any more bad news."

Then her cell phone rang. Alice glanced at the screen. Her heart sank. Jeanie Boone.

Chapter Six

There Was An Accident

"Alice Greer?" The voice trembled.

"Yes?" Already Alice could feel the words "Oh, no" forming in her throat.

"The police called me. Charlie—Charlie's dead." She gulped. "There was an accident."

Alice closed her eyes, unable to make her voice work for a moment. "I am so sorry. Can you—do you know what happened?"

"He was asked to go visit a building site somewhere in southwest Coffee Creek. He—the police say he slipped off a girder and fell."

"Oh, no." Alice closed her eyes again, trying to block the vision—that young man's body, falling. "Oh, Jeanie—when?"

"Late yesterday. Now I know why he didn't show up for the hearing. I was so worried last night, I stayed with a friend here and kept trying to call him. But he never answered. The police say they didn't know who to call until this morning. They say they still haven't found his phone."

That's weird, Alice thought, frowning. Charlie had to be constantly accessible to Apex and his bosses. He would always have his phone with him.

"Jeanie, was he taken to a hospital here?"

"An ambulance came from the hospital, but the police say he was already dead, and they sent his body to Austin. I don't understand where...."

To the Travis County Medical Examiner, Alice thought. That's what the police would do, for an unexplained death at a work site in Coffee County. And right now his little sister shouldn't be alone. "You're still here in Coffee Creek? Could you come by my office, Jeanie?"

Jeanie's voice was thick with tears. Alice heard her blow her nose. "I—I guess so. If you have time, maybe you could help me figure out what to do. After the police called me, I called Mom. She's devastated. Couldn't even talk. I called my aunt and asked her to go stay with Mom." She paused. Alice heard her swallow. "I need to go home, but I've got to find out what happened."

Alice groaned inwardly, thinking of Jeanie's mom. Death of a child...every parent's worst nightmare.

*****

From her office window, Alice saw a young woman pull up to the curb in a battered old blue RAV and climb out, slinging her backpack over her shoulder. Jeanie Boone again reminded Alice of Charlie—same mobile face, same reddish curls. Alice met her at the front door. Silla took her in hand: a hug, a mug of hot tea, a box of tissues, a chair in the conference room.

Alice sat down with Jeanie. "Tell us again what happened. You talked to the Coffee County police, right?"

Jeanie nodded. "I had classes yesterday morning at Texas State in San Marcos, then I drove up here to take Charlie to lunch, before the big public meeting. I picked him up at noon outside that old hotel where his office is, and we had lunch at La Tapatia. I asked why he was so distracted, and he said some contractor had come by the office and left some plans and Charlie had had a weird conversation after that with the agency, but he wouldn't say more. It was a hurried lunch—I had to race back to San Marcos for another class, and he said he needed to pick up his blazer at the dry cleaners and then prepare to answer questions at the hearing.

"Anyway, I dropped him off at his truck, parked at the office, and was almost to Wimberley when he called me back. He said he'd left some of his stuff under the seat in my car and could I get to the hearing early to give it to him. I could tell he was upset. He said that Weathers, the project manager for the venue, had just ordered him to go check out the roof coating on a new baseball facility under construction on the south side of Coffee Creek. Some kind of liquid coating, he said. Charlie asked why, because the concert venue roof's supposed to have a foam coating. Weathers told him, 'Who knows, we might change the specs for our roof.'" She stopped, took a breath. "Charlie told me he hoped to keep the ballfield trip short so he could finish preparing. And he said we could go for beers after the hearing. Then he said the weirdest thing—'Hey, maybe I could just resign?' Then he said, 'Just kidding.' I thought he was freaked out, having to handle this public hearing."

She wiped her nose with the tissue Silla handed her. "That was the last I heard." She burst into tears. "The last time I'll ever hear his voice."

"He died at the construction site?" Alice asked again.

Jeanie nodded and took a shuddery breath. "The police said he was apparently climbing up an unfinished sort of walkway or beam that led up to the roof. They said he might have slipped and couldn't catch himself." Another shuddery breath. "But Charlie was in great shape. We went climbing in Colorado last summer. He was very surefooted."

"Where was this site?"

"I'm not sure. South Coffee Creek's all I heard." Silla poured her more hot tea. Jeanie gave her a grateful look. "Charlie was already in a knot over some calculations from the guy who'd showed up. He said at lunch he'd already called TCEQ about them. Imperious...no, impervious, that's the word. He wanted to be able to answer any questions at the hearing about impervious cover. He sounded worried."

I don't have a good feeling about this, Alice thought. Apex itself had designated no representative to the hearing other than a baby engineer, and then they'd sent the baby engineer out to look at a construction site instead of letting him prepare for the hearing. Construction specs often change. So what was the urgency of getting Charlie out there yesterday?

"Was he alone? Who called the ambulance?" she asked.

"The police said they got the same call as EMS did, then a second EMS call from some man with the company Charlie was working for," Jeanie answered. "The man told the police he was supposed to meet Charlie there, but Charlie beat him to the job site. He said that when he got there, he saw Charlie's truck and then saw his body."

"Hang on a minute, Jeanie. Let me make a phone call, see if we can get more information." Alice slipped out of the conference room, went to her office, and closed the door. She called George Files, chief detective at the Coffee County Sheriff's Department. The two had what Alice considered a cordial but wary relationship: each had information to protect—and sometimes, carefully, to share.

To her relief, Files was available. "George, I'm calling about Charles Boone, the young man who died yesterday at a ballfield construction site," she began. "He'd asked me to help him with his will this week. Right now his sister Jeanie's here at my office. You can imagine how upset she is. Can you tell me more about what happened to him? Like, where he was, and who else was there?"

"Alice. Glad to know someone cares about that poor kid. Well, you know who first called 911?"

"Who?"

"Apple. His watch reported a 'fall' incident. There was another call later, from some guy named O'Leary."

"Conrad O'Leary? He's with Apex, the outfit that's managing the proposed concert venue construction."

"Yeah, that's who called. Said he didn't see the accident, got there after it happened."

"Where is this construction site?"

"It's the new ballfield getting built by the folks who run the batting cage business, down toward the end of Windy Lane—that one-lane road that dead-ends into the back side of the new post office. As you know, the police as well as EMS have to respond to an unexplained death. Since the boy was dead, we called the justice of the peace, who came right away. And if it's a job site accident, OSHA will also investigate."

"And no one but Charles Boone was there?" Alice asked. Hard to imagine....

"The ballfield contractor said his workers were waiting on the roof coating to dry, so he'd closed the site and sent everyone home. And yes, before you ask, the site is fenced."

So was Charlie made to trespass? Other questions popped into her mind, but before she could ask, Files said, "What's your interest, Alice? Doesn't sound like this boy was your client, yet?"

"His mother just learned her only son died in a weird accident. His sister's here in my office, trying to learn where his body is and what happened. She's asked me to help. In addition, I'm a fellow human being." Well, not a direct answer, but surely Files would relent.

"Yeah, okay. Tell her the Travis County Medical Examiner has to be involved on an unexplained death like this. That office should be able to tell the family more later."

"But right now the family's desperate for answers. You know that."

He sighed. "Always. Yes. And I never have them all. However—"

he paused—"you can tell that young woman that we've impounded her brother's truck. It was locked. It's been checked. We've got his wallet and keys. She can pick those up here and take the truck with an okay from her mother."

Well then, thought Alice. I'm on a mission.

When Alice re-entered the conference room, Jeanie looked up, eyes red. Alice sat down next to her. "I've asked George Files, chief detective with the Coffee County Sheriff's Department, what he knows. He says that when one of the Apex managers, Conrad O'Leary, got to the site, no one was there but Charlie, and Charlie had already fallen."

"I just hate it that no one was there, no one to help him!" Jeanie's face crumpled.

"According to Files, the construction crew had gone home, waiting for the roofing sealant to dry. When Charlie fell, his watch apparently called 911, so EMS came, and also the police. O'Leary also called EMS. I'm not sure about the timing." She took a breath. "Jeanie, when there's an unexplained death, two more things happen: the police have to come, and the justice of the peace, and in this case the body had to go to the Travis County Medical Examiner for further determination of the cause of death." She paused. "Coffee County's too small to have its own medical examiner. Also, OSHA investigates workplace fatalities. And Texas Workers' Comp investigates any reimbursement owed the family."

Jeanie nodded. "All right. Thank you. So what happens next?"

"Detective Files said his office has Charlie's truck, and also his wallet and keys. They'll want your mom's okay to release them to you. But won't you also need to pick up his belongings at the place where he was staying? His studio apartment at the old Coffee Creek Hotel?"

Since the police hadn't found his phone, Alice was hoping those belongings might include Charlie's computer.

"Yes. But before anything else, Mom and I need to know what the medical examiner says."

"Would you like me to check for you?" Alice asked.

"That would be great. And I guess Charlie never had a will, right? So will you let me know what else I—or Mom and I— need to do about his—his estate, I guess you call it?" She stood up and turned to face Alice. Alice waited, watching Jeanie's young face grow more and more determined. "I also want to find out why his bosses sent him out to such a dangerous place. I still don't understand. And why did they do it the afternoon he was trying to get ready for the hearing? That makes no sense either."

"Those are good questions," Alice said. She wanted answers to the same questions, plus others. And she intended to help Jeanie and her mom, whether as paying clients or pro bono, if necessary. "It will be easier for me to get information if I'm representing you or your mother in dealing with Charlie's estate. Silla will send over an engagement letter to sign if you want us to help. Will you let us know as soon as you can?"

Jeanie nodded. "We will." She picked up her backpack, slung it over her shoulder. "I've got to get back to New Braunfels and be with Mom. But I'll be in touch."

Alice walked Charlie's sister to the door, hugged her goodbye, watched her climb into the battered RAV, imagined the sad drive home to comfort a grieving mother.

Her cell phone beeped. She checked the screen: Merry Givens. Message: "Need some advice. Any chance you could come by this morning?"

Merry had never asked for help before.

Surratt's appointment was after lunch, and the vet wasn't due at Alice's until five.

"Yes. On my way."

Like I'm Losing My Mind

Alice sped back up the creek road from town. No wildflowers yet, but pastures were turning green in the early March sun. Merry's text, though, didn't sound sunny.

She pulled into the parking lot at Goat Hill—empty except for Merry's old green van. The old ranch house offered blank windows. The creamery didn't open to visitors until noon. Alice knocked on the creamery door, with its hand-painted sign—"Coffee Creek Cheese."

When Merry opened the door, Alice tried not to gasp. Merry still looked dreadful from her encounter with the out-of-control Jersey bull—she still had black stitches on her forehead, and the bruises across her cheekbone, though less purple, were still greenish, yellowish. In addition, Merry had dark circles under her eyes, hadn't brushed her hair, apparently hadn't noticed that her flannel shirt was buttoned askew. And her usual smile was gone—just a downturned mouth.

"Come on in."

Merry locked the door behind Alice. Alice, noticing Merry was still limping, followed her into the cheese shop, then into a small office off the hallway leading to the big creamery room.

Merry sat down at the desk, pulled up a second chair and beckoned Alice to her side. She opened a small iPad and turned it so Alice could see it. Then she looked up at Alice.

Alice peered at the screen at a typescript with blanks. "'Transfer on Death Deed,'" she read aloud. "Looks like a free legal aid draft." She frowned and looked at Merry. "Why are you showing me this? Do you want me to help you draft a transfer on death deed?"

Merry's bleak face looked back at her. "This is not my iPad," she said flatly.

Uh-oh. Alice waited. Finally she asked, "Is it Denny's?"

Merry nodded, eyes full of tears. "I found this on Denny's desk last night, while he was out."

"Where's his desk?"

"Both of us used to work in here. But a few months ago he told me he needed quiet space to study. So he moved his desk into an empty bedroom he calls his office, in the house." Alice noticed her dry tone. "I don't think he's studying much, though."

"You haven't told him you've seen this?"

"No. He was out last night. I just—I just looked in his—his office."

Alice waited a little longer while Merry groped for a tissue and blew her nose. Alice took a breath. "What's going on, Merry? Has he asked you to sign a transfer on death deed?"

Merry slowly shook her head. "No, he hasn't used those words, much less asked me to sign anything. What he's focused on is cash. He tells me that Teena Ann Traynor is going to get almost two million dollars when she sells her thirty acres to the venue investors."

Wow, Alice thought. Tempting....

"This place is my family's! My parents bought this place in 1976 and named it Goat Hill. I grew up here and inherited this land from my parents. My daughter, Francine, grew up here too. She wants to take over the cheese business. I need every acre for the goats and the Jerseys. I don't want to sell a single acre!" Merry said.

"Does Denny want you to?"

"He says Teena Ann needs five more acres to get her deal done. She wants four acres on my northeast corner and one more acre just south of those. He swears he could get us $500,000 for five acres."

Alice had her calculator out. "So they're offering her over $63,300 an acre? But maybe more per acre for her five frontage acres on Old Hays, less for the rest?" Commercial frontage on Hill Country roads usually commanded a higher price.

"I think so. But Alice! Teena Ann doesn't own any creek frontage. We do! Right on Coffee Creek! It runs under the bridge over Old Hays Road onto my land and then flows south almost to the end of my property before it turns and runs over onto the Winthrop land. You've never been in the house, right?" Merry picked up the iPad and stood up. "Let me show you."

Alice followed Merry out of the creamery into the portico leading to the house. It opened directly into Merry's kitchen, which felt welcoming: old cabinets, but a big new stovetop, and a long granite-topped island with stools around it.

Merry left the iPad on the kitchen island and opened the double back doors.

Alice followed her outside onto the wooden planks of a porch that ran the width of the house, and felt the prevailing southerly wind lifting her curls, touching her forehead with cool air.

"Oh!" Alice said, before she could stop herself. Below the porch steps lay a small green lawn, bordered by a flower bed with clumps of iris and blue salvia, and a vegetable garden with tomato plants, a fig tree, and dill and basil showing green in a mulched bed.

Off to her left, below rocky limestone banks, the blue-green waters of Coffee Creek ran bubbling past the house and on downhill into the pasture until, in the distance, the creek turned right and disappeared into the trees.

"Wow, Merry. I had no idea. What a magical spot." She stood, listening to the music of the creek and feeling her shoulders relax.

"You see how I fenced off the back yard and the creek from the goats?" Merry asked. Below the steps to their right, a hogwire fence, with a protective strand of barbed wire on the top and bottom, ran from the rear of the house past the lawn and gardens, then turned sharply left until it met the rocky banks of the creek. Then the fence, still outside the creek banks, followed the creek almost to the end of Merry's pasture, where the creek bent sharply right, as did the fence. "See where the creek runs into the trees?" She pointed off to the right. "The Winthrops and I share a boundary fence on the west side of my pasture. That boundary fence runs from Old Hays to the end of my land."

"So from the house you get into your pasture through that little gate by the flower bed?"

"Yep. That gate works for humans, not goats. I can't have goats invading the creek. They don't need it for water. See the stock tank and pump house down where the creek bends?"

Alice nodded. Far out in the pasture, some of Merry's multicolored Nubian goats—black and white, reddish tan and white—were moving toward the silver metal stock tank.

"I pump creek water to the stock tank for the goats. But here at the house, I can walk straight down my back steps and then down the path to the creek and go floating naked as a jaybird, if I want. Yet Teena Ann wants me to sell her some of this creek frontage. I've told Denny, no way! This place is my life!"

Alice loved her own house, high on the bluff above a different creek—although she had to hike down to the water. No one could make her sell her place, either. She understood Merry's feelings.

"Where's the boundary between your place and Teena Ann's?"

Merry pointed left. "Look that way across the creek, into the clump of cedar." Past the banks of the creek, Alice spotted fencing with five strands of barbed wire. "That's my barbed wire east boundary fence you see. It runs from Old Hays Road all the way down to the end of my property. Teena Ann Traynor's thirty acres are entirely on the other side of that boundary fence."

"Did she tell Denny why her venue deal requires five more acres?"

"She said something about needing space for more concrete or cover. He didn't explain it very well."

Hmm, Alice thought. More concrete or cover? Maybe the investors now fear thirty acres isn't enough to allow the amount of impervious cover they want for buildings and parking. Maybe to get their projected profits from parking and facilities, the venue investors have a back-up plan?

"Are the venue people telling Teena Ann they want the same five acres Denny mentioned, the ones with creek access?"

"Denny said not necessarily, but maybe."

Alice frowned at a worrisome thought. "Merry, if the venue owned frontage on Coffee Creek, the investors might apply for a water discharge permit so they could discharge treated sewage effluent directly into the creek instead of fighting over a land application permit."

"That's all I need," groaned Merry. "Sewage effluent discharging straight into the water my goats drink. Goodbye, cheese business. And I'm not the only person relying on this creek. What about my downstream neighbors?" She checked her watch. "Not time to open yet. Let's have some iced tea."

Alice nodded and followed Merry back into the kitchen. But she was bothered by more than the sewage issue. What was Denny's real interest here? "I thought you said you need all your acreage for hay, for pasture, for the goats, and now for your Jerseys?"

"I do!" Merry put ice in tall glasses and added iced tea from a pitcher in the refrigerator. She brought lemon slices and sugar and spoons to the kitchen island and sent Alice out to the garden to cut mint sprigs.

The nicest job for guests, Alice thought, smelling the mint as she sipped her tea.

"Is Denny saying you'd get enough money from selling five acres to give up your cheese business?"

"He says we could invest the $500,000 and live on the interest. He says he could get over five percent on it."

"But that's only, what, $25,000 a year? Assuming you actually get paid $500,000. How can that replace your cheese business?"

"He keeps saying the interest would exceed our profits from cheese production. He also doesn't get it, that if we lose our agricultural exemption we'll be sunk, because without that exemption I can't afford the taxes. So we'd still need to keep raising goats. I use every bit of my thirty acres—I even grow hay on the far side of the creek to feed the goats. I don't think Denny grasps the balancing act I operate on, doesn't see it would be uneconomic to run all this machinery, advertise, hire someone to help in the creamery, if I had less milk to turn into cheese, less product to sell." Merry shook her head, stirring sugar into her iced tea. "He even said we could buy milk from other producers. That would make nonsense of our marketing—'homemade cheeses from our own herd!'"

Alice remembered the old covenants—didn't they permit sales but only for agricultural products from the property itself? "I think you're okay selling cheese you make here on your own turf, with milk from your own herd. But it's not clear your land restrictions, your covenants, would let you sell cheese here made from milk coming from land you don't own."

Merry's face brightened. "Really? That's good news...at least it's an argument I can make. But he seems absolutely determined to make me agree to sell some of this land to Teena Ann. Which she will then sell to the venue investors."

"It's your land, though, right?"

"Yes. Under my will, when I die, Goat Hill goes straight to Francine. Denny knew that when we married."

Alice's eyes returned to the iPad.

"So why do you think Denny has this draft deed on his iPad?"

Merry's face fell. "I guess he's hoping I'll agree to write a new will and sign the land over to him instead. He sort of raised that a couple of months ago, but I reminded him it goes to Francine."

I'm not her lawyer, I'm her friend, Alice kept telling herself. But Denny's interest in this kind of deed—a transfer on death deed—made her nervous. Also, if Merry wanted to keep her land and her cheese business for her daughter—and didn't want the venue next door—why transfer valuable creekfront property to Teena Ann for Teena Ann to sell to a concert venue?

"How do *you* feel about the concert venue, Merry?"

Instant reply. "I absolutely *hate* it."

"So you shouldn't be the one who helps Teena Ann—or the venue—get another five acres while you lose a chunk of your creek. Especially when your neighbors oppose her proposed venue and support your cheese business!"

"I hadn't thought of that. I'll tell Denny we can't help her. And that'll be the end of it." Merry finally smiled.

I've got to ask, Alice told herself. "Merry, forgive me this question. Denny doesn't—he wouldn't—do you any harm? Hit you?"

"Oh, Alice!" Merry said. She lowered her eyes for a moment, then said, "Denny's not the hitting kind. It's just—I hoped this marriage would work. No, Denny just nags."

"Hey, how's that Jersey bull doing?"

"He's settled down," Merry said. "After I called and told our vet what happened, she came out and got a blood sample. She's waiting for results. It's Dr. Annabelle Duncan. Do you know her?"

Alice nodded.

Merry gave Alice a lopsided grin. "Thanks for coming out here today, Alice. All this mess—the bull, the venue, seeing that deed—lately I've felt like I'm losing my mind. Like, one afternoon two weeks ago, I drove to the Coffee County tax office to re-register my van. But when I got there, I couldn't find my driver's license in my wallet, so I couldn't register the van. Came home, couldn't find it anywhere. Next morning, I looked again in the pocket of my fleece vest, hanging on the coatrack. And there it was." She shook her head. "I thought I'd checked there the day before but—did I? Nutty."

Alice laughed. "For me it's always my phone. Where'd I leave it?

Car? Kitchen counter?" It was good to see Merry smile again. "You've got so much going on with the creamery. Your life will be easier once Francine finishes culinary school and pitches in here."

The two sat at the kitchen island for a few more minutes, talking and sipping tea, until Alice remembered Merry had to open the shop at noon and she herself needed to prepare for James Surratt's rescheduled appointment.

"Hey, it's starting to rain," Merry said, opening the front door for Alice. "Hallelujah. My pasture's so dry." Alice gave her a quick hug, then dashed through the rain to her Discovery and headed toward town again down the creek road, windshield wipers on high. She was feeling more cheerful about Merry until an unwelcome thought popped up: maybe Denny wouldn't want to have a different neighbor sell five acres to Teena Ann. Maybe he had an interest himself—a personal interest—in helping Teena Ann?

And maybe she should have warned Merry that her neighbor, Teena Ann Traynor, was rumored to treat rules as "mere suggestions." Note to self, Alice thought—what else does Silla know about Teena Ann?

But sufficient unto the day were the evils thereof. Right?

Chapter Eight

What's He Got?

Alice parked in the office driveway and abandoned her wet jacket in the kitchen as Silla pointed her down the hall to the conference room. "Surratt got here early," she whispered. "I got him ice water, got him settled."

James Surratt stood up from the far side of the conference room table as Alice opened the door. He was tall—nearly six foot three, she guessed, and about sixty, according to her file. Thinning gray hair, tired face, but attentive eyes, and a good handshake. Alice could not abide a limp male handshake or—even worse—the partial crusher, where a man grabbed only her fingers, but not her palm, and crushed the defenseless digits. Surratt passed the handshake test.

"Thanks for seeing me," he said. "I'm glad to meet you in person. I've heard good things." Rain was drumming on the office roof. "Glad to hear it rain, too. Our watersheds need a good soaking."

Alice nodded. "Hey, I appreciated your comments at the public meeting last night."

"Criminal, that project," he said, shaking his head. "I'm serious. People who would put a Hill Country creek at risk—a creek is helpless. Ruining a creek? It's like committing murder! Killing something beautiful! The wildlife, aquatic life...the joy we take in it, and its sheer beauty—we'll all be hurt. We were talking about it this morning at the coffee shop in the old Coffee Creek Hotel, me and some other master naturalists. We have breakfast there every Wednesday."

"Nice." She sat down in the chair across from his.

"I brought our old wills along so you could look them over." He removed a stack of papers from a manila folder, leaned across to hand her the stack, and sat back down, picking up his glass of water.

Alice began paging through what he'd brought: wills, powers of attorney, and advance directives for him and his wife, Cynthia. Alice quickly glanced at the beneficiaries—children, grandchildren—then flipped to the last pages to see signatures and notarizations, all dated ten years earlier. "Ah. You mentioned you'd worked with Sonny Bonway before." Alice knew Bonway, who'd died the year before, as a careful lawyer.

"Right. But we'd like you to review everything, given current tax laws."

Alice nodded. "Happy to help. I'll also need to hear about any potentially significant changes since you signed these—like the current situations of children and grandchildren. And your thoughts on health care, charitable plans, any big lifestyle changes."

"Sounds good. I need Cynthia here for that." Surratt began coughing, pulled a bandana from his pocket, stood, walked to the window, still coughing. Alice jumped up, grabbed the pitcher from the credenza, poured more water in his glass, and set it back on the table. He stood at the window, back to her, trying to stop coughing. Sounded painful, she thought. Watching him hold the red bandana to his mouth, she found herself thinking of John Keats, Robert Louis Stevenson, and others, coughing blood and dying young, likely from tuberculosis. She shook her head, trying to clear away the deathbed portrait of Keats stuck in her mind from college art class.

"Sorry," he said, returning to his chair. "Allergies. Must be pollen or something. Maybe this rain will clear the air."

"Cedar season's nearly over," she said, watching his face. "I understand you're the local water testing guru. Are you retired?"

"Yes, as of last week. But I'll keep working with the master naturalists. Good thing, getting volunteers involved in our waterways. I enjoy those folks." He smiled slightly, then pointed to the stack of documents. "I don't really have any issues with what Sonny did. Cynthia may want to specify additional gifts—there's a church orphanage we usually help. Talking to you, we may think of something else. I just want to be sure these are—are in good shape."

Alice nodded, noticing again the tiredness in his face. "I also always suggest reviewing your Advance Directive with care. Our ideas can change about medical care...."

"Good idea. Also"—he pointed to the stack—"I hear there's a new form besides the Advance Directive. POST? Or POLST? Something like that?"

"Right. Physician Orders for Life-Sustaining Treatment. It's helpful in specific situations, like if you can't make your own health care decisions."

He nodded slowly. "Let's make another appointment to discuss your thoughts on our existing documents. Maybe you could give me a copy of that new form so Cynthia and I can be thinking about it too."

He stood abruptly and turned back to the window, again coughing into his bandana.

Alice sent an email to Silla, attaching a copy of a current POLST form used in Texas: "Please print for the Surratts."

He turned back toward her, with a small smile. "Sorry about the cough, and thanks for your help, Alice. Cynthia and I are anxious to get these wills updated."

Alice looked up from her calendar. "What if we meet again next week?" she offered. "Would Wednesday at ten work? Let Silla know. She's also got a copy of that POLST form for you."

She stood. He thanked her and retraced his steps down the hall. Silla handed him a brown envelope, then carefully shut the door behind him.

"Hope you didn't catch anything," said Silla. "What's he got? Croup? Whooping cough? TB? Covid?"

"Lord, I hope not," Alice said, handing the Surratt documents to Silla. "Listen, he and his wife can come back next Wednesday at ten. I need to review their old wills."

"I've already set up the file," Silla said. "Hope he's not as whoopy next week. Maybe I'll leave a pack of masks in the conference room." She tilted her head, lifted an eyebrow. "Don't want you getting sick now that you've finally set a wedding date."

Alice rolled her eyes.

Silla continued. "Call Jeanie Boone. Her mama does want us to help find out what happened to Charlie and figure out what to do with his estate. I've drafted an engagement letter."

She put it on Alice's desk and stood waiting for her to scan the draft.

Challenging assignment, Alice thought. What *did* happen to Charlie? Why did Apex need him to check that particular site on that particular afternoon? Was Apex negligent, sending him up something like an iron girder, all alone, with no safety harness? On property Apex didn't own? She inserted a short phrase in the otherwise vanilla tasks set forth in the engagement letter: "...and review applicable circumstances with respect to his estate." Including negligence...which might apply to Charlie's employer, Worth Engineers, and their client, Apex. And was there a potential conflict with the City? Not as far as she knew. Nevertheless...she tapped her pencil on the desk, then added a condition that permitted her to withdraw in the event of potential conflict with the City of Coffee Creek.

She handed the engagement letter back to Silla, who scanned the additions, gazed at Alice and nodded. "I'll send it back right now. Inquiring minds want to know..." She swept out the door.

Alice's cell rang. Mayor Wilson plunged in before Alice could finish saying "Good afternoon...?"

"Alice! What the hell is going on with this Apex deal? We've got no one showing up for the public meeting and now a dead engineer. On the ballfield our city kids might be using!"

"Mayor, the Apex guy, Conrad O'Leary, told the police that when he himself reached the site, the young engineer was already dead. The police told Jeanie he apparently slipped off a beam leading up to the roof."

"But that doesn't explain why Apex had him out at that site—which is not Apex property—in the first place. Especially given the public meeting just hours away? We need to know. I don't like being ignorant when we may have to take a position on this permit at some point. How're you gonna find that out, Alice?"

Alice paused. "You know, Mayor, Charles Boone told me before the hearing that he was going to talk to the TCEQ guys about impervious cover. He'd come across some contractor plans that didn't match what he remembered had been submitted. He said he might be wrong, though." Her answer might sound like a non sequitur to the mayor's question—why Charles Boone was sent to the site in the first place.

But the mayor got there fast. "Impervious cover could be the key," she growled. "How much you can build under your permit depends on the amount of impervious cover."

"Mayor, why don't we send an Open Records Act request for the entire TCEQ file? There could be a phone record of Boone's call. And I'll follow up with the Travis County Medical Examiner, see if he can tell us anything more about what happened to that poor boy."

"Good. Keep me posted. And Bradley Ott." The mayor hung up.

I always do, Alice thought, walking to Silla's desk. "Silla, per the mayor, let's send an open records request, on our usual form, asking

TCEQ for a complete copy of their file on the Apex venue permit request, specifically including all phone records. Can we send that request today? By email? And ask TCEQ to expedite it?"

"Electronic or paper?"

"Electronic, I think. Easier to search," Alice said.

"Got it. Charge the costs to the City?"

"Yes. And you know who to call if the agency slow-walks us, right?"

Silla fluttered her eyelashes. "I'm on it." Then she scowled. "But, Alice, there is absolutely no excuse for what happened to Charles Boone. Is there?"

Alice slowly shook her head no. "I don't think so. As safety-conscious as that boy was? I'm having trouble grasping why he would do something so dangerous. Which reminds me, we also need a letter to the medical examiner, requesting a copy of the autopsy report, including all photographs."

But would there be an autopsy? Or would the busy medical examiner just decide that yes, the kid had died after falling from a height— no autopsy warranted?

"I'll get that letter ready," Silla said. "Surely someone saw more of what happened than whatever the Apex guy told the police."

Alice nodded. "Maybe... not much traffic on Windy Lane, though."

Back at her desk she called the Travis County medical examiner's office and learned no decision had yet been made about an autopsy. She told the examiner's office to expect a letter; she'd want the report. Would that slow down any speedy decision not to do an autopsy? Maybe, maybe not.

On my way home to meet the vet, she thought, I'll just swing down Windy Lane.

Chapter Nine

A Glint Of Gold

Rain had stopped, but muddy stormwater was still rushing into the storm sewers as Alice turned onto Windy Lane. When she reached the construction site, she pulled over to the curb—no trucks, no workers, no one in sight.

Farther down the road, where Windy Lane dead-ended, she could see the employee parking lot behind the new post office. It was past four-thirty—the post office closed at four.

She climbed out of her car. In the vacant lot across the street, a large dumpster labeled "construction waste" sat on the ground, along with some big metal drums. An orange tarp, flapping in the wind, partially covered a stack of iron girders. Must be their staging area.

At the construction site itself yellow crime scene tape flapped along the chain-link fence. Alice stood at the curb, staring through the fence at the partly-finished ballpark construction. On the ground, concrete tiers rose in a semicircle for future seating, with no seats yet installed. Four groups of iron girders supported the central section of the metal roof, which projected partway over the seating area behind home plate, with short extensions extending over future seating behind first and third bases. A pair of apparently temporary iron girders, about four feet apart, slanted up from the bare ground just inside the construction fence, then above the bare concrete tiers and up toward the edge of the roof. A makeshift rope handrail began partway up the twin iron girders, about twenty feet above the ground.

She noted the printed signs wired onto the chain link fence every forty feet or so: "KEEP OUT – AUTHORIZED PERSONNEL ONLY." Close to the curb, where the ground was torn up by heavy equipment entering the site, someone had wired closed the chain link sections. Had Charlie had to twist open the wire to enter? Or climbed over the fence?

Looking up at the two slanted girders, Alice shuddered, imagining trying to climb up them to reach the roof. Then she wondered: where exactly had Charlie fallen?

She heard an engine and turned to see a UPS truck slowing, then stopping. The driver waved. She recognized the same guy who delivered parcels to her office. To her surprise he climbed out of the truck and walked over. "Hi, Rich," she said, glad to have remembered his name.

"Hi, Alice. I just finished my last delivery of the day to the PO," he said, thumb pointing over his shoulder and back toward the post office. He stared at the construction site.

Was this his daily route?

"Rich, were you here on Tuesday, when that young man fell?"

"I didn't see him fall. But I did see him starting up one of those girders."

"And he was all alone?"

Rich turned to her, eyebrows drawn together in a frown. "No. Not alone. When I drove by, I saw two trucks here. Another guy was standing inside the fence. Kind of a big guy."

"And the young man was up on a girder?"

"Uh-huh. About ten feet up, but he'd stopped." He shook his head. "I don't always love my job, but I sure didn't like what he was having to do." He looked at his watch. "Whoops, got to get my van back to the office. See ya."

And he was gone.

Another truck? "Kind of a big guy"? She'd better call Files again.

Alice moved closer to the fence. Partway to the roof one of the temporary girders showed a shiny patch, glittering with raindrops. Inside the fence the rain had turned the ground, chewed up by heavy equipment and work boots, into sloppy mud. As she turned to leave, a glint of gold caught her eye. Just a bit of gold, in the mud by the construction fence, uncovered by the rain.

She reached for her phone.

Beep...beep...beep.... Files didn't pick up. Finally his phone instructed her to leave a message.

"George, it's Alice Greer. I stopped by the Windy Lane ballfield site. Have you—" how to put this?—"has the department finished its site investigation? Because I see something in the mud here, after all this rain—not sure it was visible before. Might be a shell casing. And before you ask, yes, I'm outside the fence!"

She hung up and looked at her watch. Oh lord, nearly five o'clock. The vet would be heading for her place, expecting to find the burros secure in their corral and ready for their shots and de-worming. Alice climbed back into the car and sped home, realizing only after she turned off Old Hays into her property that she still needed to tell Files about Rich.

As she clicked open the solar gate, she saw the vet's truck heading back down the drive toward her. Dr. Annabelle Duncan, the new vet who'd joined her old vet's practice, braked and climbed down from the driver's seat, leaving her assistant in the cab. Jeans, hat, vest with useful pockets, blonde hair in a ponytail—not only elegant but an animal whisperer—and an exceedingly savvy vet, with special expertise in lab analysis.

Alice parked and climbed out to talk to Annabelle.

"Alice, we're all done," Annabelle began. "Big Boy and Queenie behaved well. They made Princess stand still too."

"How do you do it? Do you give off calmness vibrations? Wait, that's an oxymoron."

"They're used to me. Also...the treats, you know." She gave Alice a wry look. "Princess doesn't need more treats. She's getting...um...a little pudgy."

Alice squinted at Annabelle. "What am I supposed to do? Put her in the corral?"

"No, she's fine. Burros are efficient at fat-building. Princess is preparing in case, you know, she has to lead a caravan from Egypt to Syria like donkeys used to do."

"How's the practice?" Alice asked. "I keep imagining you riding English and competing in dressage back in Georgia. And now here you are in your boots and jeans and cowgirl hat."

"I'm liking it," Annabelle responded. "Huge variety out here in the Hill Country. Besides...." Her face turned pink.

Alice grinned. "You've met someone, I hear. Tyler Junkin's cousin Eddie, from Wimberley, right?" Alice liked and respected Tyler, a seasoned criminal defense lawyer she'd met when she first came to Coffee Creek. "Tyler says Eddie's pretty smitten."

From Annabelle's face, she too was smitten. "He's a great guy. I'm—I'm really glad we met." Then she said, still blushing, "This was my last call today. I've got to change. Eddie's taking me to Tillie's for dinner."

"Very nice!" Alice grinned, imagining the two lovers in that romantic venue. Annabelle climbed back into her pickup and waved goodbye; Alice returned to her used green Discovery, remembering how Kinsear had found it for her after her own beloved old pickup got shot up. Heading down her driveway for a lonesome evening in an empty house, she couldn't help remembering the fizzy feeling she'd had when she first re-encountered Kinsear after moving to Coffee Creek. But at the moment, the man was 1800 miles away in New York, four long hours by air. Probably busy resolving some dispute for his old partners. He wouldn't get back until Friday.

She couldn't stop herself. She picked up the phone and punched his number.

"Hey, I was just about to call you," he said in a low voice. "Hang on." Then, a little louder, "Meeting's finally over. At least I've escorted myself out of the room. How's it going?"

"Did you hear about the concert venue public meeting here where the applicant didn't show? And about the venue team's baby engineer falling to his death off a girder at the ballfield, just before the hearing?"

"Wait a sec, counselor. What's your role here?"

"The City asked me to attend the public meeting, and the baby engineer who was supposed to represent the applicant asked me to help with his will. Oh, Ben, he was a nice young man. He loved bridges. Wanted to go see the Arkadiko Bridge in Greece. He shouldn't have died."

"What do you mean, fell off a girder?"

"Too long to explain on the phone." She realized she wanted Kinsear's insight, his take on this weird week. "But I really need to talk to you about it so I can understand why it's so—so unbelievable."

"I'm on the 1 p.m. flight from JFK on Friday. Back a little after 5. Traffic will be horrible, so I've made us reservations for early dinner in Austin, at Wink. I like the way that guy picks out wine. I'll catch a ride from the airport if you'll meet me there and then you can tell me all about this venue business. Maybe after dinner we could swing by Sam's Town Point, listen to some music, do some dancing. What do you think?"

"Sounds great." What a relief, to tell him everything that had happened, watch his face change, watch those eyebrows rise as he picked up the details, the possibilities in her story—some, she realized, she

may not have recognized yet.
    Plus she loved dancing with Kinsear.
    "I miss you," she added. "It's too quiet out here."
    "You can't hear the bluebonnets growing?"
    She grinned. "Love you. See you Friday."
    Two days felt like forever.

Chapter Ten

A Disgusting Display

Seven a.m., Thursday: Alice was in her car, ready to leave for the office, when Files called. "You're right, it was a shell casing," he said. "Gotta say, you've got sharp eyes."

"Just happened to be there after it rained so hard," Alice said. "But why was it there?"

"That's the question, isn't it?" Files's deep voice answered. "Looked pretty new. Also, it's the only one we found. Still, so far as we know, Charles Boone wasn't shot. So, is it relevant?"

"That shell casing was right inside the fence," Alice said. "Also, while I was there, the UPS guy came by—Rich. He said that on Tuesday afternoon he saw Charlie—Charles—partway up an iron girder, maybe ten feet from the ground. But Charlie wasn't alone, according to Rich. He said he saw two trucks, not one, and a second guy standing by the fence."

"Who's Rich? Why'd he stop to talk to you?"

"He'd just finished his last delivery at the post office and saw me. I know him—he delivers our packages at the office."

"I need his full name and contact info."

Silla would know. "I'll call you right back."

Alice called Silla, explaining the early call from Files. "Woodworth. Rich Woodworth," Silla said, and reeled off the UPS office phone number.

Alice called Files back immediately with Silla's info, then asked, "Any word from the Travis County Medical Examiner yet about Charlie Boone? I know his family's anxious to hear."

"Not yet."

Driving into town, Alice wondered why Conrad O'Leary had lied to the police. When had he called 911? Had he arrived at the construction site in time to see Charlie fall but not wanted to get himself—or Apex—involved? Was his call to EMS an attempted coverup, intended to suggest that Charlie himself had decided to climb the girder alone, without help, without waiting for any supervision?

Had O'Leary noticed the passing UPS truck, or not? If he saw the truck, did he assume its anonymous occupant would never remember seeing him?

And that shell casing? The south side of Coffee Creek was only now beginning to see development. The ballfield site was part of an old ranch. Owners—and neighbors—could've used the property for target shooting, for hunting. A shell casing could've been lying there in the dirt for years. But Files thought this one looked new. Alice had questions for him: what time did Charles's watch call EMS? What time did O'Leary call 911? Had anyone heard any shots?

When she reached the office, Silla had already made coffee. Alice followed the aroma to the kitchen, filled her favorite mug, and added some milk. As soon as Alice reached her desk, Silla marched in and laid down a stack of papers. "Okay, here are your client bills. If you'll review them, I'll mail them today. And where's your letter to Henry Winthrop about the covenants that apply to the venue?"

"Thanks for the reminder. Give me a sec. Then we'll send it to him by email and regular mail."

Alice found her draft letter and typed in a paragraph offering to discuss the covenant research at Henry Winthrop's convenience. If she had to guess, he might be leery of the stress and expense of litigation. With Coffee Creek running through his ranch, he was directly in the line of fire if sewage effluent from the concert venue polluted the creek. That alone gave him reason to challenge the proposed permit, and maybe he could save money by joining with the plaintiffs represented by Sandy Graves.

But unlike his downstream neighbors, under the existing covenants Winthrop also had the separate legal right to prevent commercial use of the venue property. She'd remind him that he shouldn't "sit on his rights": he should move promptly to enforce the covenants before the investors spent substantial money on construction. She forwarded the revised letter to Silla and sent herself a reminder: call Winthrop later.

Then, thinking about Charles Boone and the venue permit, Alice left her desk and found Silla. "Where are we on our open records request?"

"I called the agency yesterday and then again first thing this morning. They say it's a lot but they'll have it done by noon."

In any disputed case, Alice felt the same buzz from opening a new cache of documents as from picking up a hot new murder mystery, especially when she spotted a document offering a potential path to victory. She was anxious to see if the TCEQ file contained any records of discussions on impervious cover standards, any queries or promises from Apex about proposed impervious cover, any evidence Apex was pressing for slacker standards.

But the main driving force?

The haunting thought of Charles Boone plunging from an iron girder.

Everything was hanging fire: the open records file, the medical examiner's report....

Trying to calm her restlessness, she'd just sat down at her desk when her cell rang. Jeanie Boone.

"Alice, hi. Listen, my friend Maggie is driving me up to Coffee Creek today so I can get Charlie's truck from the police and pack up his apartment. And I wondered if you'd heard any more...?"

Alice explained the wait for the medical examiner's report. "I'll put in another call," she said. "Maybe you and Maggie could stop by the office later?"

"Okay. Oh, and my mom's back at work, but she asked me to tell you we do want your help. She signed your engagement letter, and she's mailing it today." Jeanie hung up.

Silla stood in the doorway. "Alice, last night I went dancing in Luckenbach. With Bender."

Bender, an archeologist, was the reason Silla had begun flying lessons—so she could recognize stone age ruins from the air. Which was how Silla had helped save Alice, months earlier, from being left to die in a shed, hands bound, her red bandana over her eyes. Alice still hadn't been able to wear that bandana again. Blue, gold, okay—and she'd bought a new black bandana to try.

Mentally she shook away the memory. "Can he dance, Silla?"

"He's coming along. But listen. You know who else was there?"

"Tell me!"

"Teena Ann Traynor!"

"Can *she* dance?"

"Oh, please. Know who she was waggling her fanny at?"

Riveted, Alice shook her head.

"The husband of a local cheesemaker."

"Denny...?" breathed Alice.

"The same. I mean, a disgusting display. They were hanging all over each other."

Pieces began falling into place.

"But if you ask me—" Silla paused. "Part of it was a put-on act. *He* is smitten. But when he'd go get more beers? She'd lose interest, start looking at her phone, make eyes at the band, know what I mean? *He's* head over heels. *She* wants something."

"Like five acres of Merry's property?"

Silla nodded. "That's my guess."

"Did she see you?" Alice didn't want any more accidents, like the ones Merry had suffered.

Silla shook her head no. "Don't think so. I wasn't in rodeo garb. And I kept Bender dancing around the back of the dance floor where those two couldn't see us—she was twirling around in front of the band." Her eyes narrowed: "Listen, I could take Teena Ann any time." Then she leaned forward, hands on her hips: "But wait, there's more!"

"Tell me!"

"*Well*," said Silla, "The word from Houston—this comes from a rodeo buddy so it's pure gold—latest word on the Traynors is that after Daddy remarried last year, he started spending big dollars on his new wife. They bought a place in River Oaks—you can guess how expensive—because new wife wanted to start married life with a totally new house, new furniture, new everything. I guess that means Teena Ann will have to decorate her own room—if new mommy saved one for her. Also, their honeymoon was a round-the-world-on-private-jet affair. But wait—there's more!"

"More spending?"

"No. Despite his big show of dollar-power last year, more recent news is that Daddy Traynor made some bad fracking bets in Oklahoma and had to sell some assets to cover those bets. Word is he's trimming his sails. Which means less largesse for Teena Ann. She may really need to cash in on her thirty acres on Old Hays Road."

"Aha. So if the venue deal fails?"

"She won't be happy. But meanwhile, she'll try anything to get what she wants. I mean anything." Silla made a face and swung back out the door, leaving Alice to think about Merry, Denny, and Teena Ann.

*****

Toiling away at her desk, reviewing client bills, Alice saw a Ford 150 truck pulling up to the curb, followed by a battered blue RAV. Jeanie and friend?

She met the two girls at the front door. Jeanie had the drawn, sleep-deprived look of someone who'd been socked in the stomach by a loved one's death, someone still trying to figure out how to manage facts that could not be managed. She introduced her companion—"This is Maggie Simon, my best friend since kindergarten. I couldn't deal with any of this without her." Then, prodded by Maggie, she blurted, "Alice! We think someone searched Charlie's apartment! You should see it!"

Alice walked them back to the conference room; Silla brought coffee. Alice leaned forward in her chair. "Okay. Tell us everything."

"Well, first we went to the Sheriff's Department. The officers gave us Charlie's keys and wallet and helped us find his truck in this big fenced lot," Jeanie said. "Maggie's going to drive it back to New Braunfels for me. The police said they were keeping his garment bag in the evidence room and that was all there was in the truck. They said they'd already taken a look at his apartment and it was okay for us to go up there. They said no problem, they'd left it neat. Then we set off for the old Coffee Creek Hotel. We had the key to his apartment, but we didn't know which one it was, so we had to ask at the desk."

"The guy there gave us a funny look," Maggie added. "Then he said, '4-C,' and up we went."

Jeanie continued: "Charlie had sent me and Mom pictures of his apartment, so I knew what it looked like. Plus, I grew up with Mom asking me why I couldn't keep my room as neat as Charlie's. He's— he was a neatnik. Born engineer. He sent us pictures when his firm sent him to Coffee Creek for this gig." She pulled up photos on her phone—shipshape closet, tidy kitchenette, perfectly made bed.

"But when we walked into apartment 4-C—drawers were pulled out on his desk and the bureau, the closet doors were wide open, kitchen cabinets open—the lid was even off his garbage bin and on the floor. Like someone was looking for something."

Alice frowned. Maybe the police needed to hear this.

Jeanie went on: "We packed up all his clothes, got his belongings out of the bathroom—filled up three big cardboard boxes." She teared up. "I couldn't bear it, having to box up his toothbrush, his shaving cream, his books."

"Another weird thing—" Maggie added—"when we got out of the elevator downstairs, Jeanie led the way. We were carrying those boxes. The guy at the desk nodded at Jeanie and asked me, 'She's Charlie's sister, huh?' I said 'yes,' and he said, 'So does he have a big brother too? Older guy?' I said 'no,' and he got a really funny look. Then he said, 'Oh, I hear the phone,' and he hurried back into the office behind the desk. So we couldn't ask him if the 'older guy' had wanted to get into Charlie's apartment."

Jeanie said, "Anyway, now we've got Charlie's beloved new truck— he bought one with a big center console. The office package, that's what he called it."

Alice stood. "Let's go look." The police wouldn't have missed a computer, though....

Charlie's truck still gave off the faint scent of new leather and Charlie's after-shave, faint and citrusy. Alice watched as Jeanie lifted the center console lid and peered inside. "Not much here, just a blank sticky pad and pens," she said.

"What about under the seats?" Alice asked. "Any sign of his computer?"

Jeanie opened the back door, clambered onto the rear bench seat, and leaned over, peering under the driver's seat, then the passenger seat. "Nothing here. Just like the police said. But wait!" Her eyes widened. "I just remembered!" She slapped her forehead. "What a dunce!"

She hurried to her blue RAV, yanked open the door and peered under the front passenger seat. When she stood up, she was cradling a silver MacBook Air laptop. "I guess my head's been so messed up about Charlie, I forgot. He'd left his stuff in my car when I picked him up for lunch that day. I guess I blanked on everything after the police called us." She stopped on the sidewalk, looking down at the laptop. "To think that lunch date was the last time I saw him alive. He thanked me again for that new messenger bag Mom and I gave him for his birthday. Then she blinked away tears. "He coveted one from the Manready store in Houston but said it was too expensive. Mom and I saved up and surprised him. Typical Charlie, too disciplined to spend money on himself."

With Jeanie carrying their prize, the three returned to the conference room, joined by Silla. Alice said, "Jeanie, you remember Charlie was concerned about the amount of impervious cover the concert venue would need? And the limits under the rules?"

Jeanie nodded. "Yes. He wanted to understand in case there were questions at the hearing."

"It's possible his computer contains important evidence," Alice said. "We need to be sure nothing is added, subtracted, or lost. For example, the police don't have his phone. But if someone else does, and they delete some of Charlie's notes or records, those might also be deleted from this computer. We don't want that to happen. So we need to get someone to make a mirror image of this computer, immediately."

Jeanie's eyes were huge. So were Maggie's. "You know someone who could do that?"

"Roddy Ratliff, aka Minor Genius. He's helped me preserve some—well, pretty critical evidence, in the past. He's only two blocks away." Alice found Roddy's contact info on her phone. She put him on speakerphone and called; he answered; she gave a brief summary.

"Can someone bring it over?" he asked.

Alice looked at Silla, who nodded and said, "I'm on my way, Roddy."

"Okay. Don't touch a single button on that laptop."

With Jeanie and Maggie finally en route back to New Braunfels, Maggie in the truck, Jeanie in her RAV, Alice left a message for George Files: Charlie's sister and her friend thought his apartment had been searched, the girls had found Charles Boone's computer under the seat in his sister's car, and Minor Genius was making a copy before he delivered the computer to the Coffee Creek Sheriff's Department.

Silla stuck her head in the office. "Barbara Winthrop called; she says it looks like her dad wants to go forward. He'll call you later today to confirm."

*****

Alice's phone rang again.

Merry, her voice a controlled fury.

"Alice, remember you told me I should have received a letter from the environmental agency telling me about the draft permit for the venue and the public meeting date? And I told you I never got one?"

"I remember," Alice said, listening intently.

"I can't leave the creamery right now, have to watch the temperature gauge on the milk. Do you have time to come by?"

"I'll be there in ten minutes." Then a vision of Merry's bruised face flashed before her. What if Merry's discovery had triggered another confrontation? "Is Denny there?"

"No, he's not."

"On my way." Alice grabbed her keys, told Silla where she was going, and hurried to the car, the fury in Merry's voice still ringing in her ears.

Chapter   Eleven

What The Hell's Going On?

Too early for customers at Merry's. Alice parked by the door to the creamery and rang the bell.

"Come in." Merry's face was grim. The stitches were out, Alice saw, and the bruises fading.

Alice followed Merry into her office in the creamery, where Merry picked up an envelope and thrust it toward Alice, lifting up the flap with her thumb. "This was buried in Denny's sock drawer. See, the seal looks wrinkled like the envelope was steamed open, but someone got impatient and pulled the flap open too fast. One spot's torn."

Alice took the envelope—TCEQ return address—and pulled out the letter, clearly addressed to Merilee Givens. The letter was TCEQ's standard notice of public meeting for permits, inviting recipients to attend and comment.

"*HE HID MY MAIL*," Merry hissed. "*MY* mail. He knew I had a right to get notice of the hearing. And he *hid* it."

Alice waited.

"Alice, I still have the right to protest that permit, don't I?"

"That's not clear—you didn't submit comments. But you have something even more important, Merry," Alice said. "Your land, and your neighbor Henry Winthrop's land, and Teena Ann's land, are all subject to a covenant that prohibits commercial use except as you and I discussed—products made on your land from your agricultural uses."

"I remember...."

"And each of you three landowners has the right to prohibit commercial use on any of the three parcels."

A pause. Merry's face changed. "You mean I can *prohibit* the venue?"

"Yep."

"Will you help me, Alice?"

"I can try," Alice said. "There'll be some expenses. Are you sure you're ready? Stress, cost, time spent dealing with discovery and experts?"

"Alice, I've got to save my business. For myself and for Francine."

Merry's phone rang. She looked at the screen. "Got to take this, Alice, it's the vet." Then: "Hi, Annabelle?" She lifted her head, listening, then frowned and asked, "What's that?"

Meanwhile Alice stood wondering if she had an obligation to tell

Merry where Silla had seen Denny and Teena Ann last night. Maybe Merry already knew? Maybe she'd guessed?

Merry was still on the phone. "But how did it get that stuff in its blood?" A pause while she listened, then thanked the vet.

"Well, Alice," she said, "the Jersey bull's blood test puts a new twist on things. Annabelle Duncan says the test showed the bull had something called 'hordenine' in its blood. She was really surprised."

Alice had never heard that word. "What did you call it?"

"H-o-r-d-e-n-i-n-e. Annabelle had to spell it for me. She says it's a stimulant, barred at rodeos and so on."

"So your Jersey bull already had the drug in its blood when you were unloading," Alice said. "When and where could that have happened?"

Merry looked at the ceiling, remembering. "On Monday morning after milking, I took my truck and trailer and picked up the bull about ten, then left him in the trailer out in the parking area, with water and a pile of feed, to settle down. I planned to drive the trailer into the pasture to let him out. But I also needed to start a big batch of cheese, and I wound up watching the milk thermometer like a hawk for a couple of hours. Must have been about one when I went back to get him out of the trailer."

"But you saw the rancher load him into the trailer. Did he behave then?"

"Uh-huh. The rancher called the bull 'Mister Tractable.'"

"And when you unlocked the trailer?"

"The bull started madly thrashing around, banging the bars, tossing his head. I assumed Mr. Tractable was tired of being cooped up and needed to get out."

"Merry, after you parked his trailer in the courtyard, someone could've driven up, and—what? Poked a syringe into him? Put something in his feed? What did Dr. Duncan say?"

"She said it must have been a pretty big dose. She also said she couldn't imagine how we'd have gotten the bull into the trailer in the first place if he'd already been doped with that stuff. Plus she'd already contacted the rancher, who said he'd never even heard of hordenine, much less used it."

Merry's entire demeanor had changed. Squared shoulders; set jaw; flashing eyes. "Anyway, back to this letter. No more Miss Nice Guy, Alice. I've got to protect everything I've got. In case you're wondering, that no longer includes Denny."

Alice loved "Miss Nice Guy." She was wondering whether that meant Merry already knew about Denny's outing with Teena Ann, when Merry continued: "Alice, I've got a confession. I don't think Denny's really working on a Realtor's license. When he says he's studying at the Coffee Creek Library? Or when he says he's attending a workshop in Austin on the law of homeowner associations, for goodness' sake?" She tilted her head. "I know where he is. I stuck an AirTag in his car."

"Ah," said Alice. "I was wondering if I should tell you—"

"Where he was last night? Luckenbach, Texas, per that AirTag."

"Silla saw him there with Teena Ann."

Merry snorted. "Nice. Everyone calls her a cheater, who'll do anything to win. Even abuse her horses." Then her face changed. "So do other people know, Alice? Is Denny making me look like a fool in front of everyone in Coffee Creek? I mean, I've got a business to run. And a reputation to think of! And what about Francine? I don't want her mortified!"

"I honestly don't know if anyone but Silla has seen him out with Teena Ann."

"Doesn't matter. I knew Denny was a bit of a lightweight, but I'm done. I had a friend who got married too soon to a young college prof who turned out to be the wrong guy. When she found out he was bonking the grad students in his department, she cut the crotches out of his boxer shorts and threw them out on the front lawn for all the neighbors to see." Merry snorted. "I don't have a good front lawn, just that parking lot. But I can sure throw his stuff in some contractor bags and load them in the garbage. He's out of here."

Alice couldn't think of a response worth making. She wasn't about to stick up for Denny. But now she was wondering about Teena Ann's horses. "Do you know who Teena Ann's vet is?"

"No, I've never talked to her about that. Or anything, really."

"She doesn't drop in for a chat? Come over and buy cheese?"

Merry shook her head no. "She's got a big cedar thicket on her side of the fence from my property. I can't really see what goes on over there."

I'll ask Silla, Alice promised herself. She can probably find out about Teena Ann's vet…. Time for a serious talk.

"Listen, Merry," Alice began.

But Merry was already talking. "I want to stop that venue. That has nothing to do with Denny or Teena Ann. I can't afford the risk that project poses to my creek, my property. So can you help? What do we have to do?"

"File a petition in court, asking to prevent violation of the covenant. It's possible your neighbor, Henry Winthrop, will join in. Also, courts disfavor plaintiffs who sit around and watch the defendant spend money on a project before the plaintiffs try to stop it. We'll need to move fast."

"Okay. Even better if Henry Winthrop participates."

Alice agreed. "A suit to enforce applicable covenants won't be a vendetta against—against any romantic activity. It's just protecting your property. Okay, we'll start work on it, Merry. Silla will email you an engagement letter." What a relief, she thought; maybe Merry's not feeling like she's losing her mind any longer. Maybe she's taking charge of her life again.

*****

Driving again to the office, Alice called Henry Winthrop to see if he would join Merry in a suit to prevent commercial use of the proposed venue property. "I think we've got to," he said. "Barbara agrees. Can't sit around and let that Teena Ann ruin life out here. I'd never forgive myself. You think we'll win?"

"No guarantees. Teena Ann may argue the covenants are outdated and overly restrictive, but she could face an uphill fight, assuming her neighbors have respected the restrictions. Plus, didn't you buy your ranch only on condition the seller imposed those restrictions?"

"Right."

"That's got some appeal."

*****

At the office Silla said, "Are we on? Gonna sue Miss Teena Ann?"

"Yep," Alice said. "I'd like to confirm the buyers haven't yet closed on Teena Ann's property. Can you doublecheck? She's our primary defendant, though we may add the proposed buyers as defendants—I presume that's the permit applicants. We'll need exhibits: copies of the original covenants; the deeds for the acres owned by Henry Winthrop, Merry Givens, and Teena Ann; and affidavits from Merry and Henry Winthrop. Also, I'd like to keep the lawsuit quiet until we serve the defendants with the petition."

"Got it," Silla said. "Whoo-ee! Can't wait to hear what Teena Ann says."

Hmm. What about TCEQ, which had to rule on the permit? Maybe, Alice thought, after we file the petition, I'll at least send those folks a courtesy copy; they're already overworked and might prefer to stop working on, or at least slow-walk, the permit, pending the outcome of our lawsuit. And what about those open records documents? They might reveal some reason the agency wouldn't be ready to issue the permit.

Silla stuck her head in Alice's door. "Check your email. Our open records documents are here. I've sent you the link."

But before Alice could plunge into the document trove, she needed to take care of Charlie's family. She picked up her phone, called the Travis County Medical Examiner's office, and identified herself.

"Susan Quarles, examiner's assistant. Let me put you on hold for a moment; he said he wants to talk to you."

Alice waited. She'd heard the medical examiner speak at legal ed seminars but had never dealt with him in a case.

A different voice began. "Alice Greer? So far, I've found no evidence of injury from a bullet or knife wound or from a blow, other than what we'd expect from a fall from height onto the concrete tiers below. No suspect drugs in the blood sample. But before I finalize, I want to mention one issue. We found some semi-liquid material on the victim's jeans, on the right knee and shin area, on the heel of one shoe and on the fingers of his right hand and palms of both hands. Slick stuff, colorless. Can you shed light on this?"

"The Apex manager apparently told him to go to the ballpark site and inspect the silicone liquid material being applied to the roof."

"That stuff's notoriously slick."

Alice started to say she'd read online that silicone liquid required special safety measures—but didn't. Instead she asked, "So, did the liquid on his leg and hands contribute to his fall?"

"Has any eyewitness come forward? My report raises a question about the slick stuff, including on the decedent's hands and leg. I've drawn no conclusion yet about causation." He paused, then made a comment Alice didn't expect. "His background makes him sound like a bright young engineer."

"Yes," Alice said, surprised. "He'd worked two jobs to put himself through engineering school and was helping pay his sister's tuition. In fact"—she wondered if this would seem relevant—"because his civil engineering prof told students to get their wills done, given risks at construction sites, he'd asked if I would help him write a will. But" —she didn't want the ME to think Charlie was suicidal—"he also told me he was looking forward to designing his first bridge, taking his first trip to Europe, and seeing some specific historic bridges, like the Arkadiko in Greece."

"If he was so safety conscious, why was he up in the air with no safety equipment?"

"That's my question. The man who called EMS apparently lied to police when he said he didn't arrive until after Charles fell. And it's concerning that the police didn't find the victim's phone, either." She waited, then asked, "Will there be an autopsy?"

"Given that slick material, I believe so."

"Okay, thanks. I'll watch for our copy of the report." Alice said an internal thank you, hung up, and called Jeanie Boone to tell her what she'd just learned.

"So what does it mean, that he's doing an autopsy?"

"I'm not sure. It may mean he and the police are concerned about why Charlie was up on one of those girders and why he fell. That's unexplained at the moment, though they could decide it was simply an accident...."

"I know he would have been as careful as he could, Alice!"

"I agree. Okay, I'll keep you posted. You're passing all this along to your mom, right?"

"As soon as we hang up."

Alice sat for a moment, remembering Charlie's excitement about seeing those bridges—Seattle, Boston, Greece.... She looked at the computer link Silla had sent, thinking she should tackle the open record documents.

Then she imagined Merry staring at her phone while an AirTag showed Denny carousing with Teena Ann while plotting to maneuver Merry into selling part of her property. Task one: file suit against Teena Ann to stop the venue.

Silla stuck her head in the door. The woman might be clairvoyant, Alice believed.

"Silla? Let's get going on this petition to bar commercial use of Teena Ann's thirty acres."

"Sounds great. It's three-thirty—I'll hit the probate office for certified copies of the deeds and the original covenants. Right?"

"Yes, but Merry inherited the property, so we'll also need to find the executor's deed to her. And get a copy of the will the executor was dealing with."

"Got it. I'll run over there now."

Alice began drafting a petition to enforce the covenants barring commercial use. She listed key details of the proposed permit for land application, including the designated venue site and its owner. Next she described the covenant prohibiting commercial use and the specific parcels subject to that prohibition, referencing the deeds as exhibits. Then, hoping to stave off any defense that the Winthrop and Givens plaintiffs had themselves violated that prohibition, she asserted they had been and remained in full compliance.

She'd be requesting an injunction. What about the bond the court would likely require? She called Henry Winthrop to discuss. He cautiously agreed that he could provide a reasonable bond.

Alice re-read her draft. Okay, she'd got the bare facts down. Now for legal authority. She dove into Westlaw for relevant cases, sending them to the printer. Some good cites here, she thought, highlighting the best cases with her yellow highlighter. ("Never use any color but yellow," she'd been taught as a baby lawyer....) She printed out her draft and read it with some satisfaction, feeling pretty good about her case.

The front door crashed open. Silla strode into her office, waving a document, "Holy cow, Alice! What the hell's going on?" She slapped two short pages down on Alice's desk.

Chapter Twelve

What Do I Do About This?

Alice picked up the document and stared at the title: "Transfer on Death Deed."

By whom? She searched for the name of the property owner making this transfer.

Merilee Tarlton Givens.

The primary beneficiary?

Denson Ward. Denny....

Alice's stomach heaved. Why hadn't Merry told her? And when had Merry signed this? Maybe Merry *was* losing her mind. She looked at the notarization: "This instrument was acknowledged before me on the 18th day of February...." About two weeks before the Jersey bull incident. The notary's signature: Olivia V. Street, in Burnet County. Likely Marble Falls.

"Silla! Can you find where this notary works? Burnet County somewhere."

When an owner signed a transfer on death deed, that deed trumped that owner's will. Under this document, at Merry's death, Francine wouldn't get her mother's property as promised in Merry's will. Instead, Denny would.

What had Merry said when Alice visited just this week, about losing her mind? But surely to goodness she wouldn't forget signing this.

Alice looked up at Silla. "She's been under a lot of strain. Told me she sometimes feels like she's losing her mind."

But this document looked properly signed and notarized. No, not in Coffee County, but Texas notaries could notarize documents involving property in other Texas counties.

Stunned, disbelieving, Alice picked up the phone to call Merry. Busy signal.

Silla stood shaking her head, eyes on the deadly document.

"Did you ask who brought this in to record it?" Alice asked.

"I did. It was mailed in with the required recording fee in cash."

"Huh." Legal, but weird. The notation at the end of the deed instructed the probate court, after recording, to return the deed to Merilee Givens and gave her mailbox address on Old Hays Road.

Alice frowned. That detail supported the idea that Merry indeed had signed this document, if it was to be mailed back to her...except Alice knew that Merry couldn't even see her mailbox from the house. Merry's street mailbox stood in a cluster of mailboxes across Old Hays Road. Consequently, Merry, like Alice, had most of her mail sent to her paid-for mailbox at the post office, safe from strangers and kids knocking down mailboxes on Friday night.

Bite the bullet. "Make me a copy, would you? I've got to talk to Merry," she told Silla, and stalked out the door, keys in hand.

*****

Alice drove too fast to Merry's, slid into the parking area, throwing gravel. She climbed out and banged on the front door to the creamery.

She heard the familiar clink as Merry unlocked the door.

"Thanks, Alice." Merry took a deep breath, let it out, looked into Alice's eyes. "I feel so much better now that you're going to help me stop that venue. What's up? Want some tea?"

Alice didn't, but she nodded anyway. "Whatever you're having."

She followed Merry into the creamery kitchen area, trying to calm her anger while Merry busied herself with cups. Because Alice wasn't sure yet who deserved her rage. And this might not be Merry's fault.

Tea in hand, Alice took a sip, then slid the deed across the table. "Merry, I was drafting the petition to enforce the covenants. I needed to attach the current deeds for the properties owned by you and Henry Winthrop and Teena Ann's thirty acres. Silla went to the courthouse to get certified copies. And concerning your fifty acres? Here's the most recent deed she found."

Merry ran her finger down, reading.

She looked at Alice, face stark. "I swear I never signed this."

"You're sure? Absolutely sure?"

"Absolutely." Merry's voice was unsteady. "I know I've been a bundle of nerves. But I swear I never signed this!"

"Never drove up to Burnet County to appear before a notary?"

"Never!"

Alice looked hard at Merry, then said, "Okay. Let's think this through." She pointed at the notarization. "The property owner has to sign a transfer on death deed in front of a notary. Doesn't matter if it's in another county than the property itself. So this was signed in Burnet County. Recently, too—February 18."

Merry shook her head. "I haven't been to Burnet County since—I don't know when."

"Where were you on February 18?"

Merry looked up at the calendar on the wall. "That was a couple of weeks ago, on Tuesday, right? Creamery was closed. I did the morning milking—that takes almost two hours. I finished about eight. I remember because that day I summoned up courage and called Antonelli's—you know, the Austin cheese store in Hyde Park. I want to expand my sales there and got invited to bring in more small chèvres. I was thrilled! So I showered, got into something presentable, packed up the cheese in a cooler, and got there by ten-thirty or so. I delivered my cheeses, talked a little cheese with the owners."

She leaned back, stared at the ceiling. "On the way out of the house I'd remembered Francine had given me a birthday certificate for a massage at Viva, in Austin. I stuck it in my purse, just hoping, and called on the way in. Amazingly, they had an opening at one-thirty. I also called my old college roomie, Lucy. She'd offered to treat me for my birthday back in December. First we went to a local poetry bookstore called First Light. She made me choose a book. Do you know how long it's been since I opened a new book of poems?" Merry shook her head. "Then she took me to lunch at a place called Foreign & Domestic. We gossiped, we laughed, we drank some nice wine. I loved every second. Then I drove over to Viva for my massage. First time in—I don't know. Two years?" She shut her eyes. "Heaven, getting my neck and shoulders massaged. All that milking.... The masseuse said I was just one big knot."

No surprise, given Merry's current life, Alice thought. "How long did the massage take?"

"A blissful ninety minutes. I didn't want it to end. Then I got dressed and dragged myself back out to the car to head home. I thought, hey, if traffic's not bad I've got just enough time before the evening milking to stop at the Coffee County Tax Office and re-register the van. That office closes at four-thirty. I got there maybe ten minutes before closing.

"But that was the day, Alice, I couldn't find my damn license, remember? You have to have your license to re-register your vehicle. I hadn't had to pay for anything all day, hadn't even had to pull out my wallet. But at the county office I couldn't find my license, in my wallet, in my purse, or anywhere in the car. I was running low on gas so I filled up the tank and drove home praying the cops wouldn't stop me. When I got home, I looked everywhere for my license. No luck."

Alice remembered. "The next morning you found it in the pocket of your fleece jacket, right?"

"Right."

"You don't usually keep it there?"

"Nope. But I've been so frazzled...."

"You may be frazzled...but you're not going nuts."

"What am I going to do?" Merry's voice broke.

The two women stared down at their tea cups.

The amorphous dark cloud of suspicion that had entered Alice's mind took on a new shape. "But if you didn't sign it.... Let me see your license."

Puzzled, Merry produced her wallet and handed her driver's license to Alice. In the photo Merry's dark curls were shortish and slightly mussy, with bangs over her forehead. Her eyes, wide, stared at the camera. No smile. She looked like she'd been in a hurry that day.

"Issued in late 2017, after we changed to black and white photos," Alice muttered. "And almost time to renew. The picture's kind of—old."

Merry's brow furrowed. "What do you mean?"

Alice didn't say what she was thinking—Merry's tired face did look older now. "Just wondering—what would it take to fool a notary who doesn't know you? Because no licensed Texas notary wants to be accused of a false notarization."

She pointed at the tiny photo on the license. "Okay, Merry, you've got dark curls. The license reports your eyes as 'hazel' though they're also greenish. Licenses can say only 'HZL' for hazel, or 'GRN' for green. In the picture, you've got dark eyebrows, your bangs are thick, and we can't really see much of your forehead. It looks like you have eye makeup on."

"Those were the days. So?"

Alice sipped her tea, then began. "Well, Silla showed me a picture of your neighbor, Teena Ann Traynor, in which Miss Traynor had dark curly hair and, as I recall, hazel-ish eyes. She looked expertly made-up. Also, you didn't smile for your license photo—that could make it easier to imitate. So I guess my question is,"—Alice looked straight at Merry—"was Teena Ann alone, up there in Marble Falls? Or did she drive up there with the beneficiary of the new deed? If so, did the notary also see that person?"

"You mean—was Denny there too? He wouldn't have to sign, just her?"

"Right. She would forge your signature on the deed with the notary watching. He wouldn't need to appear...could have just waited in the car...but it's hard to imagine Teena Ann doing this without having him along for the ride, you know? If you think my dark suspicions are unwarranted—tell me why! If we challenge that deed, at some point we might need to drive up to Marble Falls to talk to the notary. If she sees the *real* you—maybe she'll turn into a solid witness for us. But if she denies you are you—or contends you are the person who showed up on February 18 and signed that transfer deed in front of her—we need to know that soon. The good news is it sounds like you've got a decent trove of witnesses for your whereabouts on February 18—at least until about four-thirty that afternoon."

Alice scrutinized the license again. The signature reproduced under the photo—"Merilee Tarlton Givens"—was minuscule. Even the capitals were less than a millimeter high. But Alice could see the upward stroke Merilee used to begin the initial M, and that the "G" on Givens was written with a single stroke that made a swirl to end the "G" and then continued straight on to the following letters. The dot over the "i" in both "Merilee" and "Givens" turned into a stroke that merged into the next letter. Hard to duplicate that, Alice thought. The top stroke of the "T" slanted up and right.

Alice asked Merry to write her signature a few times on a piece of note paper without peeking at her driver's license or the forged deed. She did so and handed the note paper to Alice. The "i" wasn't a neat dot—instead, a line, or a stroke that connected to the next letter. In every signature, the "G" was never a neat stand-alone; the horizontal stroke always continued into the "i." The top of the "T" was a single stroke slanting up to the right.

Alice compared the signatures on the note paper to the signature on the transfer on death deed. On the deed, the "i" in Merilee was neatly dotted. The "i" in Givens was a small dash. The M looked similar to Merry's signatures, but the top of the "T" in Tarlton was level, not slanted.

"I still fear we'll need a handwriting expert," she muttered. Maybe she'd hire the expert she'd used before. Even an abusive barrel-racer like Teena Ann was used to long hours of practice. She'd probably practiced hard before signing the deed in front of the notary.

But what if the notary worked late on February 18 and the deed was signed late in the day? Milking goats alone from six p.m. on didn't provide Merry much of an alibi.

Merry said, "Oh, Alice, what do I do about this? This fake deed?"

"Obviously, you didn't get a mailed copy in your mailbox across the road?"

"No, but I don't usually check that one since Denny's the one who mostly uses it."

"We could file a cancellation document," Alice began. "But that feels like admitting that this deed was valid, and if anything happened to you—if you died before the cancellation was granted—God forbid—we'd be screwed. Denny would get your property." She thought for a second, worrying about community property rules in Texas. "Your cheese business, it's a separate company?"

"Yes. It's an LLC. I'm the only member."

"Denny has no part in it?"

"Nope. All the money stays in the LLC account. Denny keeps his own bank account for whatever he makes. The accountants gave me a 'come to Jesus' talk about making sure I always treat my cheese business as my separate property."

With an internal sigh of relief, Alice said, "That's great. So one thing we could do is file a new transfer on death deed, from you to Francine. That should supersede the forged deed, but we'd separately file an action for fraud and forgery on the deed that purports to leave your property to Denny."

Alice's mind raced through her to-do list: (1) Contact notary, get whatever facts she'll share. (2) File a new transfer on death deed from Merry, leaving her land to Francine. (3) For a petition for fraud as to the forged deed, get affidavits from Merry's contacts on February 18—Antonelli's, Lucy, the masseuse, and from Merry, and, Alice hoped, the notary.

But most important—and hardest: she had to protect Merry and Francine. How could Merry take refuge anywhere but home—especially when someone had to milk the goats twice a day? Alice puzzled for a minute and then thought—Tonio Ramos. He'd always helped Alice with fence repair and anything else she needed. His kids were grown; he was single; he'd moved up to assistant manager at the auto repair shop in Coffee Creek; and she'd trust him with her life. Maybe he could move in and take the night watch....

But during the day?

"Here's the first thing, Merry. You've got to stay alive. So does Francine, your beneficiary, but you're the prime target. For their plan to succeed, Denny and Teena Ann need you dead. You're not safe here anymore."

Merry looked out the window and downhill, at her small cheese empire, the groves of live oaks, the goats in the pasture.

"Can we take a look at your house?"

Merry nodded. They left the creamery by the portico, which led to the kitchen. Alice toured the rooms opening off the kitchen—entry hall, dining room, den, laundry room. Down another hall she took a quick look at the master bedroom and bath and another bath plus two other bedrooms, including the one Denny used as an office. "Other bedrooms upstairs?"

Merry nodded. "Just Francine's."

"I saw smoke alarms. You don't have any video cameras, any burglar alarms? Here in the house or the other buildings?" Alice asked.

Merry shook her head. Her face was stark. "Never thought I'd need them."

"Guards, then." Alice called Tonio and put him on speakerphone so Merry could hear.

"Hey, I'm just leaving the shop," he said. "Are you okay?"

"Yes. But I'm here with my friend Merry...." and Alice explained Merry's predicament—property, goats, milking....

"I can do nights," Tonio said. "Be glad to. But listen. Remember my little brother, Ernesto?"

Alice had a vague recollection of a plump-cheeked high school kid who'd helped Tonio repair her fences one hot summer day. She remembered only his dimpled smile. Tonio continued, "He just got out of the Army and is back in Coffee Creek. In June he'll start summer school on the GI Bill, but right now he could jump in and help watch the place during the day, or spell me at night."

"Does he know anything about goats?" Merry asked.

Tonio laughed. "More than he ever wanted. Back in 4-H days he got a blue ribbon for his goat. A Nubian, I think."

"You're on," said Alice. "Tell him to bring his toothbrush."

Waiting for the two men to show up, Merry announced she'd put her new bodyguards in the guest room. "It's got twin beds," she said. "Denny's also got a couch in his office. Well, I admit he and I haven't been sharing a bedroom lately. But what am I going to tell him?"

Time to confront the elephant in the room. "Let's face facts," Alice said. "So long as that transfer on death deed is hanging over your head, you're not safe. But you can't lock him out unless you file a petition for divorce and ask for protection. Are you ready to do that?"

"Yes. No question." Merry took a long breath, expelled it. "I can't live like this."

"We need to nail down some facts before Denny learns our plans," Alice warned. "So for God's sake don't tell him what we've found out about the transfer on death deed. Don't tell him you're about to file suit to enjoin commercial use of the venue. Telling him any of that could cost you your life! Also, he mustn't get any idea we're going to talk to the notary—I don't want her frightened or interfered with. So if Denny shows up tonight, tell him I insisted you hire guards because Denny's been absent, studying, and you need stronger security to protect your goats, your equipment, your cheesemaking investments. He may think that's over the top. But Merry, you have no security alarms, no video cameras, no guard dog, and your place is easily accessed from Old Hays Road—your whole operation's pretty vulnerable. I've been wondering...."

"What?" asked Merry, frowning.

"How's your Jersey bull?"

"Oh, he's settled down now, made himself at home. Calm, collected—what was it the rancher called him, 'Mr. Tractable?'"

"Right, and when you and the rancher loaded him in the trailer, he was fine. But you left him locked in the trailer in the courtyard so you could monitor the cheese process. While he was out there in the trailer, he wound up full of hordenine. Anyone could've driven in, parked, and messed with his feed, or stuck a syringe in him. Two minutes would be enough, while you were inside watching the goat milk temperature gauge!"

"But who—" Merry stopped.

Alice just lifted an eyebrow. "I'd like to know." Then a beep on her phone: text from Tonio, "arriving in two minutes."

She and Merry walked out into the courtyard, watching the western sky turn sunset pink. Then the two brothers pulled in—Tonio, tall, serious-eyed, climbing down from his beloved old GMC pickup, and Ernesto, in what looked like a brand-new tan Jeep. Alice introduced Tonio, then Ernesto. She couldn't keep from smiling: the plump-cheeked teen had morphed into an impressive broad-shouldered man, ramrod straight, exuding competence. But he still had that infectious grin. Tonio explained to Merry that he would take the night shift, starting that night, and Ernesto would appear promptly at six a.m. "Ernesto can help you with that early milking."

"Wow," said Merry. "A guard who can also milk goats? Okay, Alice, I think I'll be fine with these guys on board!" A small smile brightened her tired face—the first real smile Alice had seen on Merry for weeks. She looked up at the two men. "Gentlemen, thank you for coming. Let me give you a tour. Show you the place. And it's nearly six—time for the milking!"

In growing darkness Alice whizzed back down the creek road. She faced a long night at the office. She'd draft the new transfer on death deed from Merry to Francine and get Merry into the office tomorrow morning to get it signed, notarized, and filed at the courthouse. She'd work on the petition to enforce covenants, barring commercial use of the Traynor property. Next, a separate petition challenging the forged transfer on death deed as a fraud. After that, she'd draft Merry's petition for divorce and protection. Good lord, her to-do list included a new deed and three lawsuits.

Alice grinned to herself, imagining Denny's face if he came home to find Tonio guarding his living room or Ernesto's big shoulders following Merry around the milking barn. She also wondered—could Merry somehow eavesdrop when, as Alice fully expected, Denny sneaked off to telephone Miss Teena Ann Traynor about his new situation at home? That was a conversation Alice would love to overhear.

Then the thought of Francine, at school in San Antonio, sent a cold shiver down her spine. Had Merry warned her yet? If it were her Ann, her own daughter, Alice would be on a plane to Boston so fast .... Merry was the prime target. But if something happened to Merry,

Francine would still be in the way. And if Francine was in the way—Alice needed to make sure it wasn't worth Denny's time to get rid of her. So maybe Francine needed a will too.

Her phone beeped. Kinsear. "Almost done here. Hoping my flight tomorrow's on time. Still okay with dinner at Wink? And possibly some dancing?"

What a relief to hear his voice. "Yes, and yes. And another yes."

She previewed the late night that awaited her at the office. "Can't give you details yet, but I sure would like to pick your brain."

"While observing client confidentiality, of course," he replied. "So if we're close-dancing, you will whisper lurid details in my ear?"

He could make her laugh, make her melt.

"Okay. Gotta go. Final dinner meeting with these folks—they all think they're the smartest human in the room. It's wearing. And wearying." He hung up.

Feeling momentarily merry herself, Alice parked in the driveway behind Silla's truck. Lights shone from her office window. Time to turn to, as her father used to say. She marched up the steps, tugging her keys from her pocket.

To her surprise, the front door was slightly ajar.

She took a step inside.

Chapter Thirteen

Pretty Damn Hard-Headed

"Silla? Silla!"

On the floor Silla was pushing herself up to a sitting position. The air smelled faintly of pizza. Silla put her hand to her forehead.

Thank God, no blood anywhere. Halfway down the hall, an unopened pizza box.

Alice bent over Silla. "Silla, what happened?"

Silla shook her head. "Not sure." Eyelashes fluttered as she touched her temple. "Got hit."

Alice punched in 911 on her phone, gave the EMTs the address. Then she called again, asked for the sheriff's office.

"We'll be right there."

Alice knelt by Silla. "Don't try to get up yet," Alice warned. "The EMTs will want to look at you."

Outside, red lights whirled in the street. Heavy boots hurried up the sidewalk. Alice opened the door.

Silla turned toward the EMTs. "Hang on, miss," said a kind but authoritative voice. "Let us take a look at you. Do you remember what happened?"

"The lights were on inside. I was carrying the pizza. Trying to keep it level. I elbowed open the front door."

"And then?"

"Something heavy hit my head, right here." She patted her forehead, above her right eye.

The EMT lifted her bangs away from her forehead. "Yep, you've got a bruise forming there. Kind of square-ish." He gently palpated the area above her eye. "I don't think it's fractured," muttered the kind voice. "But X-rays, of course. We'll get you over to the ER, let someone take a look."

Silla looked up at Alice. "I figured we'd need to work tonight, after your trip to Merry's. So I ran to Sally's Pizza...."

Alice felt tears form but blinked them away.

Officer Joske arrived—red-headed, smart, slightly mistrustful of Alice—but very interested in Silla. Alice filled him in while the EMTs went back to the ambulance for a stretcher.

He knelt down. "What happened, Silla?"

"I had the pizza. I elbowed open the front door. Then bam, whacked on the head."

"Could you tell what hit you? A hand, a cane?"

She touched her head above the right temple. "Felt squarish and cold. Metallic."

Alice cringed at the image of a gun butt.

Silla shut her eyes, frowning. "I knew I'd be back with the pizza in ten minutes so I didn't set the alarms or lock up. Could kick myself."

"Never mind," Alice said softly.

"Ostrich skin," muttered Silla. The EMTs lifted her gently onto the stretcher, carefully supporting her head.

"Ostrich skin?" Joske sounded puzzled.

"Boot." The stretcher team took her out the door.

"I'm going to follow her," Alice said. "She means she saw an ostrich-skin boot. Like a cowboy boot."

"Ah. Could be helpful," Joske said. "Alice, before you leave, can you tell if anything's missing?"

Alice scanned Silla's worktable, then the conference room, then her office. "Drawers are pulled out, but Silla's laptop and mine are still here. Conference room closet's been opened, but the safe's still shut." She picked up her purse and her laptop. "I've got to get to the ER."

"So maybe they were looking for something specific and didn't find it? Or maybe Silla interrupted them. When you got here, did you see anyone? Or any vehicle?"

"No. Well, a truck was going down the street, toward town. Couldn't see make or color. Gotta go follow Silla." She reached down and picked up the pizza box in her free hand.

"Tell her I'll come visit again after she gets checked for concussion or fracture. And I'll get the crime scene people in here to check for fingerprints."

"Okay. Tell you what," Alice said, "I'll call you as soon as I know anything."

His face cleared. "Great. Thanks."

She handed him the pizza box on her way out.

It was only two minutes to the ER. Alice met the EMTs as they carried the stretcher in from the portico and down the hall to a cubicle.

Silla asked Alice to stay until the doctor released her. "I am *not* spending the night."

"We'll see."

*****

While they waited in the cubicle for the ER doc to finish examining her and for X-rays to be read, Silla demanded to hear the saga of Merry and the forged deed. Alice described the situation. "Tomorrow morning I intend to get a transfer on death deed signed by Merry and filed at the courthouse. Tonio's on watch tonight, and he can bring her in first thing, when he has to go to work. Then we can 'turn to' on our other pleadings. But getting that new deed on record is key."

"I'll be there."

Alice looked at her sternly. "Let's wait to hear from the doc."

Ten minutes later the young scrub-clad doctor pulled open the cubicle curtain.

"I hear you're a hotshot legal assistant in Coffee Creek."

Silla nodded, with a shadow of her irresistible grin. "I don't feel too hotshot right now."

"Pretty damn hard-headed, I'd say. No fracture." He took a long look into each of her eyes. "I don't think you're concussed. I do think you're incredibly lucky."

Silla closed her eyes and took a deep breath. "Thank you." Then, curious, "Any idea what hit me?"

"We've been wondering. Can't be sure. Could've been the butt of a gun; the bruise suggests that's a possibility. In some ways you were fortunate—it's hard to get much leverage when you hit someone with something short. But something longer, like a swinging nightstick? Whoa." He peered in her eyes again, nodding to himself. "Come back right away if you have headache, dizziness, nausea, anything whatsoever. Hear me? And try not to lean over. Keep your head up. Okay?" And he was gone.

Alice helped Silla into her street clothes. They climbed into Alice's Discovery.

"Gonna file that transfer on death deed tomorrow. Don't worry,"

Silla said.

"I'm not worried. While you were being X-rayed, I called Tonio. He'll bring Merry to the office tomorrow before he goes to work at eight. We can get this deed signed, sealed, and recorded, and get a certified copy. Ernesto can run Merry back to her place. He'll be there all day."

"That's a relief," Silla muttered. "I don't want anyone bashing her."

When they pulled up at the office, Silla gave Alice what Alice called The Look. "I'm fine to drive home, and you don't need to follow me!"

Alice raised an eyebrow and retaliated with her own version of The Look. "Your mama would never forgive me if I didn't follow you home." Silla lived with her widowed mother—also red-headed and as independent as her wheelchair allowed. "Get over it."

Once Alice reached home, she worked late, wordsmithing the transfer on death deed and what she thought of as lawsuit number one: the petition to enforce covenants barring commercial use.

But what was she going to tell Kinsear? *Was* she going to tell Kinsear?

Chapter Fourteen

Stayin' Alive, Stayin' Alive

Alice finally finished drafting, emailed the new transfer on death deed and the draft petition to enforce covenants to the office, and crawled into bed. She slept hard, dreaming of trying to land a punch on some unknown man but not being able to connect. When she woke, one detail remained—a glimpse of a boot.

Cowboy boot toe. Ostrich skin. Who?

When she got to the office, Silla was already there.

"How are you? How was last night? No dizziness? No nausea?"

"I'm fine." Silla had arranged her red hair so it hid most of the bruise on her forehead. "Fine and dandy." She handed Alice fresh copies of the short crisp transfer on death deed from Merry to Francine.

Promptly at eight, Tonio and Merry appeared.

"Everything okay last night?" Alice asked Merry.

"All serene. In case you're wondering, Denny texted late last night that he was going to stay in Austin to study for the real estate class he's taking. So he hasn't met Tonio yet."

Alice watched with anxious anticipation as Merry, still in her morning milking togs, reviewed the transfer on death deed, slowly running her finger down the text. She looked up. "Ready."

Silla watched Merry sign, then notarized her signature. "Stay here, Merry, and have some coffee with Tonio. I'll be right back. Twenty minutes, max." She turned to Alice. "Lock the door behind me, okay?"

Alice included the dead bolt, with its satisfying clunk, as she locked the front door. She felt even safer with Tonio staying with Merry until Silla got the deed filed. Merry needed to stay alive....

*****

On her return, Silla triumphantly waved a certified copy of the newly filed transfer on death deed. "All done. Here's our copy, and I'll make more. Tonio can head to work. I'll run Merry home while Alice starts on petition one, to enforce covenants. And then petition two, charging forgery. And then—" she glanced at Merry—"petition three, divorce."

Merry stood, a smile of relief on her face, and picked up her purse to leave.

"Wait," Alice said. She faced Merry, holding her arms, gazing into her eyes. "Remember, Merry. Not a word to Denny—or *anyone*, with one exception—about the three petitions we're going to file. Or about the transfer on death deed you've signed. Or that you found out about that damned forged deed and the notary in Burnet County. Not one word, until we nail down the notary's sworn testimony and get it on file. Only exception to your silence: warn Francine to take precautions and also not to disclose what we're doing. Maybe when Denny knows you've filed your transfer on death deed leaving your property to Francine, you'll no longer be in danger. On the other hand, both you and Francine might still be at risk."

"I hear you."

"And I assume Francine has no will, right?"

"Not as far as I know."

"So I'll call and ask her at least to sign a simple holographic will, so we can tell Denny there's no chance whatsoever that he gets anything if he gets rid of you two." She raised a warning finger. "Meanwhile, I worry about Denny spying on your email, your computer, your iPad. I worry about him peeking at your phone. And passing along the information to other inquiring minds."

Merry snorted. "He would, too."

"So for now, Silla and I will stop sending you emails or messages, stop calling you directly, until we know you've re-secured your electronics. You can always call us on Tonio's or Ernesto's phones. So, can you get Ernesto to take you to visit your neighbor Henry Winthrop at about eleven this morning to review the first petition, to enforce covenants? You and Henry both need to be on board with that pleading. We'll tell him you're coming. We'll need you back here on Monday morning too."

"I get it," Merry said. "Makes sense. I'll be very stern with Francine about being safe, and I'll try to change all my passwords. Meanwhile, thanks for Ernesto and Tonio. At least I feel safe!" Merry did a little jig as she left with Silla, singing "Yeah, yeah, yeah, yeah, I'm stayin' alive, stayin' alive!" But there was an edge to her voice.

Alice began a final edit on her petition to enforce covenants on the proposed venue parcel. After Silla returned from Merry's and worked her magic, Alice reviewed the document once more. Then Silla emailed it to Henry Winthrop with the accompanying affidavits. Alice called him to explain why his neighbor Merry would visit him at eleven to review the documents. "Right now we don't want Denny to see this. Looks like he's not on Merry's side."

"She's welcome to come over any time! I wish she'd get rid of that deadbeat she married," said Henry.

Just after eleven, Henry and Merry called. Alice put them on speakerphone. "Everything looks good," they confirmed.

"Henry, Silla will drive up today to watch you two sign your affidavits and to notarize them. But listen: we may not file until Monday, and we don't want to broadcast the existence of the petition until we're sure it's been served on the defendants," Alice said. "If someone at the grocery store asks you why you're looking so smug—just smile. Don't say why."

Silla left for the Winthrop ranch. Thirty minutes later she stuck her head in Alice's door clutching the original, complete with all exhibits. "Alice, that Apex Partners project manager, Jerry Weathers, is authorized to receive service for Apex, per the LLC records. I'll tell the court clerk he can be tracked down at their office in the old Coffee Creek Hotel. Plus, just in case, I got his license plate number, never mind how. Once he and Teena Ann have been served, you want to send TCEQ a courtesy copy, right?"

"Right." Alice reviewed the stack one last time, signed the petition, and took it back to Silla.

"I'm making copies, then off to the courthouse again. Whoo-ee, this is gonna ruffle some serious feathers!"

"That's an understatement." Alice laughed at 'serious feathers,' imagining Jerry Weathers' pink tie. "Okay, next we've got Merry's petition two, to declare the forged deed a fraud, and petition three, for divorce and protection. But we still need affidavits from Merry and the witnesses to her whereabouts on February 18. So maybe we file those two petitions on Monday."

While Silla was gone Alice called Merry's daughter Francine and left a message. "To deter Denny from further mischief (hopefully), I need for you to have a will. Can you draft a simple will in your handwriting, leaving your property to—whomever you want? And sign it? We can help you do something more formal later. It's important to help keep you safe. Please call if you have any questions."

She turned back to her computer, eyes glued to the screen.

Silla returned from her second trip to the courthouse and sailed into Alice's office, waving her certified filed copy of the petition to enforce covenants. "Here you go, filed and stamped. But now I'm thinking about that Burnet County notary. I found out she works at the UPS office in Marble Falls. The clerk there said she's working today. But I couldn't find out if she works on Monday."

"Yikes." Alice sat up, mind whirring. "What if we zip up there right now? We'd have to hurry." Alice didn't want to be late for her date with Kinsear that night. "We need to lock down the timing. You think we could get a look at the notary's record book?"

"We can always ask for a certified copy, of course," Silla responded. "But I've got another idea." That irresistible grin...

"Your head's really okay?"

"You know how many times I've hit my head barrel-racing? I'm fine. Just give me five minutes. Here's my idea..." and Silla rolled out her plan.

Alice was struck speechless. Mentally, she reviewed risks. "You're on. We've barely got time to get to Marble Falls and back by four. I'll drive."

Five minutes later Silla, holding a folder, and Alice, full of anxiety and exhilaration, roared north toward Marble Falls.

Chapter Fifteen

Like It's All Tied Together

The UPS office sat in a strip mall on the highway leading into Marble Falls. Alice parked off to the side and watched Silla, in boots and jeans, head high, swagger into the store. Alice waited a moment, then followed, stopping by the display of mailing tubes and tape. Out of the corner of her eye she saw Silla engage the desk clerk, who nodded toward a young woman with blonde pigtails and thick glasses, standing several feet further away, behind a name plate that read "Olivia V. Street, Notary."

Alice took her time nearby, choosing some package tape and mailing envelopes, then made her way to the line waiting for the desk clerk. Meanwhile, Silla handed a credit card and a document to the young woman, then leaned her elbows on the counter: "I'm a notary too. Came to see you because I didn't think any of the notaries in Coffee County needed to know my business."

Alice moved up one spot in line. Now she could eavesdrop even better. The young notary smiled as Silla continued. "I'm a barrel-racer. Anything happens to me, now I'll know my mom's protected." Her voice took on a confiding tone. "A fellow Coffee Creek barrel-racer was up here two weeks ago to get a transfer on death deed notarized. February 18. That's what gave me the idea—I've been worrying about my share of this stable property." She paused, holding a pen. "You remember her, at all?" Then Silla signed the document and handed it to the notary.

The young notary stamped the document. "Transfer on Death Deed. Let me check." She flipped open a notebook and went back two pages. "Oh, here it is. Merilee Tarlton Givens. Nice name. I remember her, she came in right at lunchtime. High noon, I made a note here. I was supposed to be on break."

"Lunchtime?" Silla said. "You're making me think of barbecue. Think I'll go get some after we get through. Hey, did she have her sweetheart with her?" Silla took back her credit card from the notary and carefully slipped the executed deed into her folder.

"Maybe. Some guy was standing around watching her, and they went out the door together."

"Brown hair, not bad looking?"

The notary nodded. "He'd parked right in front. I saw them drive off together, because I got her taken care of before I left for lunch. You're a notary, you know how we remember people, right?"

"No kidding," Silla said. "Okay, now I need to pick your brain on barbecue. You have a fave?"

"Inman's closest, so I'm there a lot, but if you have time, try Holy Smokes! Other end of town, but hey, the brisket's worth the drive...and there's homemade cobbler. Not even kidding."

Alice finished paying, took her receipt and her purchases, and walked out the door. Oh, that Silla!

The two skipped barbecue and headed back to Coffee Creek. Alice was thinking, she'll give us an affidavit—along the lines of "I never met the customer before...she presented a driver's license and signed the deed at noon"—and we'll attach a copy of the fraudulent deed.

"Brilliant work," she told Silla. "Perfect phrasing, if anyone questions how you extracted that info."

"Yes indeed. Every word I uttered was true." Silla smirked. "I've got my own notary rep to protect! Plus, it turns out she does work on Monday...."

*****

Kinsear was already standing at the front door of Wink when Alice squeezed her Discovery into the tiny parking lot off Lamar in Austin. He swept her into a hug that made her close her eyes, then kissed her long and thoroughly. Finally he loosened his grip, but she still held his shoulders, burying her nose on his chest, and inhaling. Yes, that reassuringly familiar scent. Kinsear.

Through the window she could see diners grinning at them. Let them look.

Inside, the tall wine steward seated them, smiling. "Good to have you here again. And to begin?" Kinsear ordered an old fashioned, Alice a glass of Spanish cava. When it arrived, she heaved a sigh of relief, took a sip, and gazed at the man across the table. "I'm thinking crab cakes."

Kinsear, still studying the menu, gave her a lopsided smile. "I love it that your first words to me, after I stagger home from the big city, involve crab cakes. I'll go with the mussels." In typical fashion he quizzed the wine steward at length about the wines. The steward made some suggestions—wines Alice had never heard of, much less tried—and hustled away.

"Don't worry. I've learned to rely on that guy. Okay, tell me about the cheese business in Coffee Creek. Pretty hot, I hear."

Alice took two more sips of cava, then began. "Client confidentiality rules, as usual."

"Of course."

"I feel like I'm in the eye of a hurricane, but things could get stormy fast." She recounted Charlie Boone's request that she help him with his will, local outrage over the concert venue application involving Teena Ann Traynor's thirty acres, and Charlie's horrifying death. "Then Merry found a draft transfer on death deed on her husband Denny's iPad. And while we were assembling deeds to attach to our petition to enforce covenants against commercial use, with Merry Givens as one of the complainants, Silla found there was *already* a transfer on death deed on file leaving the land to Denny—a deed Merry swore she'd never signed."

The server appeared—two exquisite little raku bowls of bay scallops in aromatic liquid.

Kinsear's eyes met hers. "Nourishment first."

The clear liquid absorbed her mind for a moment. "White vermouth with a little butter and thyme?" guessed Alice.

"And shallots? Okay, what did you do about the forged deed?"

"First we filed a new transfer on death deed that Merry actually signed. But we needed to know when the forgery was notarized. Silla should get an Oscar for her performance." She described the scene at the UPS counter, then spooned the last bit of liquid from the scallops. "Now Denny's pressuring Merry to sell five acres to Teena Ann—and Silla saw Teena Ann prancing around Luckenbach with Denny."

"The thick plottens," said Kinsear. "Worrisome, with Merry still wearing a big bullseye."

"Which is why Tonio and Ernesto Ramos are signed on as day and night protection."

Kinsear nodded, eyes thoughtful. "And your stop-the-venue petition?"

"Your basic petition to enforce covenants, because existing covenants preclude commercial use." But what rose in her memory was Charlie Boone's face. "What I really care about is finding out—"

"Why Charlie was on one of those girders and fell off."

"I feel like it's all tied together—what happened to Charlie, the threats to Merry." She hadn't told him yet about the attack on Silla. Maybe she'd already said enough. Might upset his dinner.

The server appeared with tall wine glasses and the thoroughly discussed wine. "Please taste! Let me know."

They obeyed. "This requires another sip." Kinsear contemplated the wine, then smiled. "All right, all right, all right."

When his mussels and Alice's crab cakes appeared, by mutual agreement they abandoned the concert venue topic. Alice demanded details of Kinsear's week in the big city, including character sketches of the main actors. He obliged, leaving her grinning at every portrayal.

"But you got them all to gee and haw, finally?"

"Yeah. In exchange for a mussel, may I have a bite of crab cake?"

"Yes. But Silla will kill me if we don't decide a few—a few details so she can plan our—our—"

"You can say it! Come on!"

"Wedding!"

Diners at the next table peeked at them, then looked away.

By the time dessert arrived, Kinsear had staked out clear positions. Smallish wedding, late afternoon, four-ish; just their minister, Laura, plus family and the wedding party. A big reception to follow at the Beer Barn with a Mexican buffet and M.A.'s wedding cake and champagne and toasts. He'd already asked Floyd Domino and Bill Kirchen to play piano and guitar. Later, the Beer Barn would open to the public as usual. Kinsear had also asked the Beer Barons to hire a local band everyone could dance to, for the rest of the night, and he'd pay the freight.

"And you will be wearing—?"

"Texas tux, of course, for the wedding. Remove jacket and bolo, unbutton collar, and add black vest for dancing."

"My dream come true."

"And you?"

"Just wait and see." Goodson Kells boots, with coral stars....

*****

Kinsear retrieved his suitcase from behind the restaurant's bar and followed Alice to her car. Heading west toward Coffee Creek, she thought how comforted, how relaxed, how safe she felt, riding home with Kinsear. "Poor Merry!" she blurted.

"Because?"

"Because—what's it like to marry someone, live with someone, who turns out to be planning to kill you?"

"Like living with Henry VIII, repeat offender. Ernest Burkhart, the Osage murders."

"An endless sequence of days with a rising sense of impending doom."

He snorted. "Plus bouts of self-criticism—'how could I have been so stupid?'"

They turned onto Alice's drive and reached her carport, where he'd left his ancient Land Cruiser.

"You are not saying goodbye tonight. You're staying with me. Right?"

"Even if I have to leave early? I hoped you'd say that."

The chilly night breeze hurried them into her house.

"What if I build a fire?" he asked.

"Absolutely. Maybe later." She turned to hug him, found herself patting his cheeks, his hair. "Never leave."

"Certainly not. We still have to decide on a honeymoon. And then the rest of our lives. Thoughts?"

She held his hand on the way to bed.

Chapter Sixteen

What Shooting?

By sunrise on Saturday, Kinsear was dressed and at the door, ready to leave for Fredericksburg. "Gotta go. We've got a big scout troop coming out early to ride today." She followed him to the driveway, waving as he backed out.

Alice made another small espresso, poured it into her reliable go-cup, spooned hot frothed milk on top, and, thus fortified, headed for the office. Duty called; check out the open records documents and finish Merry's pleadings. A long, lonesome afternoon.

Live Oak Street was quiet. She unlocked the office door and peered down the hall, still fearful after the shock of finding Silla on the floor two days before.

At her desk she opened the link Silla had sent with the TCEQ documents and began scrolling. Application, correspondence, meeting notices, the usual. She searched for "site coverage" and found an info dump of construction plans with roads, parking, and building area calculations. She punched numbers into her calculator. Thirty acres times 43,560 square feet in an acre—hmm, 1,306,800. What site coverage limit applied? Was it 65%?

And what about Charlie's call to the TCEQ engineer? She searched staff emails and spied one phone record dated the morning of the permit hearing: "Apex engineer called, said contractor had provided plans not yet submitted to agency; site coverage nearly 75%. He felt plans were in error. Warned him plans would be noncompliant. Agency would inspect to confirm compliance."

She'd call the TCEQ engineer Monday, see what else he remembered about his conversation with Charlie. Had Charlie also alerted Apex about receiving the noncompliant plans? And where are those plans? Did they disappear when Charlie's room was searched?

What about that mirror image of Charlie's computer? Alice managed to open the link, then typed in "Weathers." Hmm, only a couple of entries. One read, "Note to self. Do not badmouth clients where anyone can hear you. I hate it when Weathers says things like 'Coffee Creek's a dump' or 'Mayor's a dumbass...' or 'Who'd live in a place like this?'" Alice remembered her first encounter with Weathers, that first handshake, those unsmiling eyes. Maybe Charlie had read the man pretty accurately? Weathers felt he was just dealing with a dump?

Well, nothing she could do for Charlie now. Job one was protecting Merry. As morning stretched into afternoon, she left a message for Merry on Ernesto's phone: "Help! We need affidavits confirming where you were on February 18. Can you send me contact info for your friend Lucy and the person at Antonelli's and the massage folks? Can you alert them that I'll be sending drafts to them?"

Merry called back almost immediately. "Alice, I'm on it. I've told them you'll be sending a short affidavit and that they need to call you right away about any changes. Gave them your cell number."

Already one o'clock on Saturday afternoon. She knocked out affidavits for Merry's friend Lucy, for the person Merry had dealt with at Antonelli's, and for the masseuse who'd tried to unknot Merry's shoulders, then forwarded copies to the three, thanking them and requesting any comments asap. Shouldn't be a problem – just that "Merry was at this location from approximately (insert time) to (insert time) on February 18...."

Then she drafted two more affidavits for Merry, one describing her whereabouts on February 18 and declaring the forged transfer on death deed a fraud, and the next supporting the petition for divorce/ protection.

Alice's phone rang again—this time it was Charlie's sister, Jeanie Boone: "Alice? Another weird thing happened Thursday. I meant to call you yesterday but had to take my mom to the doctor. Anyway, on Thursday morning a guy knocked at our door and said he was from Apex and needed to pick up Charlie's computer. I said the only computer I know about was his Apple MacBook that he paid for himself. I know because I was with him when he bought it."

"What did he look like?"

"Big. I mean, burly. Gray hair. No smile. Sport coat. I didn't want him taking even one step into the house. He argued with me, said, 'You need to give that computer to me anyway.' I said absolutely not, and anyway I don't have it. Then my mom yelled from the back, 'Our lawyer has it!' And I shut the door."

Ah. No wonder Silla got bashed on the head on Thursday evening. But whoever it was couldn't find the computer. "Jeanie, remember we gave it to the Minor Genius for a mirror image? Afterward he took it to the police. So if anyone asks for it again, the police have it, and you haven't seen it since. Where'd you put Charlie's truck? Is it safe?"

"Yes, it's locked in our garage."

"Did you see what this guy was driving?" She thought of Silla on the floor. "Or his boots?"

"No to the boots, and I did look up and down the street for a vehicle. Then I closed the door and chained it shut! Okay, thanks, Alice." Jeanie hung up, leaving Alice to wonder what Apex wanted from Charlie's computer. But she needed more. Where were those noncompliant plans?

Plus, she still hadn't heard back from Merry's daughter, Francine. One more loose end. She called again, left another message.

Time to go home and check on the burros. Alice locked up, more carefully than usual. The western sky was turning golden orange. Along the office driveway the Lady Banksia rosebush that had climbed over the hedge was showing off its first yellow blossoms, and the mysterious fragrance of wintersweet, the *Chimonanthus praecox*, with its tiny flowers, enchanted her as it did every spring. She shut her eyes, inhaled...exhaled...repeated.

Speeding up the creek road toward home she considered the contrasts. Such hatefulness, the big guy with gray hair, maybe Conrad O'Leary. But such sweetness in the spring air. Humans. Plants. What a world.

*****

Sunday morning: church, with Laura preaching and a soprano leading the choir in "Sheep May Safely Graze," supported by two recorders and a cello. Alice, in the back pew, felt uneasy, felt she should be watching her own flock. For wolves? Rustlers? Mountain lions? Thank God for Tonio and Ernesto standing guard, keeping watch by night and by day. Merry was a lucky sheep. But still, the buck stopped with Alice. The sheep she needed to protect included Merry, and Francine, and now Jeanie, and Charlie's mom.

That afternoon, with the petition declaring the forged deed a fraud now ready to file on Monday, as soon as she got notarized signatures on all affidavits, Alice distracted herself with chores: wash clothes, vacuum floors, clean the bathrooms, and assemble the welter of tax documents she owed her accountant. When she finished, she poured a glass of fizzy Spanish cava to celebrate and began wrapping packages for her daughter, Ann, and for Gran, Jordie's mother and her children's beloved grandmother.

Gran's package would fly across the sea to her farm on the coast of southwest Scotland—piano sheet music plus a down vest from a Colorado brand Gran admired. Alice loved Gran for her wry wit, her warm hugs, her long view of the past, and her ability somehow to surmount tragedy. For Ann, who'd promised to make a Mexican breakfast for her northeastern roommates, the package included butter tortillas from the H-E-B grocery and four cans of Rotel for salsa and to pour over the pan of chilaquiles Ann envisioned.

Alice grabbed a new mystery and sank into a bubble bath, seeking an escape from shepherd worries.

*****

But when she woke early Monday, Charlie's face was still center stage in her mind. He'd wanted her help but didn't live long enough to get it. Why had a contractor delivered the noncompliant plans Charlie had called TCEQ about?

The question haunted her all the way to the Coffee Creek Post Office, where she and her packages were first in line. As she walked toward the exit, she was buttonholed by Georgia Green, the long-time postmistress who ran the postal service with an iron fist and plenty of laughter. "Any word on what happened down the road at the baseball construction site? To that poor boy? Nice kid. I met him when he mailed stuff for his company." She turned, facing Alice. "I never heard who was doing the shooting."

Alice stopped dead. "What shooting?"

Georgia Green glanced up and down the empty corridor, then tilted her head. "C'mon." She pushed open the door marked "NO ENTRY" and ushered Alice back through the bowels of the mailroom—shelves of boxes, bags of mail—and toward the door that led to the loading dock.

Alice couldn't stop swiveling her head back and forth, staring at the forbidden territory where her mail landed before being slotted into her mailbox.

"Haven't you always wanted to see this?" Georgia Green waved around at the mysterious piles of boxes and bags.

"Oh, yes!"

The postmistress led her out on the concrete loading dock. "Here's where I come for my cigarette."

"Singular?"

"Yes. One a day. No smoking inside, and besides, these young kids look at you like you're a woolly mammoth with a bad habit. They vape, of course." She strolled to the end of the loading dock. "I quit long ago. But once a day, at least the days I'm here, I come out to the loading dock after closing time and light one cigarette. There's almost no traffic on this road, so no one sees me. I still love the smell of that smoke. I lift my one cigarette to toast the bad old days. And I hold it while it slowly burns down. Sometimes there's still one driver out here—late with his afternoon delivery. That was UPS, the day that boy died at the ball stadium site. Rich Woodworth was driving. I enjoy that man. Then he left. It wasn't yet raining. I pulled out my pack, lit my cigarette, smelled the smoke, looked at the sky, enjoyed being alive. And then?"

Alice was mesmerized. "Then?"

"Five bullets. BAM! BAM! Then a second or two, then three more. BAM! BAM! BAM! Then silence."

"But the police said no one at the post office heard anything!"

"Huh." She looked at Alice. "Well, they never asked me. I'd have told them. That boy got hurt late on Tuesday afternoon, right? I had lunch early the next day. Girlfriends, at Thyme and Dough. Maybe that's when the cops came by here, and I was gone. And of course, we close at four. Most employees were already gone by the time I went out on the loading dock that day."

"What did it sound like? The shooting?"

"Sounded like a handgun. But also, the bullets hit something, something solid, maybe metal. I heard a couple of shots kind of go

WHANG when they hit something. Like a ricochet."

Holy cow. "And you haven't told anyone?"

"Nobody asked. I just assumed the police knew everything."

"Nope."

*****

Alice drove straight to the Sheriff's Department and asked for George Files. The desk sergeant acknowledged that he was in the office. She paced up and down until she spotted him walking down the corridor, brown eyes on her. "Alice. What's up?"

She lifted an eyebrow, glancing around the crowded corridor.

"Okay, come on back." He beckoned her into his office and sat behind his desk, one foot resting on a drawer he'd pulled out.

Alice perched on what she called the "penitential metal chair" in his office. "George, the Charlie Boone case. Remember when you asked if anyone heard shots that afternoon? Someone did. Georgia Green, at the post office. Five shots, that afternoon. After Rich Woodworth left the post office and drove by the ballpark site."

"But we had someone go check with the employees, and no one heard anything!"

"No one talked to her. She says she never saw anyone from your department and must have been gone when your guys came by. George, you need to hear her describe what she heard. Pistol shots, she thinks, and some of them hit something and went WHANG."

Silence. Then, "You found that one shell casing. We found none. But the victim wasn't shot so we didn't look for bullets." He rose, opened the door and yelled down the hall. Alice heard "metal detector."

"One other thing. Joske told you about someone breaking into our office and hitting Silla on the head?"

"Yeah. Joske said you gave him the pizza she'd bought."

"Remember Charlie's sister, Jeanie, in New Braunfels? She says some guy showed up that morning at their house–big guy, gray hair—demanding Charlie's computer. Which you've got. Right?"

"Right."

"I understand Charlie kept a running memo on every project. If you took a look at his computer file on the Apex concert venue project, did you see anything about some new plans delivered to Charlie that exceeded the permitted site coverage?"

The deep frown lines on Files's face grew deeper. "We'll double-check. What are you thinking?"

"I'm wondering if Charlie found out that Apex used one set of plans for the application but might be planning to build something a bit different, with more site coverage. And Charlie was a straight shooter. The day of the hearing he called the TCEQ engineer about seeing revised plans. That engineer described the phone call in the file we got from the agency."

"What does this have to do with his death? And how about giving me a copy of that TCEQ file?"

"Sure. Silla can send you the link. But the phone call timing's important. According to Charlie, that phone call happened the day of the public meeting. What if later that day, at the public meeting, Charlie had disclosed any of that discussion—or been confronted by the TCEQ representatives about it? Especially in front of that audience—a pretty anti-venue group? How would the permit applicants react to that possibility?"

"I see what you're saying." Files was making notes in one of the small spiral notebooks he always carried.

A crime scene officer stuck his head in the door. "You got a minute to fill me in on this Windy Lane deal, George?"

Alice stood. "I'm leaving. But what I want to know is—why did he fall?" She couldn't bear the thought of Charlie on the slick girder. And then bullets—WHANG!

Chapter Seventeen

Full Of Holes

Silla called from the road while Alice was returning to the office. "Just reporting," she said. "I've already been to Austin to collect and notarize the affidavits about Merry's whereabouts on February 18. Got 'em from Merry's friend Lucy, Antonelli's, and the masseuse who'd noticed Merry's knotted shoulders. Then I drove to Marble Falls to acquire a very brief affidavit from the young notary—to quote, 'The person who presented the transfer on death deed that I notarized at approximately noon on February 18 presented a Texas driver's license bearing the name Merilee Tarlton Givens. I had never before met the person who presented the license.'"

"Oh, excellent!" Alice exclaimed. Perfect testimony. Short, crisp, definitive.

Meanwhile, Ernesto had driven Merry to the office. Alice settled her in the conference room to review two more affidavits—one for the petition concerning the forged deed, detailing Merry's movements on February 18 and declaring she'd never signed any transfer on death deed in favor of Denny, and one supporting her divorce petition.

Alice asked Ernesto to join her in her office. "Any sign of Denny yet?"

He shook his head. "Merry says he texted again yesterday that he was staying in Austin to study for that exam. That's not where his AirTag was, though."

"Next door, at the Traynor place?"

"Yep. Listen, Alice, Tonio and I are worried about Merry's safety. Even with one of us there night and day, it'd be too easy to pull into her parking lot and do mischief. From the parking lot someone could sneak into the creamery, mess with her equipment. Or go through the gate or over that little fence—nothing but three strands of barbed wire—and mess with the barn. So—how about we set up some security cameras, put in some alarms?"

Ernesto's face—still young, still appealing— now bore a distinctly adult expression: knowledgeable, serious, determined. "I know how to do this, Alice. I worked security details in the Army. Roads, fences, buildings, labs, computer systems. Alarms, night vision cameras, monitors, repairs. Tonio and I made a list of what we think she needs."

He handed her a list in small, neat handwriting: security cameras on the parking area, inside and outside the creamery and the barn, including the loft. Hardened chain and keyed padlock on the big gate from the parking area to the barn and pasture. Window and door alarms. "Plus," Ernesto said, "more smoke alarms—the only ones she has are in the house—and night-vision cameras. And the alarm system should alert fire and police."

Alice thought about Merry's fall climbing down from the barn loft, where—perhaps—someone had messed with a ladder rung, and about the Jersey bull, tractable at home, but full of hordenine after sitting in the trailer in the parking lot. Would've been nice to have cameras in place....

"Also," Ernesto went on, "She changed her password for the wi-fi system but should get new locks for the doors into the house and creamery. We'll work on the barn doors too."

"Good idea. I'm all for this, Ernesto. Does Merry agree?"

"She does."

"When can you start?" She handed him back his list.

"I'll swing by and get as much equipment as I can while she's here with you, if that's okay. Tonio and I can start installing the new toys as soon as he gets off work." He rose and gave her a quick wave on the way out the door.

Alice took a deep breath, let it out, closed her eyes, let her head lean back. What a relief. Though maybe she was jumping the gun, letting Merry change the locks without warning Denny and without a protective order in place? Although he hadn't been home to get any warning, had he?

Voices down the hall—Silla and Merry. In a moment Silla appeared and laid documents on Alice's desk. "Here's our petition alleging fraud concerning Teena Ann's forged transfer on death deed. Ready to go with all exhibits, including from Merry's friend Lucy, the guy at Antonelli's, the massage technician—and the notary. Miss Olivia V. Street was nervous, but she signed. And also Merry's affidavit, which supports the petition and attaches a copy of her own transfer on death deed leaving her land to Francine. And like you wanted, after it's filed, I'll mail a courtesy stamped copy of the whole shebang to Denny."

She laid two more stacks on Alice's desk. "Here's the petition for divorce, also with Merry's affidavit. And here's the petition to enforce covenants, ready to go."

"Great." Alice began her usual hyper-attentive final review—had she covered all bases? Once she was sure, she'd be in her usual tearing hurry to get these filed. She worked her way through the petition, read the very convincing affidavits, decided no further changes were needed. Ready to rock. And she was hungry.

She looked out the window. An old gold station wagon had pulled up.

*****

Silla had ordered lunch from M.A.'s Tea Garden House. M.A. herself—a vigorous seventy-nine-year-old, with her white hair still braided like a coronet, and wearing the frilly Tea Garden apron (available for high prices at the Tea Garden shop), burst through the front door and delivered lunch herself. Alice escorted her to the kitchen.

M.A. unloaded a venerable wooden picnic basket onto the table. "You have here my pimento cheese sandwiches on home-made multi-grain bread, toasted." She stacked the waxed-paper-wrapped sandwiches, cut into triangles, on a china plate. Alice began to salivate. "But you also have my devilled eggs, as requested, with tiny sweet gherkins and tiny sour gherkins, home-pickled." The devilled eggs, with a light sprinkle of paprika, rested on a classic white devilled-egg plate, with the pickles in a small china bowl. "Of course you'll bring the china back to me."

"Of course," breathed Alice. Devilled eggs first—her fingers were already itching to pick one up—or the pimento cheese?

"But wait, there's more," M.A. announced, reaching into the picnic basket. "Here's your jar of fresh-made lemonade, with mint. And here—" she reached in again, letting suspense build—"here are my triple-threat chocolate cookies. Still warm from the oven." Small dark circles, with wrinkled chocolaty tops, the cookies filled the room with the most intense chocolate aroma Alice could imagine.

Silla and Merry appeared at the door, eyes riveted on M.A.'s offerings. Silla whistled. "Look at those cookies! Is this a new recipe?"

"Brand new," M.A. said smugly. "All those years in a high school lab, you think I don't know how to reach people?"

"You know your chemicals." Alice's hand sneaked toward a cookie.

"Lunch first," warned M.A. "And bring me back my basket and the china. Today."

"Yes, ma'am. Would you consider sharing the recipe for—" but M.A. was already stalking out the front door.

"You'll never get her recipe." Silla dealt out their paper plates. "Hasn't Kinsear begged for her egg salad recipe for years? Without success?"

"Mm-hmm. And she announced to Silla she's making our wedding cake, but has she asked us a single question about what we want? No. Right, Silla?"

"Right. She didn't ask me either."

Alice first encountered M.A. when she trespassed on M.A.'s land and was greeted with a shotgun. Known for her fierce temper and tender heart—especially for former students and the Tea Garden—M.A. was, as Silla put it, independent as a hog on ice. And was also, as Alice said, "a woman to ride the river with," a woman to count on when the going got tough.

Alice set aside a plate for Ernesto and told Merry that he was busy acquiring her new security systems. Merry nodded, then looked up. "My life has changed so fast. Two weeks ago—I was still trying to figure out how long I could wait for Denny to—to get traction. And now? Fraud, forgery, lawsuits, security systems...." She straightened her shoulders. "Thank you both for helping me get traction on a really slippery slope."

"I've called Francine and left a message about staying safe, and writing her will. But I haven't heard back from her yet." Then, curious, Alice asked, "How much does Francine know?"

"We talk every day. She said she'd been asking herself how long I could hold out. She knows about the forged deed and my new deed to her, and I told her to be extra careful. And to start using my new phone number and new email—just got those this morning."

The three women sat around the table, silent except for the soft sound of chewing and an occasional "mmm." The devilled eggs disappeared first. Then pickles, sandwiches, and lemonade vanished. Finally, the cookies. "Lordy, lordy," Merry murmured, picking up a last crumb on her plate.

Alice glanced at the kitchen clock. "Twelve-thirty! Let's get these pleadings out the door!"

Silla was already at the copy machine with the petitions and exhibits. "Come on, baby, I've loaded you up with more paper and new toner. Here we go!" Merry and Alice watched, riveted, while the copy machine rustled into action, spitting out paper like the runaway copier in *Nine to Five.*

Silla stapled the copies as they flew out.

Alice turned to Merry. "On the petition to declare the bogus deed a fraud—we'll try to get that served asap. Plus, we'll mail Denny a courtesy copy. Once those two know eyes are on them and that you've filed your own transfer on death deed, I *hope* you and Francine will be safer."

Silla slipped the originals and service copies of their pleadings into separate manila envelopes and grabbed her shoulder bag. "I've already got citations and checks for the filing fees. I'll call if there's any problem."

As Silla started out the front door, Ernesto was already standing on the steps. He held the door open for Silla, then leaned inside. "Miss Merry? You ready to go? I've got a project to start!"

Merry hugged Alice, grabbed her purse and the plate of food for Ernesto, and followed him out.

Alice returned to her office, feeling relief wash over her: they'd taken critical steps on the journey to protect Merry. And Francine. She stood at the back window, staring at the pecan tree's new leaves and the flowerbed along the back fence, now showing the geometric small pale green rosettes that would soon erupt into a sea of bluebonnets.

Still to be done? Think about what she needed in discovery. She still felt dubious as to whether existing facts warranted a request for divorce *and protection.* The barn ladder? No idea when or how that happened. The wild Jersey bull? Merely an unsupported guess as to who provided the hordenine. Did filing a forged transfer on death deed constitute enough "danger" to warrant protection? Even though that forged deed *did* put Merry in danger of losing her right to leave her property to Francine? Was that enough? Surely....

With Merry and Silla gone, the office sat silent as an empty church. One thing Alice loved about being a lawyer was the lonely work of putting words on paper, sometimes late into the night, citing cases, developing arguments, pruning anything extraneous until each remaining word made its specific necessary contribution...all the while knowing that silent papers, like those Silla was filing right this moment at the courthouse, would break their silence, come to life, speak on behalf of Merry, and cause a ruckus, with final arguments in a courtroom before a listening judge. Words, doing their work.

Speak, O silent words! Alice felt a laugh begin. Too silly, too romantic.

Oh, maybe not. This work was critical. Could Merry afford it? Well, maybe Teena Ann could. Alice had requested costs and damages in the fraud petition, where she'd be paying for the handwriting expert, as well as costs in the other petitions to enforce covenants and the divorce petition. The thought of deposing Denny—maybe deposing him *first*, before Teena Ann—made her sit up straight, eyes wide, brain buzzing.

Could be some serious fun. And very useful. Who knew what he'd admit? Teena Ann would lie like a rug, of course. So would Denny, but that rug would be wrinkled and full of holes.

Text from Silla: "Everything's filed. Mailed Denny a stamped copy. Heading to the stable. Text if you need me back tonight. Otherwise, see you early mañana." Second text: "Attached pls find draft list of invitees for the Beer Barn wedding reception—have added Kinsear's invitees—can you edit?" Third text: "Attached pls find draft invitation for Beer Barn reception—can you edit and decide typeface and paper?" Fourth text: "How many days until wedding? Just counting!"

Oh, Silla!—collaborating with Kinsear and making sure the wedding was on track. She had to admit it was a relief. She typed back: "Will do! Thanks!"

She blinked, realized she'd been staring at the laptop screen for two minutes, brain-dead. But she could still make the last yoga class. She unhooked her yoga bag from the back of her office door, grabbed her laptop and work bag, and hurried out the door. In the driveway she took one more deep breath of the wintersweet to clear her mind of Denny and Teena Ann.

Om. Yoga, then home, where she broke her long-standing promise to herself and all her ancestors and ate for supper a couple of crackers with cheese, over the kitchen sink, no plate, no napkin. Her ancestors crowded around her head in horror. She talked briefly with Kinsear,

then crawled into bed. Maybe, after this long day, a long sleep.
But no.

Chapter Eighteen

A Narrow Escape

At five a.m. she groped for the insistently ringing phone—Tonio, breathless. She heard a siren in the background. "Alice! Listen—Merry's barn caught fire. Don't worry, Merry's fine. The firemen are still here, finishing up. Hoses everywhere. You'll want to see what happened but no need to come right now."

By seven she was in the parking lot at Merry's, staring up at the smoldering ruins of the west end of the barn. Had the fire reached Merry's milking parlor, built into the east side? The acrid smoke made her cough, made her eyes water. Tonio and Ernesto met her in the parking lot.

"Merry's asleep, worn out," Tonio said. He looked exhausted, smoke smudges on his face and arms, shirt gray with ash.

"Tell me what happened!"

"Well, all I can say is, thank God Ernesto got us started on the alarm systems yesterday. We'd put smoke alarms in the creamery and in the barn. Looks like the fire started around three a.m., over on the far end of the barn. But it didn't get to the milking parlor."

"Oh, Tonio! And the cows! What about the cows?"

"Out in the pasture with the goats, fortunately. The smoke alarm went off and alerted the fire department," Ernesto added. His face was grim; no sign of that dimpled smile. "The hay stacked inside the west barn door burned really fast. But the firemen stopped the fire before it got to the milking parlor." He gazed at Alice, his eyes unblinking. "The firemen said they weren't sure, but someone might have lit fire starters at that barn door. Maybe used something like charcoal lighter fluid. That's where Merry started stacking hay inside the barn, after she got those Jersey cows."

The two men walked Alice across the parking lot where she could look over the fence at the blackened wreckage. Part of the roof had collapsed above the gap where the barn door once stood.

"Did you see anything? Hear anything?" Alice asked.

"Tonio and I worked on the new systems till about eleven last night, and I decided to sleep here," Ernesto said. "I thought I heard a car or truck slow down, sometime late, but that's all."

Tonio shook his head. "I got up and did my walk-around about two, checking all the doors, but I didn't see anything."

"But Alice, we did get some cameras up yesterday," Ernesto added.

"We'll check the video cards. And the fire department notified the Fire Marshal's Office and the police. They were here at dawn. I think they looked for prints and footprints, but of course with the firehoses—it was kind of a mess."

"Let me know as soon as you can, if you see anything else that worries you. Anyone." She looked at the two men, dark-eyed, stalwart, exhausted. "Thank God you were both here."

On the way back down the creek road she called Silla, who was already in the office.

"Good lord! But Merry and Tonio and Ernesto are okay? And the house? And the creamery? All the animals?"

"Yes. A narrow escape. And to think last night I was worrying whether we'd pled enough facts to back up Merry's request for protection. Now it's a burning issue, right?"

Silla snorted. "Ha. I hope Ernesto finds some fun facts on the video cards in those cameras."

*****

"Ooh! You smell like smoke!" Silla waved her hands when Alice walked in. "Call Cynthia Surratt. She looked at the draft wills you sent and says she only has two small changes, and James says he'd want the same changes on his. Charitable gifts. I've made the changes for you to review. They don't have any concerns about the current powers of attorney. Otherwise, they're ready to sign."

Alice called Cynthia, discussed her requested changes, and confirmed that James wanted the same changes on his will. "He does, but he's not feeling very well," said Cynthia. "Can we come by maybe tomorrow to sign the wills? He got his Physician Orders for Life-Sustaining Treatment form signed by our primary care doc. I'll get mine signed today.

"Tomorrow works," said Alice.

Silla swooped into Alice's office waving two papers. "Got your invitees added to our list. I'm ready to order invitations. Here's the draft." She handed one sheet of paper to Alice. "Now, which typeface and which paper?" She handed an order form to Alice.

"Hmm." The invitation included those weighty words— "wedding reception." And the date, place, and time. It was really happening. Come on, Alice! She took a breath and made check marks on the order form—"This typeface. Ecru paper with that soft sort of edge."

"Got it." And Silla swooped back out.

Now, "time to turn to." Her father's phrase again, in his voice, and how she missed that mellow timbre, the distinctive vocabulary, the humor beneath his driest statements.

And here maybe what it meant was—amend the dadgum divorce petition. Maybe something like, "Early this morning, after this petition was filed, fire erupted at petitioner's barn, causing extensive destruction. Petitioner's husband had not spent the night at home (and had been absent for some days). Security cameras at the scene recorded the following..."

Just as she picked up her cell to call and ask what the cameras had seen, it started ringing. Ernesto.

"Well, I'm emailing you what we got on the night vision camera at the back right corner of the barn, Alice. But it's hard to see who it is. Two people, dressed in dark clothes. One's a little bigger than the other. Both wearing ball caps."

"Can you see what they're doing?"

"Oh, yeah. Poured something out of a container, not big, maybe charcoal lighter fluid. And dropped a match. Then disappeared." After a moment: "Thank God it wasn't gasoline. Like I said today, it was enough to catch the hay on fire, under the barn door."

"Could you see a car? Or a truck?"

"The shape looked like a pickup. Big one. Can't see the plates, though; it pulled into the parking area sideways. Darkish, but you can't tell the color."

"Anything else that could tie the fire directly to Teena Ann or Denny?"

"Not so far."

"Okay. Thanks. And thank you for getting all this security in place, Ernesto! You may have saved Merry's life. You certainly saved the cheese business."

"Merry's got all the windows open in the milking parlor and the creamery. We'll start milking again tonight. Those goats'll be ready!" He hung up.

Alice was second-guessing herself over waiting until Monday's petitions were filed and then mailing, not emailing, a copy to Denny. If she'd emailed a copy including the notary's affidavit, might he and Teena Ann not have burned the barn?

But not only had she not wanted them dodging the process server, she'd also been anxious to protect the notary against interference by, or, worse, danger from Denny or Teena Ann before Alice could get the notary's affidavit testimony on file.

She'd finally included in the divorce petition and Merry's affidavit a section briefly describing "recent unexplained incidents" including Merry's fall from the barn ladder and the hordenine-crazed bull. She wandered out of the office and found Silla at her worktable, working on client bills.

"I'm frustrated," Alice said. "I sure hope Files can identify that truck. I want to amend that divorce petition and get Denny barred from the property."

"Agreed. Meanwhile, I'm excited about making Teena Ann pony up for Merry's costs. I'll enjoy helping with that, big time!"

*****

It was nearly eleven. Feeling at loose ends, Alice wandered out the back door of the office, checked the bluebonnet seedlings, looked at the blue sky, felt the soft southeast breeze brushing her pants against her legs. Which made her think—wedding. The dress. How was it coming?

Chapter Nineteen

Tacky And Tackier

Ten minutes later she pulled up in front of KP Cox Creations, an elderly but shipshape small stucco house, painted soft pink with green shutters, on the south side of Coffee Creek. KP met her at the door, hugged her and pulled her inside. "I am so glad you called! Time for a final fitting! And afterwards, coffee and coffee cake!"

Short and wiry, her silver hair in a punk cut, eyes narrowed in professional scrutiny, KP scanned Alice. "You look great!"

Alice took a deep breath. The pink house smelled wonderful inside—not just cinnamon and vanilla from whatever KP was baking, and not just KP's own unique faint scent—flowers? Mint?

"What's that smell that makes me feel like I'm six years old again?"

"Pine Sol. The cleaner just left. I always feel the same way...like I'm about to go out and play hopscotch or climb a tree. Okay, Alice, come to the fitting room!"

KP had made her name in LA, designing costumes for the movie industry. Five years ago, she'd moved back to the Hill Country. "Downsized my ambitions," she said. "Happy doing wedding dresses, bridesmaid dresses, vintage costumes for our drama productions." She glanced sideways at Alice, smirking. "Yours, my dear, was extra fun. Okay, off with your very practical office garb. Hope you wore a low-cut bra."

She had.

The wedding costume was on a hanger on the fitting room garment rack. The window was open; a little breeze stirred the dress, making its skirt sway back and forth. And next to the dress, on its own hanger—a petticoat, slim at the waist and gored outward, also midi-length, with five inches of ruffles at the hem.

Alice clapped her hands, thrilled. "Oh, KP! Oh, oh, oh!"

"You said you wanted to dance with Kinsear, wanted something old and something new, wanted something you could maybe wear again, wanted something in your favorite pinkish-apricot. Well, the petticoat's vintage, and here's your dress."

KP had designed a sleeveless dress with a sweetheart neckline and fitted top, sewn pleats shaping the bosom, lace around the neckline. The midi-length skirt, gored from the waist, blossomed like a trumpet. KP had used silk-linen fabric that draped and flowed. The color made

Alice think of apricots, of peach blossoms, of her daughter's cheeks when she ran in from playing outside, of her own favorite dress when she started kindergarten.

Alice stepped into the vintage petticoat and tied the waist tapes. Then she slipped the dress over her head. KP zipped up the side zipper. Alice peeked at the mirror. She turned left, then right. Below her knees the skirt flounced softly back and forth as she turned.

"Hold still," commanded KP. "Still need to blind-stitch the hem." She knelt and began pinning the fabric. Alice felt blissful, watching the skilled hands moving below. Finally KP stood and carefully helped Alice slip out of the dress.

"That peachy color lights up your face." KP looked very pleased with her creation.

"I usually feel like I'm dressing for myself. Kinsear, though—I cannot wait for him to see this. Oh, KP, it's perfect. I think it'll match my new boots too!" Alice tugged herself back into her "very practical office garb".

"I happen to know it does match. Took a swatch by Goodson Kells."

"You are coming to the reception, right? Dancing at the Beer Barn. Silla's about to send out the invitations!"

"Of course! I always enjoy taking credit in public! Okay, you can come back next week to get the finished product."

Alice glanced at the rack of other KP creations, then took a second look. "KP—is that rodeo wear?"

"You mean that highly garish revoltingly glittery cowgirl shirt? And the slinky pants with initials embroidered down the side? Last thing I'm doing for that woman. I am not putting my label in those, but she's going to have to pay full freight—in cash—before I let her have them."

"Is 'TAT' for Teena Ann Traynor?"

KP scowled. "You got it. Tacky And Tackier. Honestly, Alice, I've always prided myself on finishing what I start. But I knew it was a mistake just as soon as I bought the fabric, when she waltzed in and demanded more sequins. Then she was slow pay—I told her I was stopping work until she paid 90% of my fee." She looked at Alice.

"She's not one of your clients, is she? If so, get a big retainer up front!"

"No. She's an adversary. She owns the land on Old Hays next to Merry's creamery, where the proposed concert venue would be built."

"An adversary?"

"Yep. The covenants on her land forbid commercial use. So...." Alice lifted an eyebrow.

"Bless you, my child!"

*****

Back in the car, still exhilarated by seeing what KP had wrought, by trying on the silky, whirly dress, by coffee and coffee cake, Alice drove slowly through downtown. Which took her past the old Coffee Creek Hotel. She wondered whether Jerry Weathers had been served yet with the petition to prevent commercial use.

And what Files had found, if anything, with his metal detector search of the ballfield construction site.

She parked at the courthouse and made her way into the Sheriff's Annex. The desk sergeant looked up. "You're looking for Detective Files? He's back from early lunch. I'll give him a call."

She dawdled at the end of Files's hall till she saw him stick his head out of his door. He waved her on down the corridor. When she reached his office, he pointed her to her usual cold metal chair, pulled out his bottom desk drawer, leaned back in his desk chair, and propped his right foot on the drawer, his favorite position.

"I was wondering if I'd hear from you today. You wanta know what we found, after we talked to your UPS buddy Rich?"

"Yes."

"We sent a helpless young crime scene member up those girders to get samples and photos."

It would be a long time before Alice could get that picture out of her mind.

"He sampled that shiny spot you mentioned, on one of those girders leading up to the roof over the stands. Maybe roof coating material. While he was up there, with a safety belt on, unlike your young friend Charles Boone, he saw another shiny spot, sampled it too. So now the question is...?" He lifted an eyebrow at her.

"How did the slick roofing material get on those girders? And also, per the coroner, on the victim's 'jeans, on the right knee and shin area, and on the palm of his left hand and palm and fingers of his right hand.'"

"That's the question. One shiny spot was approximately above the spot on the ground where Charles Boone landed when he fell. While he was up there, the recruit also spotted a couple of impact areas where a bullet apparently hit the girder and caromed off. You could see the marks on the iron."

"On the girder near where Charlie fell?"

Files nodded. "I've contacted the Travis County Medical Examiner about what we found, including part of our sample of the shiny spots on the girder."

"Did you find any bullets?"

"We found two, both west of the site, where they could have ricocheted based on the marks on the girder. They were quite deformed, again maybe from hitting the iron girder. Could be pretty hard to prove, though."

Alice leaned back in her chair. "So, are you going after Conrad O'Leary? He was at the site. Or anyone else at Apex?"

"We've asked O'Leary to come in for questioning. His office says he's in Nevada but supposed to come back this week."

"What about Weathers? His boss?"

"He's also in Nevada this week, at least according to whoever answers the phone at Apex Partners. Why?"

"The TCEQ documents. Remember? They include notes from a staff member's telephone conversation the day of the hearing, reporting that Charlie called them to discuss that he'd received some documents from a contractor showing the proposed site would have 75% impervious surface coverage instead of the maximum 65% allowed."

Files frowned. "We haven't seen any documents like that. Pretty sure nothing like that was in Charlie's room over at the old Coffee Creek Hotel either. You think they could be significant?"

"Maybe. If I were Apex management, I wouldn't want my engineer admitting at the public hearing on the venue permit that an Apex contractor had sent the company those documents."

Files squinted at the ceiling. "Could've been just a misunderstanding. Contractor got the dimensions wrong."

"Be fun to ask the contractor that at a deposition." Alice wriggled on the cold hard chair, crossed her legs. "I can't stand this chair much longer."

Files grinned. She went on. "But where we started was—how did that slick stuff get on the girders? Was it the construction people?"

"They claim not. I talked to the contractor and the construction chief. Met them at the site. They were horrified by what happened to Charles Boone. They explained how they apply the roofing liquid. It goes only on the roof, nowhere else. They take all kinds of safeguards for the working crew so they won't slip. The roof over the ballpark stadium seating is pretty flat, so they didn't have to use safety harnesses up there."

"But don't they have to take all that material up on top of the roof?" Alice had wondered what the girders were for.

"Not this final coat. Know how they put it on? I had no idea. They run a long, long hose from the high-pressure air sprayer, down on the ground, up to the roof. The silicone liquid's in the tank next to the sprayer. The workman on the roof walks back and forth, spraying the liquid from the sprayer attachment to the hose."

"Where did they keep that liquid silicone material?"

"Alice, you are a persistent person. They kept it with their other chemicals in the little metal building they brought on site. You may have seen it, at the rear of the ballfield proper. Not across the road on the staging area."

"Locked?"

"Some dispute about that. They say it was padlocked when they left. But when we met them there, we didn't find a padlock on it. One interesting thing, though. Apparently this stuff gets a skin on top if it's exposed to air—from the moisture in the air. One of the tubs—the top wasn't on securely, and there was a skin. Pissed off the construction chief. That stuff's not cheap."

"Did someone get in and steal some of the liquid and use that sprayer to get it up on the girder?"

"No way. That sprayer equipment's expensive. They keep it locked in a van. Nothing's missing. Plus, each sprayer component gets cleaned with mineral spirits after use to prevent clogging. They'd notice if it had been used. And I know you're about to ask. So, yes—we got a sample of the silicone material that had developed a skin in the tub with the loosened top. And yes, we've shared samples with the Travis County Medical Examiner."

Alice sat musing, remembering the girder, the supports, the slick spot, the other slick spot....

"Someone got in their metal building, and someone squirted some clear liquid on the girders? How? Someone shot a couple of bullets at the girders? Is that why he fell? Why were those girders even there?"

"Helped the construction crew stage the roof sections."

So...who was responsible for the slick stuff on Charlie's jeans, knee, shin, hands...and for his fall?

And what was that feeling she'd missed something?

C h a p t e r   T w e n t y

Don't Touch Anything!

When Alice stalked back through the front door, Silla stood up from her worktable and followed her into her office. "What's up? Didn't you like KP's creation?"

"I did! It's great. But I stopped to talk to George Files on the way back." She told Silla what she'd learned. "I can't stand what happened to Charlie." She sat down at her desk and rubbed her temples.

Silla nodded. "I get it. Here's something else to think about now that we've got the petitions filed. Jeanie Boone asked you to call. Remember, she and her mom want your help with Charlie's estate. The signed engagement letter got here in the afternoon mail."

Alice was feeling that she hadn't helped Charlie, but she could at least help his family. And something was still nagging at her, a gap, a missing piece.

Alice grabbed a pencil and sticky pad. "Okay, let's think. Charlie's employer was Worth Engineers in Dallas, under contract with Apex Partners. Worth should already have contacted Charlie's family. Can you call their human resources folks? Tell them we represent the family and need to know what benefits he had, whether there was any insurance that might go to his family, whether he'd started investing in a 401K plan or something similar, whether they owe him any salary and bonuses. Also, ask them the status of OSHA's investigation into his death. I'll call Jeanie and see what she and his mom can tell us about his financial records, bank accounts, and so on."

"Don't forget Jeanie and her mom will want to know when the medical examiner will release his body," Silla said on her way out the door.

Alice closed her eyes and shook her head at the thought of having to ask when your son's body, your brother's body, would be released. Especially when the body was Charlie's.

She found herself imagining how Charlie felt on the afternoon before the hearing—maybe a bit nervous, but determined to be prepared for this big task. Of course he'd never have appeared at the hearing in his jeans, which he'd worn to the ballfield, so he must have planned for uncertainty. He dutifully went to the ballfield as his boss instructed but apparently took along his dress clothes in case he left that meeting with only enough time to change at the high school before the hearing, likely in the boys' bathroom. He'd have planned to wear—what? A blazer, a tie, a dress shirt, a pair of chinos?

He'd forgotten his computer in Jeanie's car. Of course he'd want his computer at the hearing. And wouldn't he have wanted more? Maybe a carefully prepared outline and key documents? Plus his perennial companion, that orange notebook? Hard to imagine someone as organized as Charlie forgetting anything, but maybe he was really rattled by the phone call he got, apparently ordering him to go check out the roof at that new ballfield. Jeanie had mentioned a pricey new messenger bag. I didn't even ask about that, Alice scolded herself.

She called Files, left a message. "Jeanie Boone says you've got the garment bag from Charles Boone's truck in the evidence room. Did it by chance contain anything besides his clothes for the hearing? I'm thinking of notes, papers, or the orange notebook he usually carried."

She got a text back in five minutes. "Not per evidence list. Clothes only."

Okay, a long shot; she took a deep breath and called Jeanie. She had a good excuse—getting started on Charlie's finances.

"I'm at home, Alice, but I've got to leave for San Marcos in thirty minutes for class." Jeanie and Alice worked on a list of Charlie's financial accounts and any outstanding bills, as well as his subscriptions. When they finished, Jeanie was silent for a few moments, then said, "It's too quiet here now. No Charlie playing his drums, shooting hoops outside on the driveway...."

"I didn't know he was a drummer!"

"Oh yes. He was terrific. It's weird, being alone in the house with the silent drum kit. I went in and struck the brass hat just to get a little echo going. Charlie was always good with his hands—he could juggle—he'd juggle oranges in the kitchen."

Silence. "How's your mom?"

"It helps that she's still at work, school secretary, you know. She loves the kids. I don't know how she'll function this summer, when school's out."

Charlie juggling oranges. "Jeanie, Charlie's orange engineer's notebook."

"Yeah, he loved those orange notebooks."

"When we looked for Charlie's computer and you found it in your car, did you find anything else? I still feel we need to see his orange notebook and the materials he'd planned to have at the hearing. Surely he planned to have more than his computer there. You'd mentioned a new messenger bag?"

"Yes! His messenger bag was stuck under the seat," Jeanie said. "I haven't opened it, though."

"I feel it's important to see any notes he made on the impervious cover issue. They may be the key to why in the world Apex sent him to visit that ballfield construction site the very afternoon of the hearing. Of course, maybe someone took his notes or other materials from his apartment, given how trashed it was. Or maybe he left them in the Apex office, but I doubt Apex will give us access." She waited.

"Hang on," Jeanie said. "I've kept his messenger bag hanging on a hook in my bedroom, where I can see it." Alice heard her footsteps, then some rustling.

"There's a zippered compartment inside." Alice heard a zipper. "Alice, there it is. The little orange notebook. Also a folded site plan or blueprint, looks like just one sheet."

"Don't pull them out. Avoid fingerprints. Leave them in the bag. But I really need to see those."

"I've got my seminar at Texas State this afternoon at three. I can't make it to Coffee Creek and back there in time."

"Why don't I just meet you in San Marcos? How about in the parking lot at Palmer's Restaurant? In about an hour?"

"Perfect." Jeanie hung up.

Her phone buzzed—message from Kinsear. "On way home from Austin meeting. Is late lunch possible?"

She called him. "How about a drive to San Marcos? We need to pick up a messenger bag and get it back here."

"Will it be like this when we're married? I'll ask if we can get lunch, and you'll say sure, but first we have to fly to Alaska to interview a witness, or you'll say yes indeed, lunch sounds great, let's grab a bag of potato chips and eat them in the car?"

"It's an emergency. Pretty much."

"I'm on. I'll pick you up in fifteen minutes."

She realized she had a grin on her face, with no one there to see it. Why? The comforting prospect ahead. She'd tell Kinsear everything she'd heard from Rich Woodworth, Postmistress Georgia Green, Files, and the medical examiner. She'd watch his face, watch the quick uptake, watch his analytical mind at work. She'd tell him how she felt about Charlie, the utter wrongness of what had happened to him, her need to punish the killer.

Rummaging in the kitchen she found a pack of string cheese, a bag of apples, a box of her favorite multi-seed crackers, and, yes, a bag of the potato chips she and Silla had jointly declared the best. A random car picnic.

*****

Kinsear backed into a parking place at the restaurant. "Can't believe we're at Palmer's when it's neither lunchtime nor dinnertime."

"The string cheese was inadequate?"

He shook his head, lifting an eyebrow. "I insist on a decent dinner tonight."

Alice spotted Jeanie, maneuvering the blue RAV into a parking space. "C'mon. There she is."

Jeanie climbed out, clutching the messenger bag. She gave Alice a one-armed hug and handed her the bag.

Alice introduced Kinsear, who said, "I'm very sad to hear about your brother. Sounds like he will be deeply missed."

Jeanie nodded.

Alice pulled out her phone. "Jeanie, I want to take pictures of the messenger bag before we touch what's in the zippered compartment. You've left things just where they were, right, haven't tried to get anything out?"

"Nope. It's just like Charlie left it."

Alice took a photo.

"I don't want to add fingerprints," Alice said, turning to Kinsear. The man always had a bandana.

Kinsear pulled a folded bandana from his pocket—pale blue.

Alice wrapped the bandana around the messenger bag and put it in a grocery tote bag. "We're not going to open it until we get back to Coffee Creek," she told Jeanie. "I'll let you know if the notebook helps us understand what happened to Charlie."

*****

What now?" asked Kinsear. The messenger bag lay in the back seat of his ancient Land Cruiser. "Your office? The Sheriff's Department?"

"Hmmph." Alice felt torn. "I can hardly wait to open it—carefully, with gloves on."

"What about Files?"

Silence while she thought. She was desperate to pull that zipper tab, find what Charlie had stashed in the messenger bag, see what the orange notebook had to say about 75% impervious cover. Could that folded blueprint be what the contractor delivered to Charlie at the office? She muttered to Kinsear, "Files says he hasn't seen anything from any contractor in the TCEQ documents, and I can't tell if he's really looked at Charlie's computer. But I can't let anything screw up a piece of evidence that might explain Charlie's death. Chain of custody should be okay— Charlie left this bag in Jeanie's car. Jeanie's had it since then. She gave us the computer, and Files has that. But still...."

Was she making the right decision? She had to see that notebook... or at least have full access to it. Wisest thing...probably to call Files.

"Tell you what." Kinsear turned onto Ranch Road 12 toward Wimberley and Coffee Creek. "I'd like to stop at that ballfield site before we go to your office. It's on the way, kind of."

When they reached the turn-off for Windy Lane, Kinsear parked next to the construction site, where crime scene tape still flapped in the breeze.

They stood at the chain-link fence. Alice pointed at the girders, then at the ground where Charlie had fallen. "You can't see them very well now—the dust has dulled them—but there're two spots that were very shiny when I stopped by the first time. The crime scene team sampled them—silicone roof coating, very slick, and clear."

"But you say the roofers used a power pump to coat the roof itself, right?"

"Right. The material was kept in that shed back there"—she pointed. "The door padlock was gone when the crime scene people got here and one tub—"

Kinsear finished. "The top wasn't completely down."

"Yep. They don't keep the power sprayer on site, so that wasn't what sprayed the girder."

Kinsear looked at the girder, scanned the site, then slowly turned around and stared across the street. "The dumpster?"

"That's the contractor's. That lot's the staging area." She turned back, staring up again at the girders, thinking about Jeanie and her mom. Why in the world did Weathers and O'Leary send Charlie out to this isolated construction site, a site they didn't own?

"You coming?" asked Kinsear

"What?"

"You never had a pool, did you?"

"A *pool*...!?" She caught up with him on the other side of the street as he strode across the staging area toward the dumpster, dodging the muddy truck tracks that criss-crossed the ground.

Kinsear helped Alice steady herself on a jutting support at the dumpster's base. The two peered into the dumpster's depths: torn packaging, empty concrete bags, heavy wrapping from stacks of lumber, broken-down cardboard boxes, strapping tape. Lunch sacks, sandwich wrappers. Some local had apparently decided to dispose of household trash as well—and had flung in at least three white trash bags, one visibly full of diapers, as well as grocery bags full of cans and boxes. Kinsear walked the length of the dumpster, peering down, then circled to the far side and stopped.

"Come around here, Alice."

She climbed off the support, hurried around to where he stood, clambered up again on the support beam.

"See that?"

Wedged under a broken-down cardboard box she spotted crumpled bright plastic. Alice read aloud, "something ending in 're' then... Electric Water Guns for Ad...and below that '...matic high pr---....'"

She looked at Kinsear. "Water guns for *adults*?"

"Sure. They've got more range, too. That label probably says, 'Automatic high pressure.' Range could be twenty to thirty feet. You haven't ever seen one of those at a pool party? What were you doing, lolling on a chaise lounge, sipping a daiquiri?"

"Seriously?" Wait, Kinsear had a small pool at the ranch. "Ben. Do you have water guns like that?"

He looked slightly sheepish. "Hey, my girls like to invite people for pool parties..."

Alice peered down at the wrapping. "So what would you do, put some of that clear silicone stuff in an electric water gun? Would that work?"

"I'll bet it would, if you shot it off fast enough, before the air got to it. Shouldn't we call Files?"

No question in her mind, especially for items at the bottom of a dumpster. She pulled her phone from her pocket, where Files's number was now a "Favorite."

He answered. "Yes?" She heard road noise.

"George, can you come to the ballfield construction site? We may have found a possible answer in the Boone case."

"Who's we?"

"Ben Kinsear. We're at the staging area site across the street. By the dumpster."

"I thought I might go home early today. Wrong again. Dumpster diving, are you? Our crime scene people already looked in there. We need them to come back?"

"Your best dumpster diver."

"*PLEASE* don't touch anything!" He hung up.

Chapter Twenty-One

He Was A Straight Shooter

Kinsear and Alice retired to the shade of a live oak, watching Detective Files brief the arriving crime scene team as they stared down into the dumpster. Then the team huddled with their leader. "What are they doing?" Alice whispered.

"Flipping a coin? This is interesting," Kinsear whispered back.

With all deliberate speed the team took assigned positions, photographed the contents from above, carefully positioned ladders for entry and exit. Three climbed down into the dumpster. Alice could see only the tops of their heads.

"Watch for nails on that scrap lumber," called the leader from the ladder leaning on the outside of the dumpster. "Jimbo got stuck on it the other day."

They heard muffled voices. Ten minutes later, Files strode over. "You guys were right. That's a wrapper off an electric spray gun."

Alice elbowed Kinsear. "You nailed it," she whispered.

"But wait, there's more. The team dug under some of the adjacent garbage and found the gun, too." Files almost smiled. "They're dusting for prints, but I'll be surprised if they find any."

"Why?"

"Whoever left the gun and the wrapper poked them beneath a flattened cardboard box, maybe using one of the longish pieces of scrap lumber. Got the gun hidden, but only part of the wrapper. Not a great job of concealment, but whoever it was apparently didn't care enough to hide it completely. So I expect whoever it was, wasn't very worried about fingerprints."

"Did they find the bag it came in? Or the price slip?"

"Why? You think we'll find those too, Alice?"

"I was just thinking: this whole trip to the ballfield, on the day of the hearing, happened suddenly, happened fast, maybe after Charlie said something to his bosses about the new contractor plans that arrived. You know, the ones showing 75% impervious coverage."

Files frowned. "You mentioned that Apex wouldn't want those discussed at the hearing, even if they were just a result of contractor confusion."

"Right. If you find silicone sealant in that gun, I'm guessing whoever bought it thought this up and then had to buy the gun in a hurry. No time to order from Amazon. Had to get the water gun sometime the same day as the hearing, after Charlie revealed his concern about the plans, and maybe about his phone conversation with the TCEQ office, but before Charlie was supposed to show up out here. So, maybe whoever used that water gun had to buy it somewhere nearby, like in Bee Cave, at the sporting goods store, or Target." She paused. "Or maybe lots of adult men travel with electric water guns?"

"I'll alert the guys to watch for a bag and receipt."

Kinsear spoke up. "Alice said you sampled the clear material on the girders above the ground where Charlie landed. I assume you'll sample the water gun too?"

Files nodded.

Alice's mind was buzzing. "I still want to know exactly when Charlie's watch called EMS and when Conrad O'Leary called. My guess is after he heard the sirens."

"We're trying to confirm that." Files turned, eyes moving across the scene. "Gotta get back to the troops."

He strode back to the dumpster, phone to his ear. Alice watched him lean over and talk to the crime scene team leader, now standing in the dumpster. In a moment a member of the crime scene team hurried to the team's truck, then returned to the dumpster with a long prybar.

"You going to share the news about the messenger bag?" Kinsear asked, voice neutral.

Feeling reluctant, Alice nodded. Files was returning.

"George, you can't go home yet," Alice said.

"Why ever not?"

She told him what was in the Land Cruiser.

"Ah." He glanced at Kinsear, then back at Alice. "I suppose you want to see it right away. And I need to be there."

She nodded.

*****

Twenty minutes later, all three stood by a table at the Sheriff's Department in a cubicle next to the property room. The evidence mavens had photographed and fingerprinted the messenger bag and the orange notebook and the folded paper Charlie had stored in its zippered compartment and then returned them to Files. Files handed Kinsear his blue bandana. "Nice touch." And to Alice, "Thanks. You didn't have to bring this to me."

"I don't want to take a single step that makes it harder for you to find out why Charlie Boone died and who caused his death. But if you keep the originals, I'd like copies of the notebook and that folded site plan or whatever it is, before we leave." She grimaced, staring at the open notebook. The last few pages contained what looked like multiple calculations in tiny, neat printing.

Files nodded. "Okay, let's see what we got." He phoned an assistant: "Get me a copy of this notebook while we take a quick look at the folded plan, then make a copy of it too." Wearing gloves he unfolded the plan, laid it flat. "Alice, this sheet already looks like a copy, don't you think?"

"I agree. I expect Charlie made that copy and put the original in the Apex files. I don't think he'd have kept an original this way."

Laid out on the table, the sheet showed a site plan of the proposed venue. In the lower right corner Alice read, "DRAFT PER REQUEST OF APEX PARTNERS, by Synergy LLC," and it was dated the day before the public meeting.

"Confusing." Files squinted at the plan. "Looks like one drawing laid over another."

"Original site plan with another on top?" Kinsear suggested.

"Charlie thought it showed 75% impervious cover, instead of the 65% allowed by the regs. That's why he called the TCEQ engineer that day. I'm thinking the dotted lines outside the solid lines show what Apex would get with more than 65% impervious cover," Alice said. "For starters, those dotted lines show a bigger parking lot, and a larger building for concessions and restrooms."

"But why would someone kill Charles Boone over this site plan?" Files looked dubious.

Alice shook her head. "I'm guessing that if TCEQ learned about it, they'd be hyper-concerned about Apex's compliance—that if they issued a permit with a 65% limit, they'd feel compelled to make numerous trips to the site during construction to avoid so-called accidental expansion by the contractors of the impervious coverage allowed. TCEQ's already stretched. The legislature doesn't give TCEQ that kind of money. They need to be able to depend on the applicant's compliance."

"But—to kill this young engineer for fear he might say something at the hearing?"

"He's—well, he was a straight shooter." Alice stared at the messenger bag, lying there on the table. Barely worn. "He worked for Worth Engineers. Apex was their client. I think someone should talk to his bosses there. And to this Synergy outfit that drafted the plan."

"Are you looking at me, Alice?"

"Yes. I'd be interested in what they tell an investigating officer. How does Worth train their new engineers for a first job in the field like this? Do they tell them to ignore signs that the firm's client is trying to slide past the law? I doubt it. And what was Synergy instructed to produce?"

"Sounds like something you'd ask in a deposition."

Kinsear snorted. "You bet she would. One of her favorite activities."

"I think it would get their attention if you call them first." Alice stared back at Files. "Of course I'm going to call them too."

"I don't have time to deconstruct these—these squinchy little calculations in his notebook."

"Give us tonight, and Alice can study her copy," Kinsear said.

Files nodded. "Okay. Sometime in the next couple of days, we'll also get test results from whatever's in that water gun. Oh. I owe you some other results, Alice. First, on that break-in at your office? We found some prints that don't belong to you or Silla, on your desk and drawer pulls and hers, and in the conference room, on the closet door, and on the safe. But we haven't located any matches in the records."

"I guess the print records don't include whether the person wears ostrich skin boots?"

"No. Meanwhile, we do have other crimes to investigate."

"Of course you do." Alice lifted her chin. "*Meanwhile*, of course, the mayor herself told me she's very interested in this particular crime. Very interested. Is anyone checking out what's up at Apex's Nevada venue? Why are Weathers and O'Leary out there?"

Kinsear elbowed Alice, none too subtly.

"Later," she said, and they made their way out of Files's office, down the corridor, toward the entrance hall.

The desk sergeant was leaning back in his chair, reading the *Coffee Creek Caller.* He looked up at Alice. "Hey, you made the paper!"

He handed her his copy, pointing to a letter to the editor: "Concert

Venue Challenges Recent Lawsuit."

"Feel free to keep that. How'd you make the man so mad?"

Alice and Kinsear stared down at the first paragraph of the letter signed by Jerry Weathers, Apex Partners.

"'Opposing landowners will fight a losing battle in opposing our proposed concert venue, a project that will bring significant benefits to a town in great need of the stimulus we will provide,'" read Kinsear.

Well, well. Obviously, Apex had been served, Alice realized. Had Teena Ann, the other defendant?

Kinsear continued: "'Apex has extensive resources and will vigorously contest the misguided lawsuit filed by lawyer Alice Greer.' Alice, misguided? But wait, there's more. 'Coffee Creek lags far behind the curve in seizing the reins of music culture. With its state-of-the-art construction and landscaping, our concert venue will become a vital center of new music, with thousands of eager fans bringing prosperity to Coffee Creek. As mentioned, we have staying power. We're determined to finalize this venue. As we all know, you can't stop progress! That's what Apex offers—an exciting magnet drawing thousands, instead of stagnation.' Gee, Alice, when were you last called stagnant?"

Alice pursed her mouth like she'd just sucked a lemon. "Jerry Weathers. What a jerk..." she breathed, scanning the rest of the article. "Looks like the paper just printed this without getting a response from the mayor, the plaintiffs, me, or anyone who protested at the hearing." She jammed the paper into her work bag.

"Interesting he claims big resources. Let's get to your house, pour a particularly good wine, and take a squinty-eyed look at Charlie's cryptic little notes," Kinsear said. "May take hours, so it would be wise for me to spend the night, don't you think?"

"So wise!"

With Kinsear's car behind her, Alice headed up the creek road towards home. Her cell phone rang. She looked at the number—local, but unfamiliar. With misgivings she said, "Hello?"

Chapter Twenty-Two

You're Kidding, Right?

"Richie Farmer here, with the *Coffee Creek Caller*."

"Yes, Richie?" Silla had heard at the Camellia that Richie, the newspaper owner's new wife's son, was on a short leash at the paper—"not likely to win us any Pulitzers," was the whisper.

"You filed this lawsuit against Apex Partners and Teena Ann Traynor, trying to stop the concert venue on Old Hays." Accusatory tone.

"Yes, Richie, I filed a lawsuit on behalf of nearby property owners to prevent violation of existing covenants that restrict commercial use on the proposed venue site."

"Why do they oppose the venue?"

"Because the proposed venue would be on land that's restricted from commercial use, and these plaintiffs have the right to enforce that restriction. But I expect you'll see multiple other efforts to stop this venue."

"Why do you think that?"

"Richie, did you come to the hearing on the concert venue permit application?"

"No, I was covering the Blanco County Commission that night."

"So you didn't hear any of the protests from numerous Coffee County speakers about issues including traffic on Old Hays Road, the potential that their water wells would be contaminated, and potential pollution of Coffee Creek?"

She reached the intersection of the creek road and Old Hays and slowed, turning west into a fading orange sunset.

"No, like I said, I wasn't there."

"You haven't interviewed any of those folks?"

"Look, I can't be everywhere at once!"

"The *Caller* published Jerry Weathers' letter on the lawsuit without talking to me or the plaintiffs or any of the many hundreds of citizens protesting at the permit hearing?"

Silence. "I hadn't been able to finish my research."

Alice translated that mentally. He'd been assigned a story and hadn't finished it...but the letter was ready to go.

"Now you're asking me why people protested. Have you looked at the draft permit?"

"Um, no."

"I assume you're aware that there's no sewer system out by the proposed concert venue?"

"You're kidding, right?"

Glad Richie couldn't see her face, Alice rolled her eyes. "Richie. There's no sewer system there. Under the proposed permit, the proposed concert venue, built to hold five thousand people, would store thousands of gallons of sewage effluent, then land-apply it onto the soil."

Silence. "How many gallons?"

She told him.

"What does land-apply mean?"

"Just what it sounds like. Like a giant septic system."

Silence.

"I don't understand what's wrong with that."

"What if there's an accident and sewage effluent drains into Coffee Creek?"

"How could that happen?"

Alice rolled her eyes again. "Various issues came up at the hearing. What if the storage tanks leak, or a worker makes a mistake, or the drain-field doesn't absorb enough wastewater? Also, have you looked at a map of Coffee County? I'll bet you have a water fountain at the *Coffee County Carrier*, right?"

"Yeah."

"Do you know where the water in your water fountain comes from?"

No answer.

"You might want to interview the city water engineer, just down the block from you. He's got some cool maps in his office. He could show you the water system." She tried to quell the sarcasm in her voice. Honestly...he ought to know how to cover the news, but it wouldn't hurt to point him toward some people to interview, maybe get their side into the paper.

"Um, you know the names of any of the protesters?"

"The names are all in the hearing record. If you like, you can ask Silla, at my office, to show you how to get that record. She'd be glad to do that." She wouldn't pass along contact info for her client James Surratt without prior permission, though he'd give a good interview.

Maybe, she hoped, Richie Farmer would start working on an article describing the concerns people had raised at the hearing? "Richie, you know local people enjoy seeing their names in the news and seeing their local paper take note of their concerns."

A pause. "Okay. Gotta go."

He hadn't asked about the death of the Apex engineer.

Alice turned left into her caliche drive, with Kinsear following. Big Boy brayed his usual welcome as she parked. An early spring evening; chilly now, with the sun sinking below the western hills. An evening breeze rustled the branches of the live oaks, now chartreuse with their new leaves and dangling catkins. The last birds squabbled at the bird feeder. She climbed out and stood for a moment, taking a deep breath of evening air, moist with dew, enjoying the faint grassy smell and the relief of being home. With Kinsear. Maybe in a couple of weeks she'd actually begin getting used to that feeling.

Chapter Twenty-Three

Guess Who's Gonna Go First?

Kinsear built a fire in the fireplace, adding warmth and light to the main room of Alice's house. He joined Alice at the kitchen end of the room, found a bottle of Rioja, and poured them each a glass.

Alice started warming some of Big John's pulled pork and a pack of butter tortillas. Kinsear, watching the timer, added equal numbers of tomatillos and jalapenos and a big garlic clove to a pan of boiling water. After a few minutes he sliced open the jalapenos, discarding the seeds. The jalapenos, garlic, and tomatillos disappeared into the blender, accompanied by chopped scallions, salt, cumin, and a dash of olive oil.

He held out a spoonful of the smooth green sauce to Alice. She licked it. "Strong work, Chef Kinsear."

"Butter tortillas with shreds of pulled pork and green sauce." He closed his eyes. "The best."

They took their plates to the couch by the fireplace. When the plates were empty, Kinsear said, "Okay. Let's get started."

Alice groaned but retrieved the copy of Charlie's notes that Files had provided, plus a legal pad and a calculator.

Side by side, they studied Charlie's calculations on the notebook's last few pages, beginning with the page titled "10 a.m." and dated the day of the hearing. Below his notes Charlie had drawn a chart with two columns, "Orig." and "Ctr."

Kinsear looked up. "Original, meaning original application?"

"Looks like it. And 'contractor,' because it looks like the mystery guy was a contractor with a new plan."

Alice retrieved the original Apex permit application from her work bag and found the impervious cover section. Then, with Kinsear on the calculator and Alice reading the figures for each area shown on the new blueprint, they added the sum of the impervious areas—roofs, parking, driveways, and other construction— and divided by the total square feet in 30 acres. Charlie was right: the new blueprint, especially with its additional paved parking, would result in slightly above 75% impervious cover.

"Is this plan limited to the original thirty acres, though? Or does this contemplate more acreage?"

Alice wasn't sure. "Maybe this was a backup—what Apex could

build if Denny inveigled Merry into selling five acres. But maybe it's merely the plan for a post-permit sneaky approach, starting with adding more rooftop, more seats, more paved parking."

"This calls for more wine. Because I've got some questions for you."

"Oh?" What questions? Wedding details? Where they'd live?

He gave that one-sided smile. "Nothing scary. I'm just thinking—you've now got—what—three lawsuits pending? One to enforce covenants, one challenging the forged transfer on death deed, then one for divorce, right? Plus you filed a new transfer on death deed, from Merry to her daughter?"

"Yep."

"So, depositions await, yes?"

She grinned up at Kinsear. "Right! Okay, guess who's gonna go first?"

"Hubby. Because...?"

"I lie awake thinking about how helpful Denny could be if he's first in the spotlight."

"What's he going to say?"

"Which case? Divorce or fraudulent deed? I think—start with the deed." She stared into the fire. "So, 'Denny, I hand you Exhibit 1. You actually drafted the transfer on death deed that purported to leave your wife's fifty-acre property to you?' He won't know what to say. 'You drove to Marble Falls with Teena Ann Traynor on February 18 with that deed, didn't you?' 'You waited there while she took the deed to the notary and signed it as Merilee Tarlton Givens, correct?' 'Before you drove there you had watched Teena Ann Traynor study your wife's signature, right?' 'And you had stolen your wife's driver's license so that Teena Ann Traynor could present it to the notary on February 18 and claim that she was Merilee Givens, am I right?'"

"And if he lies?"

"The notary—Olivia—might recognize both of them. She saw him drive off with Teena Ann after she notarized that signature." She thought back to the brief affidavit the notary had signed. "If something had happened to that notary, we'd be in deep trouble. Thank goodness we got her affidavit." She blinked at the thought of fire, smoke, two figures lighting fire-starters. "I wish we had a better shot of the two people lighting the fire at Merilee's barn. And I wish we could prove it was Teena Ann's truck. The night vision camera didn't show the license plate."

"Hmm. Just a silhouette? No decals on the side or rear windows?"

She searched his face. "What are you thinking?"

"Well, the Sheriff's Department can check the parking lots at the grocery and the hardware store."

"What do you mean?"

"They get access to the cameras there, the ones that look at the parking lots."

"What cameras?"

"Alice! Don't you read the signs inside the stores that say, 'we use cameras'?"

"I've seen them—but I didn't know they included the parking lots!"

"Convenient place to nab shoplifters who walk out with stolen merchandise."

"Aha." She thought about that. "And maybe we'll do some additional reconnaissance later? Silla's got her ways and means..."

Hmm. She'd need to look at that picture of the truck again. Decals?

Kinsear poked the fire alight while Alice, curled in her favorite corner of the couch, leafed back through Charlie's notes, stopping at the page where Charlie had logged his initial meeting with Weathers at the Dallas office of Worth Engineers: "Apex Ptnrs, LLC. Jerry Weathers, boss." Charlie's tiny, neat engineer's printing, with abbreviations for his expected duties at the office Apex had rented in the old Coffee Creek Hotel.

Once she'd figured out his abbreviations, she could translate the rest of the notes: "Daily reports on contacts. Monitor office. Touch base w/ TCEQ." Then a new page: "Arrive Coffee Creek. Attend City Hall meeting. Review permit application. Review plans from contractor. Review TCEQ regs on land application & hearing & hearing format. Per Jerry I'll handle hearing alone." The first day she'd met him....

Alice turned to the next page—the day of the hearing. "Arrive office 7:00 a.m. Hearing preparation. Opening comments to state application complies w/ TCEQ regulations."

Next entry: "9:00 a.m.: James Surratt at office with questions. Works w/ local master naturalists group on water testing. Lives on

Coffee Creek. Grandkids swim there. Worried re overloading creek w/ sewage effluent. Worried re fish impact, etc. Asked re Apex baseline water testing, asked re Apex calculations of soil absorption capacity, asked if Apex would withdraw if significant opposition or appeals. Said I'd pass along his questions."

Well! So her client James Surratt had visited Charlie the day of the hearing? He hadn't said a word about that when he arrived the following day at her office for his appointment. Of course, she recalled, neither had she. She'd heard about Charlie's death only that morning.

Next entry: "Checked file; no water test record or calculations re soil (amount or absorption capacity, etc.) TC w/ JWeathers. Says application's complete, no other data/calculations needed."

"10 to 10:10 a.m.: Delivery from Art Selman, Synergy LLC (Lockhart), w/ revised plans. Selman said JW wanted these, with requested overlay of dotted lines for revised impervious cover. Looks like about 75%. Called JW, no answer. Called TCEQ (Will Oxford): limit remains 65%, cannot exceed. Left message for JW re same." Below followed Charlie's brief chart for "Orig." and "Ctr."

Ten important minutes. She'd like to talk to Art Selman. And Will Oxford. And Jerry Weathers.

Then: "noon – Lunch w/ Jeanie."

The rest of the page was blank. As was the rest of the notebook, now in Files's custody. Charlie would make no further entries in this or any of his beloved orange notebooks....

She felt Kinsear's hands on her shoulders. "Bedtime?" he said. She stood, closed her eyes, melted into his embrace—so warm, so strong, so alive.

"You okay?" he asked, looking down at her.

"Just—this makes me think about my kids. And yours. I'm so sorry about Charlie. And so grateful our kids haven't faced what he did."

He nodded, glancing down at the copies of Charlie's notes she'd left on the sofa. "It's two things, isn't it? Any time any parent loses a child, we shiver with fear for our own children. But also, any time that child was growing into a good man, a good woman...for that life to be cut short feels so wrong. So unfair."

One of the things she loved about this man. He read her feelings so accurately.

"Let's go watch the moonset." Nestled in bed they watched, through the French doors, the half-moon sliding downward in the west, glowing more and more golden as it neared the western horizon. Finally it disappeared. Kinsear wrapped Alice close to him, kissing her hair. She closed her eyes, feeling so safe, so loved. For a moment she thought of Merry, dealing with Denny. Then she focused entirely on the moment at hand.

Chapter Twenty-Four

Discuss His Ethical Obligations

Alice ground the "Fredo roast" beans from East Austin Coffee Traders, added the proper level of water to the little silver espresso maker, spooned in the precious dark ground coffee, and turned on the cooktop. Next: heat some milk, froth it, and spoon it onto the coffee. Her morning ritual, rich dark coffee topped with white foam. First sip? Heaven. Would there be coffee in heaven? Alice grinned to herself, wondering if there'd be a line at the counter—surely not: maybe in heaven your cup appeared, hot and ready, just as you rose from your cloud and thought—"Coffee!"

"Not too much foam for me," Kinsear said, as he always did. Alice appreciated his decent regard for morning quiet. They sipped coffee, checked the news and the weather. He sighed, rose, and leaned over Alice to kiss her neck. "Early day for me at the ranch. Now that it's finally rained, the burn ban's lifted, and we're burning brush."

"Be careful!"

"Don't worry. We've got the water tank on the trailer, ready to go."

Alice understood what Kinsear's day would entail. Hill Country ranches accumulated brush and fallen limbs that needed to be gathered and burned occasionally, to reduce fire danger from lightning. But particularly when spring winds were blowing, you couldn't let your brush pile turn into a wildfire. Kinsear and his manager, Javier, would spend a long sweaty day, keeping the burn pile surrounded by dirt, preventing sparks from escaping, judiciously spraying water when needed, confirming at dusk that the fire was thoroughly out.

"What's your plan today?" he asked.

"Decide on deposition notices. Meet clients at ten for will signing"—James Surratt and his wife, Cynthia: she was curious about his visit with Charlie at the Apex office. Plus, ask Files about the water gun test, check on Apex's Nevada venue, and retain Ruby Michaels, her favorite handwriting expert, before Apex snagged her.

*****

Alice carried her bag to her car and followed Kinsear's ancient vehicle down the drive. He turned west; she turned right, waving out her window, then headed south down the creek road to town. Silla was standing in the entry when Alice opened the office door.

"The Surratts called and asked if they could sign their wills a little early, about quarter to ten. He's got a doctor's appointment as soon as they finish here. I've alerted our witnesses over at Madrone Bank. They'll arrive shortly. I put the revised wills and those Physician Orders for Life Sustaining Treatment forms on your desk."

Alice hustled into her office and reviewed the wills, concentrating on the changes the Surratts had requested. All in order. She turned to the POLST forms each had filled out. They differed. Cynthia Surratt *did* want CPR, attempted resuscitation. James? "NO CPR: Do Not Attempt Resuscitation." He'd selected only "comfort-focused treatments" and had checked the box for "no artificial means of nutrition desired." That would mean no IVs, no feeding tube.... Whew. Pretty definite. Pretty final.

Both clients had signed their forms, as had their primary care doctor.

Alice heard the front door open, heard slow footsteps echoing down the hall toward the conference room. Somehow this meeting felt heavier than usual. She took a deep breath, exhaled, and joined the Surratts. They both looked up at her. Alice knew Cynthia was fifty-five, but she looked older, thin, with fading blonde hair and a nice smile, but tired eyes. James was pale, still with an occasional deep cough. No smile; he looked slowly around the room, his eyes seeming to notice everything.

"Thank you for seeing us early," Cynthia said.

"No problem." And Alice began the ritual. She walked them through their wills, noting the changes they'd made, asking if there were any new gifts or other provisions needed.

"Nope. We're ready," James said. Cynthia nodded.

Silla stuck her head around the door. "Time for witnesses, right?" She returned and introduced their usual witnesses, two women employed at Madrone Bank. The witnesses watched as the Surratts signed their wills, then signed the requisite affidavits and left, with Alice's thanks. While Silla made copies, Alice reminded the Surratts: "Keep the originals in a safe place, in case you decide to revoke or amend."

James coughed into his handkerchief, then drank some of the water Silla had brought. "Saw in the *Caller* that you're representing some folks opposed to the venue?"

Alice nodded.

He continued, "Based on what that Apex guy told the *Caller*, they're planning to fight you tooth and nail. And they've got plenty of money. Lots of staying power, unfortunately. Meaning a long, expensive fight for the neighbors." Alice was about to ask him about his conversation with Charlie at the Apex office when he doubled over, seized by what sounded like an agonizing fit of coughing. Cynthia stood, stroking his back. Finally, he lifted his head, managed some deep breaths, and took another sip of water.

Unsure what to do, Alice also stood. "Would hot tea help?"

Cynthia shook her head no. Silla returned with bulging manila envelopes for each client. James Surratt pushed himself up from his chair and picked up both envelopes. Cynthia walked over and hugged Alice. "Is it okay for clients to hug their lawyer?"

Alice couldn't talk; she tried to smile and hugged her back. Not speaking, Surratt extended his hand. Alice held it longer than usual. "Hope the doctor treats you well. Keep us posted, will you?"

He gave her a small smile. The couple exited.

"Whew," Alice heard herself say, entering her office. She plopped on the desk chair, staring blankly at the computer. No, she hadn't asked about Charlie. How sick was James Surratt?

Grateful for life and health, she looked out the window at the pecan tree, now bursting with new leaves. To do: something about Nevada. What about that venue? Who would know? Online she found the Nevada Department of Environmental Protection. Aha: a Bureau of Water Pollution Control. She didn't know a soul in the Nevada state ranks.

While she dithered, her cell phone rang, just before eleven.

Jeanie.

"Alice? Do you have time for lunch? Brunch? Can we come see you?"

Who was "we"? "Of course," said Alice.

"Good, because we're outside your office. With news."

*****

"Whoo-ee! Who's the handsome dude with Jeanie?" Silla peered out Alice's office window.

"Oh, my." Alice squinted at the tall man striding toward the front door, one hand in Jeanie's, another hand carrying a heavy paper bag. Strong jaw, watchful eyes scanning the office.

Silla sped to open the front door, Alice right behind her. "Jeanie!"

"Please meet Griffin Holt," Jeanie answered. "Charlie's best friend."

Aha. And maybe yours? wondered Alice. Except for the sandy hair, he looked like a young Harrison Ford.

Griffin Holt passed the handshake test.

"We've brought lunch. Or brunch," Jeanie reported. "A whole raft of breakfast tacos. I mean brunch tacos. Redfish and avocado, chorizo-po-tato-egg, migas with the full monty."

The fragrance arising from the paper bag focused their minds wonderfully. They adjourned to the office kitchen, where Jeanie arranged the tacos on a plate, Silla dealt out drinks from the fridge, and the four settled around the kitchen table.

"These look delicious," Alice said, opting for redfish and avocado.

"Migas for me, please," said Griffin. "Umm—may I have two?"

A happy silence for a minute, plus banter about which tacos were best. Silla listened, then said—"Migas. Most comforting. Crunchy corn chips plus chorizo plus scrambled eggs with cumin and chili, tucked in-side a perfect tortilla, with a little medium hot salsa inside? The breakfast of champions."

"Mmm—migas are life-giving, it's true. But I'm voting for avocado with redfish," Jeanie said. She paused, looking at Alice and Silla. Then: "The reason we're here—" Jeanie began, "is, Griffin thinks there's some-thing you should know."

He leaned forward. "I met Charlie in engineering school at A&M. He was civil engineering, so am I. I was a year ahead of him, but we both played intramural basketball. His defense—very impressive. Anyway. He called me to talk about the impervious cover provision in the Apex con-cert venue application. He was worried about it."

"When?" asked Alice.

He looked up. "The afternoon he died. It was a little before four, and it was a short call; he was in a hurry, on his way to some ballfield."

That call's not in Charlie's notebook, so Files doesn't know about it either, Alice realized. She grabbed a pencil and a sticky note pad from the table, started taking notes.

Griffin continued, "Charlie wanted to discuss his ethical obligations under the engineering code. He'd been handed these new plans by a contractor that morning. They appeared to show expanded impervious cover. He'd talked to the TCEQ engineer assigned to the permit, who confirmed that 65% was the limit. He wasn't sure what to do next. Should he quiz the Apex partners about the purpose of the plans and remind them that 75% would be unacceptable? Or ignore the plans' existence? After all, he didn't have any proof the revised plans would be used. But what if he was asked about them at the meeting?"

"But Apex wasn't his employer," Alice said. "Charlie's employer was Worth Engineers. So did he ask if he also had an obligation to notify Worth that Apex might start playing fast and loose with the venue construction? What did you think he should do?"

Griffin shook his head. "I wasn't sure. Worth wouldn't want to be party to engineering fraud. I told him maybe he should tell his boss in Dallas that this contractor had brought Jerry Weathers some new plans with what looked like 75% impervious cover and that this would not pass muster with TCEQ."

"Would Apex really be concerned that Charlie had seen these new plans?" Alice asked. "They hadn't been submitted. They might never have been submitted. And if there were indications that Apex intended to wait for the permit to be issued and then build more impervious cover than permitted, I suppose Worth could've withdrawn from its contract with Apex."

Griffin looked uncertain. "Maybe. But when Charlie called me, know where I was? Reno, Nevada."

"You're kidding," Alice breathed. "What exactly were you doing there? But before we go much further, Detective George Files needs to hear about this phone call with Charlie—especially the timing. I'll check if he's in the office. But—Nevada?" Alice had to hear this.

Can't Afford That Today

Griffin leaned forward. "Our firm's handling design on a dam rebuild out in Nevada. Plus I know another Aggie engineer in the agency enforcement division there."

"Not the Bureau of Water Pollution Control?" Alice asked.

"Full marks. And guess what? He's been grappling with Apex on a similar Nevada project for a concert venue outside Las Vegas, where Apex pushed hard for a land application permit and got it. Then, guess what again? They've now exceeded the limits on impervious cover and are fighting the state on enforcement. He says their name should be Apex Predators, not Apex Partners. But he warned me not to quote him."

Alice frowned. "Wow. If it's such a scandal, why hasn't it been in the Nevada news?"

"It will be. My buddy at the bureau knows an investigative reporter who's doing an exposé on the venue issues."

"Did you tell Charlie about that?"

"No. I was thinking that Charlie's firm, Worth Engineers, would want to know what their client Apex was up to in Nevada. But Charlie said he was already parking at the ballfield and had to hang up."

"Whether or not Charlie knew that afternoon about the Nevada enforcement action," Alice said slowly, "he'd have found out. He's—he was too smart not to have looked it up after Jerry Weathers bragged publicly about already having a similar project in Nevada."

Griffin nodded. "True. The same goes for TCEQ. Once Charlie had actually seen those new plans for more impervious cover—and talked to TCEQ about the limits—maybe Apex couldn't take the chance that he might say something about it at the hearing and that TCEQ would sit up and take notice. I'll bet those plans have disappeared. Maybe Apex will deny ever seeing them. Deny ever ordering them."

The police never found his phone, Alice thought. Charlie's calls to TCEQ? To Jerry Weathers? To his buddy Griffin? To Apex, he'd become a threat...one they'd sought to erase.

"Griff, you're pulling punches." Jeanie looked sideways at him. "Tell Alice the rest." He frowned down at the table. "It's not bragging!" she insisted.

"Okay. Like I said, I've got an Aggie buddy in the Nevada state agency. He'd mentioned his concerns about Apex. Said he couldn't ever get an honest answer out of Jerry Weathers or Conrad O'Leary. My buddy called Weathers 'the weatherman'—as in the old Dylan song: 'you don't need a weatherman to know which way the wind blows.'"

Alice was impressed someone Griffin's age knew those lyrics.

"Anyway, my Aggie buddy called ol' Jerry a repeat offender. He'd looked into his history in California. Apparently a mining company hired Jerry to manage the cleanup required before the company could reopen an old gold mine. Turns out he released all kinds of contamination—arsenic, you name it—into the creek below."

"Why is he not in jail?"

"No, my buddy says it's a big legal mess. Jerry blamed it on his underlings, and he's still running loose. But now people in that valley can't swim, can't fish. People spoiling water—shakes your faith in the human race."

Holt went on. "Anyway, before I left Nevada to visit Jeanie, I pulled the coordinates for the Nevada construction from the plans Apex submitted with the Nevada application and put them on a map. Then at dawn on Sunday, I flew a drone over the site at an altitude that correlated with the map of the original plans, to capture the impervious construction Apex had already started building. Had to try that several times to get the right scale, but no one was out there so early on a weekend. Finally, I overlaid the outlines of the original plans Apex had submitted over the impervious construction Apex had started. And sent it to my buddy in the state agency. Gave him something to challenge them with."

"So you'll be a fact witness?" Alice asked. "And maybe an expert too?"

"I hope not, but it could happen. I created a one-man limited liability corporation that owns the mapping I did."

This is a guy I'd like for an expert witness, Alice thought, looking at the serious eyes, the capable hands currently tapping a pencil on the kitchen table. Creative, resourceful, and precise. In this investigation he's already a fact witness. I should at least list him as a potential expert. He could produce a map showing what the proposed 75% impervious cover would really mean, how close it could be to the creek, how much more contaminated water might drain toward the neighbors' properties, including their wellfields....

If I could show him Apex's original application plans, and a copy of the later plans....

Wait a minute! Alice jumped out of her chair. In Charlie's notes! About Selman, the guy who handed him the new impervious coverage site plans...maybe with a wink and a smile, saying "Jerry wanted these...."

"Silla, the suit to enforce covenants, with Apex as a defendant: let's subpoena Art Selman, in Lockhart. Video deposition, at our office. He needs to bring any and all correspondence with Apex, including plans created for the Apex venue, including a copy of those delivered to Charles Boone the day of the public meeting. Get contact info for Apex's lawyer so we can plug in a deposition date as soon as possible."

Jeanie looked up at Alice. "Meanwhile, can you update us? What's the status of the investigation?"

Alice's cell phone rang. Caller: George Files. "Excuse me," Alice said. "Don't leave yet."

*****

Alice hurried to her office, listening to Files's deep voice resonate from her phone. "The Travis County Medical Examiner confirms that the material on Charles Boone's hands is a match for the slick roof sealant in the tub we found in the storage shack at the baseball facility. Same for the material on his legs, hands, shoes. Looks like that's why he slipped, but given what the postmistress told us about hearing shots, and the bullet marks we found on the side of the girder, he may have fallen because someone was shooting. Someone who apparently intended to make him fall. We've passed our information on to the medical examiner, who confirms, based on that and the roof sealant on Boone's body, that this appears to be an unlawful death. An autopsy will be done."

"Where are the Apex guys? Weathers and O'Leary?"

"Nevada, we think. We've requested help from Nevada state police with a warrant for O'Leary's arrest. May take a few days. Here's the timing you asked about, Alice: the postmistress was pretty sure she heard five shots around 4:10. Charlie's Apple Watch sent the fall alert about

4:11. O'Leary didn't call EMS until 4:17, after the ambulance left the hospital following Charlie's Apple Watch alert. So maybe O'Leary heard the ambulance coming and called EMS to cover his presence at the site. If that's the timing, he lied about getting to the ballfield after Charlie fell." He paused. "Alice, don't let this info out—about O'Leary's potential lies or about getting help from the Nevada state police. It might compromise the investigation and our ability to get the Apex people back here."

"Got it. George, there's new information. Charlie's sister, Jeanie, showed up for lunch with her boyfriend, another civil engineer, who's been working in Nevada. Name is Griffin Holt. He and Charlie were best friends. He says Charlie called him just before he got to the ballfield. Can I send him to your office?"

"Yes. I'll be back there by about twelve-thirty. Send him on down."

In her mind's eye, Alice saw again the shiny blotch on the rust-colored girder above the spot where Charlie fell. "What about the adult water gun?"

"Lab hasn't yet given us test results on the substance in the water gun or spattered on the girder. Should get those tomorrow."

His somber voice settled like a black veil over the day. Alice stared at the floor. What should she tell Jeanie? She and her mother were clients now, entitled to confidentiality. Griffin? Not a client nor an expert. Yet.

She returned to her chair at the kitchen table, facing Jeanie. "News. First, there's enough evidence that Charlie's death might be unlawful that the medical examiner will require an autopsy. The slick stuff on the girder and on Charlie's body and clothes was silicone sealant. So the investigation's ongoing, and right now Detective Files does not want certain details divulged. I think you'll be getting more information from me very soon."

She certainly didn't mention the adult water gun to this boy's sister. Using a toy—an adult toy!— to expedite a murder seemed entirely too cold-blooded, too contemptuous of human life, for her to share. And if the information got out at this point, it could mess up the prosecution of Charlie's killer—the last thing Alice wanted.

Jeanie sat, still as a stone. Then she lifted her head, sat taller. Alice could almost see her spine stiffen. Her voice was hard as stone too. "We want the police to find every scrap of evidence. And we will see Charlie's killer convicted." She and Griffin looked at each other, then stood. "Thanks, Alice. Thanks, Silla."

Alice said, "Thanks for bringing lunch! Meanwhile, Griffin, Detective Files is expecting you."

"Oh." Griffin held out his iPhone. "Just so you know, here's when Charlie called me on his way to the ballfield. See, that's his number. 830 area code." Alice looked down at the screen. Griffin pushed the little blue circle with the "i". "3:50 p.m., 8 min." Files had told her that Charlie's Apple Watch called EMS at 4:11. She imagined him, puzzled, alarmed, maybe arguing with O'Leary, then starting up the girder—

"Listen, the police couldn't find Charlie's phone that day. Someone must have taken it. That makes the information in your phone that much more important," Alice told Griffin. "Be sure to tell Files everything about the call, and show him what's on your phone." He nodded.

She turned to Jeanie. "Jeanie, you'll tell your mom about the autopsy, and that I'll be updating you two about the investigation as soon as I have more I can tell."

Jeanie hugged Alice, then marched down the hall, Griffin's protective arm around her shoulders.

*****

A brunch of tortillas, salsa, and comforting fillings can sometimes cause a sort of waking sleep. Alice felt one coming on and thought, can't afford that today. She poured another cup of Fredo roast into her favorite mug and trudged back to her desk. Time to tackle the perennial task of entering time spent on each client matter. Not fun, but prompt billing kept the office running, and if she got behind, Silla would be on her case.

After an hour she sat back. What next?

That nagging image: the truck in Ernesto's video. Kinsear had asked—were there any decals? She found Ernesto's emailed video, blew it up as far as she could, got him on the phone.

"Everything okay? Are you at Merry's, maybe near your computer?"

"Yes. And yes."

"Ernesto, I know we couldn't see the rear of the truck that was in

Merry's driveway. What about the side of the truck? Aren't those decals?"

"Hmm. First, there's some kind of fuzzy emblem behind the front side mirror. Could include a Z. If so, I suppose it's possibly ZR2, the Chevy Silverado. Can't tell, though. And yes, on the right rear window, looks like two decals. Can't tell what they are either."

Silla walked into the office and peered over Alice's shoulder. "Did I hear 'decals'? Hey—" she leaned closer, squinting at the screen. "I've seen a big decal with that fancy shape before. Houston Rodeo sells one like that, mostly white, with scrolls on the top and bottom! But I can't read the letters on this one."

"What about the round one, underneath?"

"White above and below, crossed by a sort of wiggly line?" Silla stood up, eyes bright. "Did I hear Ernesto say Silverado? I know one woman in this town who owns a big ol' Chevy Silverado, and of course she'd slap rodeo decals on it. The round white one *might* be from the Estes Park Rooftop Rodeo!"

Alice shook her head. Just as Kinsear suggested...decals.

She called Files again.

"What's up, Alice?"

"George, the fire at the Givens place."

"Yeah?"

"I took another look at our not great video of the truck in the front parking lot. As you know, it didn't catch the license tag. I see what might be two decals on the right rear side window. Silla's got an idea about them. There also may be a letter Z by the passenger-side mirror. Could you check videos from the cameras at the H-E-B parking lot—or wherever else you get film access—for a dark-colored truck, maybe a Chevy Silverado, with two decals on the right rear side window?"

"You think the firebugs might strike again?"

"Yes. Another fire, or worse. I understand law enforcement has access to videos I don't, like parking lot videos that could help track down that truck. Could someone check and see if there's a match?"

"Send me that video again, would you? Save me a minute. And what's Silla's idea?"

She complied. "Long shot—Silla says the decals might be from rodeos." Just hints and allegations, she thought...are we just seeing what we hope is there?

"I'll see what I can do. Hey, your boy Griffin Holt is sharp." Files hung up.

"Whoo-ee!" Silla did a little two-step at Alice's door, then said, "Merry called just as you called Files. She needs you to call her back."

"Is she okay? What's happened?"

"I'm not sure."

Alice picked up the phone.

Chapter Twenty-Six

The County Would Hang Convicted Murderers

M erry answered on the first ring. "Alice. Remember we mailed Denny a copy of the petition that included my affidavit and a copy of the new transfer on death deed?"

"Right. It was an exhibit to the fraud petition, showing that deed was filed in the Coffee County Property Records."

"The point being to let him know that if he succeeded in killing me, the land would still go to Francine? Still wouldn't be his?"

"Yes. We weren't required to send him a copy, but we wanted him to realize that the fraudulent deed he and Teena Ann got notarized is now void, useless, superseded, and dead in the water. Meaning—any more attacks on you or Francine would be pointless."

"Well, when not lighting the barn on fire, he and Teena Ann must be spending their days and nights frolicking in bed. He's not check-ing his mail. You know I've got my own mailbox at the post office, right? Denny doesn't have access to that. But I do sometimes check our mailbox on Old Hays, across from our place. You remember, there's a bunch of mailboxes all together."

"That's where we sent his copy."

"It was still in the mailbox this morning, with some other mail. I left it there. But what should we do?"

Damn. "I'll email and text him a copy right now. I'd send it to his lawyer if he has one—but no one's contacted me so far." And, thought Alice, I really want Denny to know there's no benefit to getting rid of Merry. No percentage in it. "Everything else okay?"

"Yep. Still smells like smoke, though. Ernesto's tweaking the secu-rity system. I enjoy having those guys around, Alice. I'm realizing it's been kind of lonesome, with no one to talk to but the goats." Merry hung up.

Alice thought, I don't think I could live like that. Milking twice a day, mostly goats to talk to.... Maybe cheesemaking, with its rigorous cleanliness, specific temperatures, precise measurements, could be both demanding and rewarding, especially when you could sell the precious packets of goat cheese to customers who told you over and over how good it tasted, how happy they were to buy it. Hmm. Still, you'd want other interactions with humans, wouldn't you?

Well, sometimes. She herself liked controlled interactions: "I'm asking the questions, sir. Please answer the question." But she also liked sparring with Files, laughing with Silla, phone calls with her hilarious children, dinner with Kinsear, long walks with Kinsear, long talks with Kinsear, and sometimes just quietness, no talking at all, with Kinsear.

She joined Silla at her worktable. "Let's email and text Denny the petition to declare the forged deed a fraud, with all exhibits, including Merry's affidavit. Message—just the usual: 'Enclosed please find the petition filed at the Coffee County Courthouse on behalf of Merilee Givens. If you have retained counsel to whom this should go, please provide us with that name and address.'"

"Got it. Listen, Griffin and Jeanie called from the road. They've wondered about Charlie's computer. Griffin thinks Charlie might have kept some other notes there. Do you think he might've included his earlier phone calls with TCEQ and his boss about the new impervious cover plans?"

Ah. Maybe private thoughts went onto his personal computer, and what Charlie thought of as "task notes" for a client went into the orange notebook? After all, he'd taken his computer with him when he left the office to lunch with Jeanie—maybe afraid someone would look at it—and accidentally left it in her car. "Can we share our mirror-image?"

"Yep."

"Send it to Jeanie. Even if she and Griffin can't find anything, she'll want to see his—his notes."

Suddenly a wave of tiredness hit her. So many details, so many loose ends, so many balls in the air. Clients to protect, not just from legal danger, but from physical danger. "Silla, I'm going to take a quick walk."

Silla lifted an eyebrow and gave Alice a knowing smile.

Alice slipped out the front door. The southeasterly wind from the Gulf rattled the new live oak leaves and ruffled the periwinkle blue iris growing in the bed by the office driveway.   Which way?

Toward the courthouse, she decided. She walked faster, leaning into the gusts of wind, listening to the chatter of birds darting in and out of trees, admiring the flowers blooming in the yards of the small houses along Live Oak Street.

Two blocks later she crossed Live Oak onto the courthouse square. She loved walking around the old limestone building, with its dome, its ancient wooden doors, and its grove of shade-providing live oaks on the lawn. The high school forestry club had measured the girth of the live oaks and had declared the biggest—a giant that shaded half the lawn on one side of the courthouse—to be at the very least 180 years old. Alice found herself, as usual, walking beneath the shade of this giant, her favorite tree, with its wide horizontal branches, curving first this way, then that. 180 years! So it was about as the same age as Coffee Creek, which was already being settled in 1846. She thought about the early days of Coffee Creek: the livery stable, the first bank, the early churches, the first real school. When wells had to be dug, clothes had to be boiled in an iron cauldron outside, corn had to be dried and then ground into grits. When everyone planted a peach tree and a fig tree and hoped desperately for no freezes in March. And when the county would hang convicted murderers, sometimes on a branch of one of these live oaks.

Alice mistrusted capital punishment. Humans could make mistakes—both defendants and jurors. But for the person who'd killed Charlie? She turned to the tree trunk, ran her fingers across the rough gray-black bark, then looked up at the fluttering new leaves on the topmost branch. The hard tough bark, the tender green leaves, the roots, traveling underground to communicate with the roots of neighbor trees...congregated here on the courthouse lawn. Trees don't murder each other, she thought. They make their own food. They don't kill each other or eat each other. We humans? We must consume. Trees are givers; animals are takers. We're animals.

But taking lives?

She left her tree and circled the courthouse, thinking of the numerous times she'd made her way up the wide stone staircase inside, its stairs no longer quite level but gently curved from the footsteps of hundreds of others seeking justice in one of the paneled courtrooms. She'd moved to Coffee Creek and set up a civil law practice dealing with paper of various sorts—tax, commercial, contracts, wills. She'd anticipated a peaceful practice, using her mind to make words work for her clients.

But now? Charlie's mother and sister were clients; Charlie had been murdered. Merry was her client; her husband had drafted a transfer on death deed that would take effect when Merry died. Her work for other clients in other cases had unexpectedly uncovered murders—a mother, murdered by her daughter's fiancé, the body undiscovered for years; a judge, killed to hide long-ago murders.

Charlie's death seemed so pointless, so cynical, so oddly *commercial*. No passion involved. Why hadn't his bosses just fired him, handled the permit hearing themselves? But he'd already learned too much.

Alice stopped in her tracks. What if the Apex bosses also learned of Griffin's Nevada discoveries? Would *he* be safe? And what else should she do to protect Merry from the greed of her husband and neighbor?

Back under the shade of her favorite tree, she patted the bark, turned and leaned on the trunk for a while, thinking, took a long deep breath, and marched back to her office.

*****

First, a call to Ernesto, at Merry's place. "Ernesto, what's going on?"

"We did the morning milking. Then Merry started a cheese batch. It's nearly done."

"Can you get some backup for the rest of the day and tonight? Just in case?"

After a moment he said, "Yes. Got a buddy who's in town this week. I'll give him a call."

"I still haven't heard back from Francine, Merry's daughter. Do I have the right number?" She read it to him.

"Hang on." In a moment he was back. "You had it right. Merry says she's not great about returning calls. Anyway, is there something special we should be watching for?"

"We emailed Denny documents including the new deed that shows he can't inherit. If something happens to Merry, the property goes to Francine. He still may be pissed off enough or stupid enough to do something dumb—maybe even be desperate enough to go after both of them."

She hung up and tried Francine's number, got voicemail again, left a message: "Francine, Alice Greer, your mom's lawyer. I want to share some info. Please call when you get out of class."

Silla stuck her head in Alice's door. "Call the mayor. She's waiting."
Yikes.

"Alice here. Hi, Mayor."

"Listen, I need you here tomorrow night at five to update the council before our regular meeting. On this whole venue deal. And they'll want to know, after that debacle at the high school, if and when there'll be another public meeting."

"It's also on your public agenda at six?"

"Yes ma'am. So be ready." The mayor hung up.

Command performance. Alice called Will Oxford, the TCEQ lawyer assigned to the venue permit, and left a message: "Urgent inquiry from Coffee Creek's mayor—need status of TCEQ position on new public meeting." After a moment, she also sent an email, adding, "Will, would appreciate your response asap as mayor has requested that info before tomorrow at 5 p.m."

Now what? She'd filed her lawsuits. It would be over two weeks before she'd get answers from the defendants. She needed to be ready. And on the forged deed? She needed a slam dunk. She called Ruby Michaels, handwriting expert extraordinaire.

"Alice! How nice to hear from you! I'm feeling bored, in need of a challenge! What's up?"

Alice loved that reassuring voice. "Ruby, my client is a local cheesemaker, Merilee Tarlton Givens. Merry for short. Defendants are her current husband, Denson Ward—Denny for short—and his girlfriend, Teena Ann Traynor."

"No conflicts. I've never heard of any of them," Ruby answered.

Alice explained the forged transfer on death deed notarized in Marble Falls, using Merry's stolen driver's license, purporting to leave Merry's land to Denny. "Then, Ruby, we filed a valid transfer on death deed actually signed by my client, Merilee Givens, leaving the land to her daughter. What if I start by sending both deeds to you? Plus a copy of Merry's driver's license, which was stolen from her by Denny and presented with the forged deed to the notary in Marble Falls? Are you available?"

"Good start, but of course I'll need more data. And who's the defendants' expert?"

"Won't know until we get initial disclosures, thirty days after the defendants file an answer."

"I know you'll want my initial take quickly. Send me copies of the deeds, the license, and more samples of your client's handwriting. Cheesemaker, right? Some informal samples: does she have a notebook where she keeps notes on orders or on various cheese batches? Also, more samples of her signature, on contracts, or her will, or copies of tax payments, or car registrations. Also signatures on checks, if she's got an account with copies of checks. Is there any way you could get examples of the forger's handwriting?"

Madly scribbling, Alice stopped. "Hmm. Don't know. I'll ask in discovery, though. Hey—cheesemakers don't make much money... think about that when you send me your rates. Merry makes excellent chèvre! Thanks, Ruby."

Alice dialed Merry and described what Ruby wanted.

"Alice, I hope I can afford all this."

"I know. Well, the key issue we prove is the forgery. But remember, your fraud petition seeks recovery of your costs and expenses, including expert fees. Hopefully Teena Ann will wind up paying the freight. Plus, I've left word for Francine to call me—she needs to be extra careful right now." Alice explained her concerns. "Next, Denny drives a gray sedan—Nissan, if I recall? What's the year and model? And the license plate?" She scribbled down Merry's answers. "And what does Teena Ann drive, besides that truck?"

"A red Toyota Supra."

Alice promised to call back after she talked to Francine.

She left another voicemail for Francine, thought a moment, then emailed. She waited, watching the clock on the bookshelf tick the minutes past. Nearly six. Not dark yet, but it would be soon. She picked up her phone, ready to call again, just as it rang. She didn't recognize the number.

"Alice Greer here."

"Alice? It's Francine Givens. Merry's daughter. I had to borrow a phone—I saw your email on my computer while I was in cooking lab, but I lost my phone a few days ago. Sorry if you were trying to get in touch with me. I'm getting a new one tomorrow."

"Tell me where you are."

"I'm just about to leave the cooking lab class—it ends at six."

"Listen, I need for you to find alternate digs tonight. Can you spend the night with someone safe?"

Silence. "Is Mama okay?"

"She's fine. But I need you extra-safe tonight and the next few days. Here's why." She explained that, even if Denny had read the new transfer on death deed, he still might be stupid enough, or greedy enough, to try to get rid of both Merry and Francine. Then she added, "And you'll need a will yourself, Francine, so Denny has no way to grab the property."

"A will? Holy cow," breathed Francine. "I'll do anything to keep that man away from our land!"

"Well, that's why I need you to have a will. Just a short one. Write it in your own handwriting, and sign it."

"But don't you need witnesses and stuff?"

"In Texas, a handwritten and signed will is called a 'holographic will' and can be valid. I'll text you a brief form. Go ahead and write one and sign it tonight. You can do a fancier one later. But if I can let Denny and Teena Ann know that you also have a will, that no way will they get their mitts on your mom's property even if they manage to get rid of you both, maybe that will keep them on a short leash."

"I'll get it done tonight."

"Great. And send me a copy. Now, about staying safe. Do you have a friend? A boyfriend? Someone you could stay with tonight and maybe longer? Someone reliable?"

"I think so." It almost sounded as if Francine was smiling. "A handsome fellow chef."

"Reliable?"

"Oh yeah."

"Write this down. If you see a gray Nissan, a Maxima, about five years old, Texas plates—" she read off the number from her notes— "it could be Denny. Maybe along with that rodeo rider who lives next to your mom. She drives a red Toyota Supra."

"Teena Ann The Tackiest," Francine volunteered. "Can't stand that woman."

"Could be her, could be Denny, could be both of them. Can you get somewhere safe, lock the doors, and call back to let me know where you are?"

"Hang on." Alice heard muffled conversation.

"Okay, the chivalrous Raoul Cardona is allowing me to share his apartment tonight. Fully trustworthy. Here's the address." She rattled it off, along with Raoul's phone number.

"Hey—what were you working on in the cooking lab?"

"Annotating our recipes for sauces. Hollandaise. Béarnaise. Crème anglaise. Yum."

Alice's stomach growled. "I'd love to sample your cooking when you're home! Meanwhile, call me as soon as you're safely at Raoul's. Be prepared to call the police if you have to. And get that new phone!"

"Will do."

Alice called Merry. "Have you met a handsome chef named Raoul Cardona? He's offered to shelter Francine tonight."

"Hallelujah. I think I met him when I went to the culinary school open house. I had the impression there might be some chemistry...."

"Here's his address and his number. And I explained to Francine about writing a short will by hand."

Silla had left the office. Alice locked up and headed north on the creek road. As she turned into her drive, her cell rang—Cardona's number again. "Hi, Miss Alice," said a deep voice. "I've got Francine with me, and we're safely locked in at my place. We'll cook dinner here. I made her leave her car at school so she wouldn't be alone in a car."

"Great. Thank you." She liked the way he thought. "You're staying in tonight, right? And you'll take her to school in the morning?"

"Yep. We're in the same classes tomorrow. Don't worry. I'll call you tomorrow, or she will. On her new phone."

Alice sighed in relief, hung up, called Merry. "Francine's in good hands."

"Maybe in more ways than one!" quipped Merry.

"And you need to stay safe too."

"Ernesto's still here. Tonio will arrive soon for the night shift. Ernesto insists on staying to spend the night as well, on the living room couch. He's got another Army buddy, Joe Storey, who's spending the night in the barn, with a sleeping bag. We've all got our phones charged, we've all got flashlights. Pretty good, right?"

Short term but hopefully a workable safety scheme, both here and in San Antonio. But Alice couldn't feel certain of her clients' safety until she knew Denny and Teena Ann had given up.

Home, and safe. Big Boy brayed as she drove through her gate. Early dusk, still some pink in the far west. Once inside, she dropped her bags on the mesquite bench by the front door and found a bottle of Pfefferer in the refrigerator. She poured two ounces into one of her grandmother's old pressed-glass wine glasses and walked out onto the deck. Birds, silhouetted against the sunset sky, were choosing their evening perches. Alice sipped the cool white wine, feeling—what did her kids call it? "Safe as houses." She hoped Merry and Francine felt safe as houses, as well.

A light wind tickled the live oak branches by the deck. Somewhere downhill, a chuck-will's-widow made the first evening call, then repeated it, and repeated it again. The moon was up. Tree frogs chirped. Alice sipped her wine, gazing across the creek at the hills rising behind, the hills of home. Sufficient unto the day are the evils thereof, she told herself.

Stop worrying. Just breathe.

Chapter Twenty-Seven

He's Reluctantly Nodding

Alice woke at three, with the setting gibbous moon shining gold, straight through the west door and into her eyes. She checked her phone—no calls. She rolled over in relief, burrowed her face into her pillows, and didn't wake again until six.

Coffee. One egg, sizzled in olive oil. Some of M.A.'s Mexican plum jam on an English muffin. More coffee—bliss. Her phone stayed silent: no calls from Francine or Merry. She hoped that constituted good news.

Today—prepare for the Coffee Creek City Council. Call Will Oxford at TCEQ as to whether the agency would hold a second hearing on the concert venue permit, and, if so, when. Decide how much she could report to the City Council on Apex issues. She didn't trust the council members not to blab, even with a confidentiality instruction. Call Griffin Holt: she didn't want to mess up either the Nevada enforcement action or Files's investigation of Charlie's death. Finally, she was somewhat curious about who'd show up for tonight's council meeting. Would Apex appear?

Suit, boots, mascara. And her favorite perfume, which made her smell like herself, she thought. The one Kinsear also liked.

At the office she called Griffin Holt. He answered immediately.

"Griffin, I need some information before the Coffee Creek City Council meets at five tonight, concerning the Apex permit request here. I don't want to say anything that will mess up your Aggie buddy's enforcement action in Nevada. Can you tell me if your drone flight info showing illegal impervious cover is public information? Has it made the news yet? Is enforcement already underway?"

"Glad to."

He called back in five minutes. "My buddy says he's already filed and served the enforcement action and that a hearing's set. It's been in the papers too. I'll send you a copy of the article and a copy of the enforcement document."

Great—public notice, plus a Nevada legal document she could provide without breaching confidentiality.

Next, a visit with the city water engineer. He'd promised to meet Alice at the water plant at nine. Alice grabbed a brush and peeked in the mirror behind her office door. Echoes of her mama: "Honey, try to get your hair out of your eyes." She always wanted to respond—"where do you think I got these unruly bits?" Brownish-blonde hair, serious brown eyes. She straightened the jacket, straightened her shoulders, applied more lip gloss, and headed out the door to the sidewalk. Then she turned and ran back in, skidding to a stop at Silla's worktable.

"Silla, when it's time to serve discovery requests, don't let me forget we'll want copies of any documents Art Selman presented to Charlie or anyone at Apex, including any plans for additional impervious cover—on deposition notices or document requests, including for Art Selman, Jerry Weathers, Conrad O'Leary, Apex as an entity, probably Worth Engineers. Thanks! Gotta go talk to the city water engineer, then to the continuing legal ed committee meeting in Fredericksburg." She glanced up at the schoolroom clock above Silla's worktable. "Yikes!" She ran back out.

*****

Walter Bowie had served as chief water engineer for the City of Coffee Creek for twenty years. Alice recalled him as shy, taciturn, diligent. Mayor Wilson never reported any quarrel with him or the employees at the town's small water treatment plant. During the Depression, Coffee Creek had built a low dam south of town, catching enough Coffee Creek water to create a small reservoir that fed the new water plant, which delivered treated water within the city limits. Coffee Creek itself then escaped and ran south.

Alice cherished field trips. Factories, power plants, stormwater systems, landfills. She'd visited the water treatment plant only once but remembered old portraits of town mayors on the wall, old photos of the original dam construction in the thirties, old photos of the original pumps. The water engineer met her at the front desk, dressed in the same type of sturdy gray cotton uniform worn by the other employees.

Walter Bowie gave her a shy smile as they shook hands. "Okay to talk in my office?"

She followed him down the linoleum-floored hallway, blinking at the bluish fluorescent lights. She could hear the constant faint hum of large machines. Bowie pulled his door almost closed as he waved her to the visitor's seat—a depression-era antique swivel chair that reminded her of the one her grandfather kept in front of his ham radio rig. On impulse she asked Bowie if he was a ham radio guy.

His eyebrows lifted. "How'd you know that? Yes. For thirty years! Still get a kick out of talking with someone across the ocean. Anyway. What can I do for you?"

"Let's talk about the Apex permit application for that concert venue. You've read it, right?"

"Yeah."

"With Bradley Ott still in the hospital, I need to talk to the council tonight about what position, if any, the City should take on the permit. Do you have some concerns?"

A deep breath. "Yes. Many! I'm worried, Alice. I re-read the permit information last night. About those huge tanks where they'll be retaining the treated effluent, before they land-apply." He shifted in his chair, and began ticking off concerns, tapping his right forefinger on the digits of his left hand.

"One—will Apex employ adequate security? Including guards at night?

"Two—what if a tank leaks, or a truck backs into the piping? What's their cleanup plan?

"Three—what training and certification will Apex require for the employees managing the effluent treatment process?

"Four—will Apex also monitor the land application process carefully during effluent release to be sure there's no leakage, or will some employee just turn a valve and go have coffee?

"Five—what about testing and record-keeping? On behalf of the City, I'd like prompt access to their records and immediate notice of any release that gets into Coffee Creek."

He shook his head. "That last item is my big fear. The proposed land application area is awfully close to Coffee Creek. As I measured it in my car yesterday, the distance from the venue area on Old Hays to the point where our reservoir begins is only about five miles. You know how fast a spill into that creek could get into our little reservoir? Damn fast." He looked surprised at his own daring. "And those proposed tanks are huge!

I mean, five thousand people at a throw?"

"Coffee Creek is the City's sole water supply," Alice said. "Correct?"

"We have a couple of wells as backup, but they're only backup. We draw from the reservoir for water we supply within the city limits. The wells can't supply the entire City."

"So if Coffee Creek were contaminated by a spill, or by failure of the land application setup, you couldn't just let water out of the dam and use the wells?"

"Nope. No way. We could probably get clean water to the hospital, but downtown and the neighborhoods inside the City would be screwed."

"What about water tanks, water towers? How many in Coffee Creek?"

"We just have two. We're trying to get a grant for a third one." Walter Bowie looked intently at Alice. "It's the sheer size of the proposed tanks and the volume of potential contamination that's keeping me awake at night. Coffee Creek's our main water source, and it's great clean water. You know it's partly spring-fed? But Coffee Creek's not particularly large. How long would it take a creek that size to recover from spillage out of the tanks? And suppose the land application system fails and contamination keeps seeping into the creek, month after month? Then what do we do for water?"

Alice remembered what one neighbor had said at the hearing—once you spill that stuff, it's hard to pick it up....

"One more thing. The little springs along the creek supply base flow to the creek. That helps recharge the aquifer below. Which people rely on for well water."

He nodded.

"The council's comments requested a contested case hearing. You want the City's concerns raised, right?

"Yes. Yes, I do."

"I could tell the council what you've told me, but, Walter, how about coming along to the council meeting and telling them yourself? You've convinced me already."

He sat back, face pink with discomfort. "I don't mess with politics much."

"I hear you. But if the City litigates, you may need to testify as the expert on the City's water system."

He shifted in his chair, then looked at Alice. "Okay. Yes. Never had to do that before. But yes to that too."

Alice stood, extended her hand. "Thanks."

Alice grabbed her phone and called the mayor. "Mayor, I'm talking to Walter Bowie about his concerns on this permit. Would you want him to come talk to the council's executive session?"

"Hell, yes!"

Alice looked at Walter. "He's reluctantly nodding. Okay, see you at City Hall at five!"

Chapter Twenty-Eight

Give Us The Straight Scoop

Alice slid into a parking place in Fredericksburg just as her bar committee meeting started. The chairman, mercifully efficient, ended the meeting at 3:30. Alice managed to dodge a teaching assignment for the upcoming continuing legal ed conference on corporate, tax, and estate practices, after pointing out she'd taught at the last two. She did agree to serve as chair. Hallelujah, she muttered, speeding out of Fredericksburg on Highway 290, heading for Coffee Creek.

Every lawyer at the meeting had asked what Coffee Creek was going to do about the proposed concert venue permit. "We're recommending the applicant choose a property in Fredericksburg or Johnson City," she retorted.

She arrived back at Coffee Creek City Hall just before five and sat in the car to call Will Oxford at TCEQ. "Are you going to extend the deadline for additional comment after that fiasco of a public meeting?"

The TCEQ lawyer said, "Just get in line. My desk's covered with letters about this particular permit."

"You remember the chaos—so many questions and not a soul there from Apex Partners to provide any answers. That seems grossly unfair. How about extending the comment period, given the inability of the applicant even to show up?"

He sighed. "Not my decision, but we'll see what happens."

That sounded only mildly hopeful.

Alice grabbed her work bag and hurried up the stairs to the conference room the council used for executive session. Walter Bowie stood waiting outside the door, looking uncomfortable. Mayor Wilson, white hair aloft and bouffant, had already taken her chair, gavel at the ready. Alice watched the five council members straggle in: Louise Compton, a quiet and watchful CPA with her own practice; Ted Ritchie of Hill Country Appliances, in blazer and tie; Kevin Garcia, of Coffee Creek Plumbing & Heating; Martina Guerrero, of the Camellia Diner; and Sam Adams, pharmacist at the grocery store.

The mayor peered over her purple cat-eye spectacles at the group. "Okay, Alice," she announced. "According to Bradley, the City filed comments and requested a contested hearing. We need to discuss whether to authorize proceeding with litigation before the deadline. Right?"

206

"Right. Some new issues have come up recently." Alice passed around two stacks of paper—a copy of the enforcement action filed by the Nevada agency and the newspaper article detailing it. Heads lowered, the mayor and the council members read the documents, then looked up.

"They're building new structures that violate their impervious cover limit?" asked Louise Compton.

"That's the charge here." Alice explained that the draft permit allowed a certain number of square feet of coverage by buildings, roads and walkways. "After issuance, Apex began construction but went well beyond the permitted areas."

"What's wrong with that?" asked the pharmacist, Sam Adams. "It's just more construction, right?"

Louise Compton leaned forward. "More construction means more impervious cover, which means more runoff that can't absorb into the ground, can't refill the aquifer. Also, with big rains, more runoff can exceed the capacity of your storm water drains and cause flooding. More construction, more runoff, more flooding."

"But that lasts for only a bit," Adams said. "So why does it matter?"

"You live out in Coffee Manor, right?" asked Ted Ritchie. "You've got minimum six-acre lots, and you definitely have zoning limits on impervious cover. Imagine if everyone in Coffee Manor just paved their entire lot. No grass, no gravel, just hard surfaces. And then we got a big rain. What would happen to your storm sewers?"

"The water would go into a detention pond?" asked Adams.

"You know we don't require detention ponds for single-family developments! You'd be flooded."

Martina Guerrero jumped in. "Flooding's bad enough, but what I worry about is sewage effluent getting into Coffee Creek. That's our city water supply! You want me using contaminated drinking water at the Camellia Diner?"

"Don't you think these folks can manage their own wastewater? They're going to land-apply it!" Adams said.

Guerrero snorted. "First of all, Sam, didn't you grasp how many thousand gallons they'll have in storage? I went to the public meeting. People are really upset about what happens if there's an accident to those big tanks or if the land application setup can't handle all the effluent. If land application fails, the effluent will go right into Coffee Creek!"

"Don't those people near the venue have water wells?" Adams demanded.

"Yes! But at the public meeting, people with wells were worried that effluent would get into the Trinity aquifer, which provides their well water. If they aren't in our service area, they don't get our city water." Guerrero gave Adams a hard look. "You apparently missed out on hearing what your constituents said at the meeting. They are not, repeat, not happy."

"Shortsighted of them," said Adams. "I think this venue will bring lots of tourist traffic to Coffee Creek. Raise our revenue."

"What if our city water gets contaminated?"

"We've got wells! Can't we just pump our city wells into our city water system?"

The mayor looked at Alice. "What did you hear from our city water engineer, Alice?"

"Walter Bowie's quite concerned about the permit. He's here, if the council would like to hear from him directly."

The mayor: "Good. Bring him in."

Alice retrieved Walter Bowie, who stood, still looking uncomfortable.

"Okay, Walter, give us the straight scoop," directed the mayor.

Walter Bowie explained that the City's two water wells, if Coffee Creek became contaminated, might provide enough clean water for the hospital but couldn't come close to providing water for the City's entire service area. Then he turned to Apex. "My concerns are, will Apex provide adequate staffing and backup to ensure proper treatment and testing of sewage effluent in the big tanks before land application? Will the proposed land application system work properly, so effluent doesn't leave the site or reach the aquifer that serves local wells? Finally, while we all think of Coffee Creek as a reliable source of excellent water, it's not particularly big; its small streamflow may take longer to clear out any contamination in the creek and also in our small reservoir. It might cause algal blooms and greatly harm our ability to supply clean water."

The mayor: "Any questions, folks?"

A chorus of nos. Louise Compton: "Thanks, Walter. That's very helpful." Walter left, looking relieved.

The mayor turned to Alice. "Your thoughts about Apex itself, Alice?"

"The Nevada enforcement action is instructive. Apex waited until after the permit was granted, then violated it. Maybe Apex hoped a Nevada court would just give them a slap on the wrist, impose minimal fees or ignore the bare-faced grossness of the violation."

"How could that happen?"

"Well, Mayor, suppose after the permit issued, Apex began construction, but no one from the agency noticed. No one came to inspect, and no one was notified. Apex might argue—we spent all this money re-paving, and you could have seen what we were doing or notified us to stop in time, but you didn't."

"If I were the judge, I'd impose big fines and make them correct every violation before they could operate," declared the mayor. "And never grant them another permit."

Silence. The council members looked at each other, then at the mayor. She lifted her head. "We began this meeting looking at the enforcement action Nevada had to bring against the same people who want to build a similar concert venue here. What are the consequences if Apex exceeds the impervious cover limit, Alice?"

"I'm not a Nevada lawyer. The Nevada enforcement action asks for criminal fines and penalties as well as removal of the violation areas. In Texas, TCEQ can also impose criminal fines and penalties, including for felony violations. But the real penalty could fall on surrounding landowners and on the City's water system, if the permit is issued and Coffee Creek is contaminated."

Kevin Garcia spoke up. "At a minimum we need more information. But we also need much more assurance that Apex's land application plan will work and will be properly managed and that its effluent won't drain into Coffee Creek. How do we do that, Alice?"

"First, I'm expecting Bradley Ott to recover and take this over. But my own expectation is that before any hearing, during discovery the City would get the information it needs to decide whether to demand changes to the permit or oppose it entirely. The City's not the only concerned party; the TCEQ lawyer told me his desk is covered with letters about this permit. I expect other parties are already planning to pursue contested case hearings, so there should be an opportunity to get all the facts. Meanwhile, we should make TCEQ aware, if it's not already, of the Nevada enforcement action indicating that the applicant has already violated one permit. That might be grounds to demand that the applicant post a bond adequate to cover completely the cost of curing any noncompliance or damages to parties affected by noncompliance."

The mayor counted votes with her eyes. "Do we have a majority in favor of doing as Alice suggests?" The council members nodded. "Alice, at tonight's meeting, taking action on the proposed permit is the first item on the agenda. We'll take comments from the public. The agenda item includes a possible vote as to whether to authorize pursuit of the already requested contested case hearing. Walter, we may need to call on you, depending on the comments we get. If we ask you to outline your concerns, tell them just what you told Alice and told us. So you need to stay for the meeting. Alice, do you have a draft motion?"

"Thank you, Madam Mayor. I do. Of course it designates Bradley Ott as counsel for the City." She handed the mayor copies of an already-prepared draft motion authorizing the City's lawyer, Bradley Ott, to proceed with a contested case hearing upon issuance of the proposed Apex permit, with the usual language about providing timely status reports to the mayor and council on issues of potential concern. In Alice's experience council members always wanted to be first to hear of any legal developments. "Let me know of any changes." The members read, nodded, even Sam Adams. Always a pleasure working with the mayor, with her no-nonsense approach and her ability to read the room—and lead the room. Alice excused herself and Walter as the council moved on to the next executive item of business.

She shook Walter's hand as he left, thinking, great witness for any permit appeal....

*****

Downstairs in the lobby before the hearing began, she called Kinsear. "How's the brush fire project?"

"We did another huge burn pile today. All those broken branches from the January ice storm. I'm whipped. And red-eyed from the smoke. *However....*" He cleared his throat. "If I can remove my smokiness, what are you doing tomorrow? For instance, what about dinner? Or breakfast, lunch, and dinner? And what about Saturday? I'd like to...umm...have more time together."

"Yes, please! What about just sitting in the treehouse with a book? And some wine? What about feeding carrots to the burros? What about...."

"I've got a stack of books I'm eager to meet. I'll bring them. But... maybe not read them."

City Hall's lobby was filling with people heading upstairs to the council chamber.

"Gotta go," Alice said. "I'll call later." Upstairs she took a seat quietly at the end of the front row next to Walter—just in case.

Promptly at six the mayor gaveled the meeting to order. She looked around the chamber, smiling. "Thanks to all our citizens who are attending tonight. I call the meeting to order. First item on the agenda: possible action to respond to TCEQ on the pending permit application by Apex Partners for a concert venue on Old Hays Road. If you want to speak, come to the microphone in the center aisle, and state your name. With this many citizens attending, your time limit is two minutes; take less time if you possibly can. When you hear my gavel, yield to the next person."

A line formed in the center aisle. Citizens hurried to speak. The gavel rang out, rang out, rang out. Opposition to the venue was strong, focusing on possible contamination of Coffee Creek. Neighbors living in town near Alice's office were vociferous: "Our water comes only from Coffee Creek! Don't put our water at risk!" After twenty minutes the mayor asked, "Anyone have something different to say from what your fellow citizens have said?"

One man stood. "Henry Duncan. I run the QuikieStop on the creek road. I wouldn't mind having more customers, which the venue might bring. I said 'might.' But I'll take clean water over that any day."

"Thank you. Anyone else?" No one dared rise. She turned to the council members. "Do we have a motion?"

Kevin Garcia lifted his hand. "I move that the City authorize its counsel, Bradley Ott, to move forward with a contested case should this permit be granted in its current form."

"All in favor?" The ayes had it. The mayor looked out over her purple cat-eye glasses. "Next item."

Alice heard a sigh of relief from Walter, as they both rose and slipped out of the council chamber.

*****

In the car, yawning, she checked her phone before driving home. To her surprise, an invitation awaited. She phoned Kinsear. "Listen to this, from Merry's daughter Francine's beau, chef Raoul. Can we accept?"

She read him the message: "Merry's birthday is Saturday. Francine wants to surprise her with a dinner we'd make out at Goat Hill—including a fancy dessert. Merry mentioned three guys are onsite to guard the property and that she likes them, so we'll invite them too. Probably seafood and probably not until about seven? We'll need to do some shopping on the way. Please come! Bring Silla if she's free. And if you wish, bring your—as I understand—fiancé!"

Kinsear laughed. "Sounds wonderful. Of course, I'll need to spend the night. Maybe Friday night too."

"Of course."

"Tell Raoul we'll bring wine if he'll confirm seafood."

"Got it—whites? Champagne too?"

"Yep."

Alice grinned to herself, wondering where Merry would want Raoul and Francine to sleep. Oh well, not her problem. Grown children. She texted grateful thanks, offering wines. Then she thought—good grief. Merry and Francine under one roof. Is that safer? Or riskier?

What Are They Carrying?

When Alice reached the office Friday morning, Silla had already stopped at the post office for their mail. She was clutching some small envelopes, which she waved at Alice. "Look at all these RSVPs for your wedding! Whoohoo! I'll add them to the spreadsheet. Band, boots, dresses, menu. Cake! Oh, and also the trumpeter for the wedding!"

"Trumpet?"

"Of course. You think we're going to lug a pipe organ out there? Purcell's 'Trumpet Voluntary,' right?"

Alice tried to imagine a trumpet echoing across the pasture. Would Big Boy think it was a summons to join the party? Had Silla discussed this with Kinsear? Whose wedding was this, anyway?

At her desk she gazed around her office, realizing she simply craved a normal day of routine work. No dead engineers. No clients attacked by a neighbor. Instead, orderly tasks for city government, orderly work on client assets and contracts. Orderly files, orderly thinking.

She opened a new file, for a new local winery, and began thinking through the requested partnership agreement. She drafted the related documents all morning and afternoon.

Late in the afternoon her phone rang: Files. "Supposedly, I'll get the decal search results tomorrow," he said. "And I pestered the Department of Public Safety about lab results on the water gun. Might have them Monday, if not sooner."

"I assume the crime scene people never identified any useful prints after Silla got bashed here in the office?"

"Nope. Nothing in our databases."

Silla, who had declined the Saturday birthday party—"hot date with Bender, Alice"—called "goodbye" as she swept out the front door. The sun was beginning to sink in the west. Alice raced home to meet Kinsear. Should she mention the "Trumpet Voluntary"? Maybe a glass of champagne in her treehouse, to watch the sun set? Then cooking together, with dinner on cushions by the fireplace, dancing around the kitchen, then some slow dancing....

That night, they woke to low rumbles in the west, growing closer and louder. Through the west door from her bedroom, they watched lightning flicker, then flash. "Will it please go ahead and rain?" Alice whispered.

Finally, the sudden patter of raindrops on the roof, then slow steady rainfall. Alice wondered briefly if anything could be better than listening to the rain while being warm and in bed. Yes, doing so not all alone, but with Kinsear.

*****

On Saturday morning over coffee, Alice asked, "What would a cheese-maker want for her birthday?" Thinking of knotted muscles from chasing goats, she and Kinsear opted for a massage certificate at the spa Merry had mentioned, then visited Kinsear's favorite wine store, where he and the clerk engaged in long discussion.

At seven p.m. Saturday evening, with Alice driving and Kinsear carefully monitoring his curated wines, they arrived at Goat Hill and parked by the gate to Merry's house. Ernesto greeted them, followed by a rangy blond crewcut guy with a shy smile. "Alice, Mr. Kinsear, meet Joe Storey, my Army buddy from San Antonio. He's helping out this week."

After the handshakes, Alice asked Ernesto for a quick security report.

"Everything's going okay. We finished installing new cameras on the rear of the house and barn. We got 'em hooked up so we can see the views from each camera on the kitchen monitor."

"Great. No more invasions by Teena Ann or Denny?"

Ernesto stood even straighter, lips tight. "No ma'am. Not since the fire. But I think we're ready."

Inside, Merry hugged Alice, then Kinsear, then dragged them into the kitchen. Merry's daughter, Francine, dark curls escaping from her chef's toque, introduced Raoul—also wearing a toque. Alice grinned. Just as she'd thought, big brown laughing eyes and a strong jaw.

Kinsear unloaded the wines, with Raoul picking up each bottle. "Perfect!" he crowed, scrutinizing the labels. "The Grüner Veltliner will partner with the snapper crudo, and the Pfefferer with the halibut! And these champagnes to begin!"

Ernesto tugged Alice's sleeve. "Come see my present for the birthday lady." On their way through the kitchen toward the back porch, he grabbed a cellphone with a huge telephoto lens attached. Alice gaped at it. "Well, my birthday present to myself," he joked. "But this may come in very handy."

Outside, the night sky was clear, almost navy blue, with the quarter-moon glowing yellow high above. Ernesto pointed to a pair of impressive bird feeders hanging from a live oak branch above the patio. "I love birds. So I gave her those feeders. I thought Merry needed some wildlife besides goats. And I've gotten some cool pictures."

Interesting guy, Alice told herself. "How far away can you focus that thing?"

"Infinity! I can shoot close-ups from here all the way to the end of Merry's pasture. Today, from Merry's back porch, I got a great shot of a hawk landing over by the Winthrop fence." He pointed off to the right. "That's around 200 yards from the porch."

"Appetizers!" called Francine from the kitchen door.

Alice gasped. The kitchen smelled delicious—the yeasty smell of fresh-baked bread, olives, something orange-y, something garlicky.... On Merry's kitchen island sat beautiful little toast-colored puffs and a variety of tempting bruschette made of small slices of what looked like homemade rye baguettes. Raoul poured champagne into eight flutes. Alice watched with interest as Tonio handed a flute to Merry, with Merry looking up into his eyes for a moment.

Francine led them all in a rousing chorus of "Happy Birthday!" Then she said, "Help yourselves!"

Alice began with a bite of the small puff. "Mmm!?" she mumbled, raising her eyebrows at Francine.

"Those are mine. Cream puffs with a savory cheese filling. Gougères, the French call them."

"But these are mine," said Raoul. "Homemade bruschette with fresh tomato and anchovy and olives."

"Amazing," said Kinsear, reaching for another.

Meanwhile Ernesto and his army buddy Joe carried the security cam monitor from the kitchen to the dining room buffet, where it was visible from the table Francine and Raoul had set, with Merry's collection of china goats marching down the tabletop. Watching from the dining room door, Alice glanced at the dark pasture on the screen.

Nothing was moving. "The goats are gathered behind the barn, ready for milking in the morning," Ernesto told her.

Laughter. Clinking toasts. More praise for the appetizers. Finally they took seats at the table. Kinsear opened the white wines he'd brought while Raoul dealt out small plates holding the first course, a vision of white fish and green herbs in an appealing golden oil. "Crudo! Spanish, like me." Delicate slices of snapper, with herbs, olive oil, lime juice.

"This may be served in heaven," Kinsear observed. Alice agreed.

"Just wait until you see what Francine's made." Raoul began removing their small plates. "You're gonna like it."

Francine circled the table with dinner plates for each guest. A half-moon of toasted parchment paper enveloped something mysterious, something that smelled wonderful. Francine passed out scissors, then passed a bowl of mixed rice around the table. "Just cut open the paper!" she instructed. "Halibut in cartoccio! Italian style! With butter, lemon zest, fresh dill, minced tomato and chives...."

The table grew quiet. "Oh, my." Merry smiled proudly at her daughter. "Oh, my!"

Alice noticed that between bites, Tonio, Ernesto, and Joe Storey kept an eye on the monitor.

Birthday cake appeared—pink meringue frosting on a cylinder of cake that when sliced revealed six slim layers separated by a mixture of strawberries and whipped cream.

No crumbs remained. Sighs rose. Alice and Kinsear leaned back in their chairs.

Francine brought in small plates, a bowl of fruit, and a couple of Merry's prize-winning cheeses. Merry appeared with a tray of small glasses and a bottle of cognac. "Good grief!" exclaimed Kinsear, examining the date on the label. "How long have you been waiting to produce this?"

"A long time. My dad brought it back when he and Mom took a trip to France. He told me to save it for a special night. Well, tonight's special! So let's celebrate!"

More toasts broke out—toasts to Merry, to goat cheese, to victory in upcoming cheese contests, to Merry's most productive goat.... When Alice looked at the clock it was after midnight.

She watched Ernesto lift his crystal glass for a sip, then glance at the monitor. He froze.

Joe Storey and Tonio rose from their chairs, peering at the dark screen.

"You see what I see? What are they carrying?" Ernesto set down his glass, leaning toward the monitor.

Alice squinted at the screen. Two figures in black hoodies were running to the right, across Merry's pasture toward the boundary fence that separated Merry's land from Winthrop's. One figure stopped at the fence and lifted something that glittered in the moonlight. The other, one hand holding something glinting, the other hand whipping up and down, ran behind the herd of goats now crowded and milling against the fence.

"What are they doing? The fence..." Alice shot to her feet. It's so dark! But she needed evidence....

"We need pictures! Before they know we can see them!"

Watching the monitor, Tonio hissed, "Those jerks are cutting the fence! They'll try to drive the goats through the gap!"

From the buffet Ernesto grabbed his cell phone with the telephoto lens.

Kinsear said, "Flare gun."

Alice had already left the table. She ran out Merry's front door to the car and reached under the driver's seat, where she always kept her flare gun. She checked to be sure a flare was inserted, grabbed extra flares, and hurried back inside.

In the kitchen Kinsear eased open the back doors. Ernesto and Alice slipped outside onto the porch steps. Ernesto raised his phone, with the big lens trained on the figures at the far fence. "Ready when you are!" he whispered.

Alice aimed her flare gun toward the fence line, then lifted it an angle. She fired. BANG! Brilliant orange light lit the sky. A sulfurous smell settled over the porch. Goats bleated. The dark figures by the fence turned, staring up, then abandoned the fence and began running back across the pasture. Alice turned and fired another flare high above their heads. Ernesto got more pictures.

Tonio, Raoul, and Merry raced off the porch and through the gate by the flower bed into the pasture, running toward the herd of goats milling around by the Winthrop boundary fence.

Joe Storey and Kinsear pounded downhill along the creek bank to intercept the two invaders now racing toward the other side of the pasture and the fence that kept the goats out of Coffee Creek. "They've got to clear the creek fence, then the boundary fence across the creek," Alice yelled.

She and Ernesto ran down the creek bank following Kinsear and Storey. One invader had cleared the creek fence and was in the water. Storey splashed into the creek and tackled his prey near the boundary fence between Merry's land and Teena Ann's. Alice saw that figure try to hurl something metallic—silvery in the moonlight—over the boundary fence, just as Storey landed on him.

Wire cutter or lopper, she thought. She and Ernesto reached Kinsear, who'd caught the second figure, now stuck face down under the creek fence. He'd bound the prisoner's hands with his bandana. "Tried to belly crawl under the barbed wire. Didn't work," Kinsear reported. He leaned over and lifted the figure's shoulder until the face was visible.

Alice pointed the phone flashlight. The black hoodie framed an enraged face. "Hi, Teena Ann," she said. Teena Ann grunted something unprintable ending with "bitch."

"How about some portraits?" Alice asked Ernesto.

Ernesto's white teeth flashed in the moonlight. "Ready! This close I can use my phone!" Ernesto took videos and stills of Teena Ann, still struggling to get free.

"But wait, there's more," said Kinsear. "Look what she was carrying." He pointed a few feet beyond the creek fence. Alice walked closer and saw a small wire cutter, reflecting moonlight. She took several photos.

"She had something else," Kinsear said. "See that dark thing?"

Alice turned, pointing her phone flash. On the rocky bank lay something too straight to be a stick...and with a tail. "A riding crop," she said in disbelief. A long one, too, not what you'd use barrel-racing. Was this what Teena Ann had been whipping up and down at Merry's goats? "Good grief." She took pictures. "Ernesto," she called, "be sure to get shots of these two items. We need backup."

Disgusted at the very thought of Teena Ann whipping Merry's

goats toward a cut fence, Alice waded across the creek and uphill to the boundary fence, where Storey stood over his prone prisoner. Like Kinsear, he'd used a bandana to tie the prisoner's hands. As Alice approached, the prisoner turned his face away from her.

Too late. "Hi, Denny," she said.

"I hope I'll get that bandana back. Souvenir from Big Bend. But look what he was carrying!" Storey said, pointing. "These two wanted to be sure they could cut that fence."

Alice took photos of a sturdy wire cutter, a big lopper roughly two feet long, lying near the boundary fence. It looked new, with a sharp blade and a white label still clean on the handle. "Ernesto," she called. "Another subject for you up here!"

She thought heard Denny whine, "Her idea...."

The air smelled of flare gun smoke, of goats.

More evidence needed—the cut fence. Alice climbed through the creek fence and jogged back toward the other side of the pasture, where Raoul and Tonio were tackling and turning around escaping goats.

Francine, running down the porch steps, yelled, "I called the Coffee Creek Sheriff's Department. They're on their way!" She waved a spool of wire and a pair of pliers as she ran toward Tonio and Raoul.

As Alice neared the Winthrop boundary, she stopped for more photos of the men and the herd of milling goats, black and white and tan in the moonlight. Outdoor lights had come on at the barn, and Alice saw Merry pouring a noisy stream of feed pellets into an outdoor trough. Hearing the familiar rattle of food, the goats began streaming uphill toward their mistress.

Francine, carrying the wire and pliers, reached Tonio and Raoul. "Hang on," called Alice. "Fingerprints! Don't reattach the old barbed wire yet, don't touch it—just use some new wire to hook up the top and bottom corner of that one panel." She took pictures with her phone of the cut fence, wires dangling. Then she took more as Tonio, Raoul, and Francine, leaving the old wires dangling and using lengths of new wire, reattached the panel of hogwire cut by the invaders.

Blue and red lights in the sky, but no siren. Alice hurried uphill toward the barn, still clutching her flare gun. As she neared the parking area and the flashing lights, she thought better of carrying a firearm and deposited it in a wheelbarrow. Might cause unnecessary questions.

Red hair, serious eyes—Alan Joske, Files's assistant detective, stood by the Sheriff's Department SUV. A police cruiser sat nearby. Two officers stood waiting with him.

"Hi," she said. "Thank you for coming. Especially at this hour...."

Chapter Thirty

Shut Up!
Shut Up!

Joske and the officers did not look amused.

"Nobody answered the doors. What's going on here?" Joske demanded. "The woman who called said something about a herd of goats and a cut fence? Is this a joke?"

"No, it's not a joke! Two people were cutting the fence and trying to drive Merry's dairy goats off into the Winthrop land. But—we've got them. Down in the pasture, waiting for you."

"Who's we?" He and the two officers followed her past the barn. Alice pointed out Merry, who waved, then downhill at Tonio, Raoul, and Francine, reattaching the hogwire panel.

"They're only partly patching the hogwire, in case these invaders left prints," Alice explained.

"So who all was here?"

"Merry Givens—she's the owner, and her daughter, Francine, who called you. They're my clients. Also Francine's boyfriend, a chef named Raoul. Then three men who've been guarding Merry's place since she got hurt in a couple of incidents: Tonio and Ernesto Ramos and Joe Storey. Plus Ben Kinsear and me." Joske gave her a look. "We were all here for Merry's birthday dinner. About midnight we spotted two figures in black, on the security camera monitor, cutting the fence and pushing the goats through."

Joske rolled his eyes. "Well, I pulled weekend duty, but at least I'll get a goat tale out of it."

The first humorous remark she'd ever heard from the man.

"And where the hell did the flares come from?"

"Umm, I always have my dead husband's old flare gun in the car. Only gun I have, besides the shotgun my brother gave me. Detective Files knows."

She looked, wide-eyed, at Joske's disbelieving face. In a moment he said, "Okay, take us to your fence-cutters."

She led the way past the barn, pointing off to the left at the creek. The moonlight was shining on Kinsear and Storey, above two dark figures on the ground.

"Holy cow," muttered Joske, leading the officers toward the creek.

Behind him, Alice madly tapped her phone, searching the Texas penal code...for fence-cutting. Hallelujah! She pocketed the phone, then trotted downhill to catch up with Joske and the officers. She clambered over the creek fence in time to hear Teena Ann, with one officer clutching her arm, squealing to Joske that she'd "done nothing, nothing at all! It was all his idea!"

Alice interrupted. "Officers, we've got pictures of these two on the other side of the pasture, at the Winthrop boundary. Teena Ann Traynor here had that wire cutter and that whip"— Alice pointed first at one, then the other—"and was whipping the goats through the fence after they'd cut it."

She pointed across the creek at Denny, firmly in the grips of the other officer. "Did Denny mention he's Merry's estranged husband? We got pictures of him cutting the fence, and—see those big loppers?"— pointing at the hefty silver wire cutters lying on the ground—"I saw him try to throw them over the boundary fence just as Joe Storey here tackled him."

"But you got the goats back?" asked Joske.

"We did, no thanks to these two," said Kinsear. "We saw them on the feed from the security cameras, after midnight, wearing black, carrying their tools across the field, and then we saw them start cutting the fence. In Gillespie County, where I'm from, cutting a livestock fence is a serious crime."

"Yup," Alice said. "Jail felony." Teena Ann's mouth fell open. Alice held up her phone, clicking it on. "Texas Penal Code Section 28.03(b) (4)(C). And I might add, Officer Joske, this is not their first rodeo. Denny and Teena Ann have already filed a forged transfer on death deed trying to steal this property from the owner."

"It was her—" Denny's voice quavered, with Teena Ann yelling "Shut up! *Shut up!*"

"I'll need your pictures," Joske said. "*All* your pictures. Ms. Givens, the owner, will testify if required, I assume?"

"Yes indeed."

Joske nodded. "Okay. Right now, I'm going across to the other fence to wait on the crime scene team. Don't touch anything here either, hear me? Wire cutters, whip, fence—nothing. Get back up to the house and send me those pictures." He set off for the Winthrop fence while his colleagues strode uphill toward the parking area, tugging along their prisoners.

Kinsear, Alice, Joe Storey, and Ernesto gathered together, high-fiving. "Nice work grabbing Denny and Teena Ann!" Alice said.

"Mighty swift work on that felony citation," Kinsear said. "Impressive!"

"I hope the words 'jail felony' will keep Teena Ann wide awake tonight, in her jail cell," Alice quipped. But she meant it.

As the four reached the steps to the house, the moon slid behind a cloud, and the night grew suddenly darker. Someone lit a lamp on the porch, where Tonio, Francine, Merry, and Raoul stood waiting.

Alice and Ernesto went inside to the kitchen counter, where Alice emailed all the night's photos on her phone—cut fence, Teena Ann's props, Denny and the wire cutter, repairs at the Winthrop boundary—to Officer Joske, with copies to Silla for the office file. She watched as Ernesto did the same, admiring his sharp pictures, beginning with a stunning shot of fence-cutting below an orange cloud of flare gun smoke. They hurried back to the porch when they heard a pop, a fizz, then the satisfying sound of wine splashing into glasses. Raoul and Tonio handed around champagne. "Cheers!"

Alice was watching Merry as Tonio brought her champagne. His hand touched hers for a moment. Was Merry smiling up at him? Yes....

Kinsear and Alice sank onto the porch swing. He drew her close, and she moved even closer, treasuring the warmth as he slowly rocked the swing. She glanced at her watch. One-thirty in the morning!

Merry lifted her glass, looking at the gathered faces. "What would I have done tonight, without help from all of you? I'd be goat-less! Thank you, thank you! What a birthday party!"

Pretty cheerful, for a woman whose husband had forged a transfer on death deed so as to get her property when she died? A husband bent on destroying her business—and maybe her? Alice felt a sense of relief. Merry had faced facts, had finally decided to get rid of Denny. And now had let down her guard and smiled at Tonio.

Alice wondered what, after a night in the Coffee County jail, Denny's next move might be....

Or Teena Ann's?

Chapter Thirty-One

Feeling Slightly Felonious

After breakfast on Sunday—Kinsear's quesadillas with Alice's guacamole—Kinsear left for Fredericksburg to await his daughters, who were spending the night.

Alice slipped into the last pew at church in time to hear the choir sing one of her favorites, "The Call," by Ralph Vaughan Williams. Thank goodness he'd survived World War I, unlike so many in that sacrificed generation.

Despite serving in the British field ambulance corps, somehow Ralph Vaughan Williams lived long enough to be shown in the church bulletin as "composer." She mused at the oddness of the word "compose".... While composing, wasn't the artist actually excited? Quickly scribbling and changing notes? Okay, maybe putting a piece of music into final form resulted in a composition, a "composed" document—but not necessarily a composed listener. Take "The Call": it thrilled her to her core as she sat on the penitential oak pew.

But thinking of young men, dead, made her think of Charlie Boone—another whose life had been snuffed out, far, far too soon. She was still thinking about him during the benediction, when her phone vibrated annoyingly in her pocket. She peeked. Bradley Ott, lawyer for the City. "Please call when you can."

After church she made the two-minute drive to her office and called him back.

"Alice, I'm sorry to bother you on the weekend."

"Not a problem. Sounds like you're already home from the hospital? How are you feeling?" Alice crossed her fingers, hoping he'd be back in the saddle for the City.

"No rest for the weary or the wicked. I've got to prepare for the contested case hearing on that Apex permit. The mayor filled me in on Apex's violations in Nevada and gave me copies of the enforcement notice and the newspaper piece. I'm wondering—any sign that Apex might intend to try something similar here?"

He didn't know about the Selman plan, she realized. How would he? And what could she say? Where was the murder investigation?

"Their young engineer, Charles Boone, who was killed just before the hearing?" she began.

"Yes?"

"I represent his family in dealing with his estate. Investigation of his death continues—the Travis County Medical Examiner decided an autopsy is warranted. But I've also separately sued Apex to enforce deed covenants on the proposed permit site—covenants that prohibit commercial use."

"Damn this pneumonia, no one told me about the covenants. If you win that suit, that alone could save the city water system! But Alice, an autopsy—was this young man murdered?"

"It's a possibility. I can't say anything to compromise a murder investigation, and I know you wouldn't either, but definitely go talk to Detective George Files. He's investigating Charlie's death and looking into the very question you've raised about mischief related to impervious cover. If you don't already have the TCEQ file, I'll send you the link, which the mayor asked me to get. I can at least tell you that Files put out an arrest warrant for Conrad O'Leary, the Apex construction guy who was at the new ballfield site where Charlie died. And apparently *when* he died."

"Thanks. Any other thoughts?"

"You'll want your discovery requests to include deposition notices for O'Leary and also Jerry Weathers, Apex's chief honcho for the project. And of course ask for all construction plans for the site. Maybe ask if any similar permits are pending, or have been issued, in any other state."

"Will do. Thanks, Alice. Sorry about that young man's death." She heard him sigh. "One thing that bothers me about appealing the permit—if an application facially meets agency parameters, it usually has to be granted. Often the agency can react only after the fact, after violations occur. Know what I mean? You've probably seen the same thing. Neighbors can protest a permit, fearing the usual dangers—overloading the land application area, spills, leaks—but if those usual dangers actually occur, after-the-fact enforcement is always too late—after the damage is done. So I'm hoping your covenants get enforced."

Alice hung up, with Charlie on her mind. Just thinking about Apex's Nevada machinations and that adult water gun sent her blood pressure to the sky.

Her cell rang again—this time the relatively cheerful young voice of Jeanie Boone.

"Alice, kind of a weird request. I can't find Charlie's high school letter jacket. For Canyon Cougars basketball! He loved that jacket. I didn't see it in his apartment—we cleaned out everything—so I assumed it must be at home, probably in his room. But I've looked all over the house, and it isn't here. I was wondering—could we possibly check in the Apex office?"

Whoa! Alice almost gasped. What an opportunity—an excuse to prowl that space and see if the office still contained any of Charlie's other papers or belongings. "Charlie had an office key, right? On his key ring?"

"Yep, there's a mystery key on his key ring! My class in San Marcos tomorrow doesn't start until one. If I drive up there, can we go check?"

"I'll be glad to. Meet me here at the office?"

Was this legal? Ask not.... "We're just looking for the jacket Charlie left...maybe in a closet?" Unless Jerry Weathers had changed the locks?

*****

Monday morning. Feeling slightly felonious, Alice opted for a black going-to-court suit with a yellow silk blouse and pearls, then added black dress cowgirl boots. As she'd been told as a teenager, by an extremely well-regarded friend of her dad's—"Just act like you know what you're doing, and everyone else will assume you do."

Silla was just turning on the computer at her worktable when Alice marched into the office. Silla's eyebrows soared. "My, my! What's happening?"

"Well, it's Monday. Who knows? Hey, take a look at the pictures from Merry's birthday party. I sent them all to you...."

Silla opened Alice's email and gaped at the screen, then turned to Alice. "Flare gun? All right!" She clicked on through the pictures. When she reached the picture of Kinsear standing over Teena Ann, she let out a war whoop. Then she spotted the riding crop on the ground. Her eyes narrowed and she shook her head. "Just let me get near that woman with a riding crop in my hand...."

"Next, take a look at the shots Ernesto got with his telephoto," Alice said. "See what they were doing? Felony fence-cutting! Alan Joske hauled them off to the hoosegow! Though he wasn't thrilled about being there at one-thirty in the morning!"

Silla laughed. "Did she have to spend the night in jail? Oh, I may have to visit, get a picture!" Then she sat up straight, eyes wide. "Alice! She's not going to want anyone knowing about this! You will have her totally over a barrel! She'll probably agree to anything if the barrel-racing population doesn't hear about this!"

"Right you are. I'm thinking she'll be highly motivated to pay all of Merry's costs and damages—including the daily pay for Tonio and Ernesto and Joe, and our bills too. Maybe the goats have suffered mental distress, what do you think?"

"Definitely! Oh!" The smile left Silla's face. "Jeanie Boone left a message. The medical examiner has released Charlie's body to the family. She'll let us know about the memorial service. Also, Detective Files called, said he was off yesterday but got some info for you. First, one of the city video spots recorded a truck with those two rodeo decals you showed me—and got the rear end too. License plate is registered to none other than Teena Ann Traynor."

"As we assumed. That twit."

"But that's not all. He got the lab results on the stuff in that water gun you and Kinsear found."

Alice held her breath.

"The same stuff was in the water gun as on the girder where Charles Boone fell. That slick water-resistant roof material."

Stolen from the tub in the contractor's shed.

Alice could not speak, thinking of the iniquity, the cold-blooded evil.

"I can't believe someone could do that," Silla whispered.

Alice walked back into her office and stared out the back window at the pecan tree, covered now with spring leaves. Time passing, trees leafing...Charlie dead.

*****

Jeanie Boone drove up at nine in her small blue car and hurried up to the front door of the office. Alice and Silla both hugged her. "I've got the keys!" She held them up. "Here's the one to the Apex office." That key bore a small white sticker labeled 5-D. "Want me to drive?"

"Sure."

Jeanie parked on the street in front of the Coffee Creek Hotel. She and Alice walked into the lobby, passing the renovated coffee shop. Alice spotted Walter Bowie at a table by the wall, talking with Bradley Ott. Probably getting their case ready. She sped past, not wanting them to see her.

As they'd decided in the car, they marched up the stairs, ignoring the elevator. No reason to signal the desk clerk where they were going. Jeanie had said, "Charlie told us Apex wanted its office on the top floor, the fifth floor, because it had a great view of the park. It's a converted apartment, Charlie said."

They climbed up four staircases, then started down the hall, passing 5-A, 5-B, 5-C. None bore a tenant's name. At 5-D a card in a brass slot read, "APEX PARTNERS, LLC."

The hall was totally silent. No sound of phones ringing, of people talking, of doors opening or closing....

Jeanie poked the key into the lock, turned it, and slowly pushed the door open into a narrow foyer. She stepped back so Alice could enter first. Alice stopped in the foyer, gazing across a conference table at the large picture windows framing the view of the city park that Charlie had mentioned. Yes, nice view. Green grass, a white gazebo, a cluster of picnic tables.

But inside, utter silence. Alice had the oddest sense that the air in the room was wrong.

"Is no one here?" whispered Jeanie.

"Let me check." Alice took a step in, then another, then turned toward the right.

Two desks, side by side. Behind each desk sat a tall black executive chair.

In the chair behind the desk on the left sat Conrad O'Leary, slumped sideways, head hanging over, jaw slightly open. The front of his tan shirt was dark with dried blood.

At the desk on the right sat Jerry Weathers. He'd loosened the pink tie and rolled up the sleeves on his shirt. But he lay twisted in the chair, his torso fallen backward and sideways over the chair arm, eyes open, mouth open. The blue shirt was stained dark, like O'Leary's.

For a moment the blood drained from her head, but she squeezed her eyes shut and tried to breathe. How long, her brain kept asking, how long had they been dead?

Who shot them?

No gun on the desks. She peeked under the desks. No gun on the floor, either.

Behind Alice, Jeanie was gasping, panting. "Go back into the hall!" Alice ordered. "Sit down! Do not throw up! I'm calling the police."

She pulled her phone from her skirt pocket and called 911. "Fifth floor, Coffee Creek Hotel. Apartment 5-D. Two men, dead."

Then she called George Files.

"Don't move, don't touch anything."

She nodded, unable to speak. He'd already hung up.

Why Are You Two Here?

iles and Joske arrived in minutes.

Standing at the foyer entrance, Alice heard footsteps hurrying down the hall and saw Jeanie, on the floor huddled against the wall, try to stand up. Alice helped her to her feet just as Files and Joske reached them.

Files looked grim. "You didn't touch anything?"

She shook her head. "No. Jeanie didn't get past the door. I took one step out of the foyer—" she pointed behind her—"then—" She let out her breath. "Called you."

"Wait here."

He and Joske disappeared into Apartment 5-D. She heard Files tell Joske, "Call and confirm the crime scene team's on the way."

A few minutes ticked by. Alice kept asking herself questions. Who shot them? Because they were surely shot. And quickly, without warning. Were they both intended victims, or was one of them merely collateral damage? Did someone just walk in out of the blue? How did O'Leary get back to Coffee Creek with a warrant out for his arrest? Has he been hiding out, here in the office?

Files emerged, his face a study. "First, why are you two here?"

Jeanie, still pale, eyes still wide with shock, said, "My brother's jacket." Her lip trembled.

Alice said, "Jeanie's brother is Charlie Boone, remember? Jeanie can't find his high school letter jacket and wondered if he'd left it here in the office. You returned Charlie's keys to her. He had an office key."

Multiple voices as the elevator doors at the end of the hall opened, and the crime scene team emerged, carrying their equipment. They clambered into their forensic protective gear. Joske showed them into the apartment. When he returned, he and Files began the team effort Alice recognized—questioning witnesses separately. Joske led Jeanie down the hall for questioning, while Files began asking Alice when they'd decided to come, when they arrived, where they parked, whether anyone in the lobby saw them. "You can ask Silla, George," Alice finally retorted. "Jeanie called me Sunday afternoon and asked if we could look for Charlie's jacket. Silla will tell you Jeanie arrived this morning and we drove straight over here, came upstairs, unlocked the door. And you see what we found. Did you have a high school letter jacket?"

That got a smile. A small one. "Yes. Football. Twenty-five years ago."

"Do you still have it?"

"Of course. But look, Alice. I'm still investigating Boone's death."

"His murder," she said, thinking of the damned adult water gun.

"Yes. So, if Apex was responsible...you see why you've both got to answer some questions."

She had to explain where she'd been Friday, Saturday, Sunday. Who'd been with her. She recounted details of the weekend, adding, "Joske can alibi me for late Saturday night." Files looked puzzled. "Ask Joske. Felonious fence-cutting."

The Coffee County justice of the peace made his way down the hall and into 5-D, then quickly emerged to confirm that unlawful deaths had occurred. The bodies would go to the Travis County Medical Examiner...like Charlie's body, thought Alice. Coffee County's keeping Travis County busy.

The hall quieted. Files turned to Alice. "Do you have any idea who would shoot Jerry Weathers and Conrad O'Leary?"

"You mean, besides all the Coffee County residents who dislike the idea of a concert venue for five thousand people on Old Hays Road? Plenty of people turned out for the public meeting and a number spoke in opposition. They're worried about Coffee Creek getting contaminated and their aquifers being at risk." She took a breath and continued. "Also, the Coffee Creek City Council has authorized legal action against the proposed venue permit, fearing a sewage effluent spill from the venue could shut down the city water system. And how about the Nevada environmental agency, which had to file enforcement charges against Apex on a similar venue permit for knowingly expanding construction and paving beyond what the permit allowed?" She tilted her head. "More? And I should mention that I'm representing two nearby landowners in a suit against Apex and the current owner of the proposed venue site, Teena Ann Traynor, to prevent violation of land covenants that forbid commercial use."

"I see." He stared off down the hall for a moment, then said, "You'll both need to make a written statement."

Jeanie, eyes red, was released by Joske and walked back toward Alice. "I'm done," Files said. "For now. Hang on a moment." He nodded at Joske to follow him. The two disappeared into 5-D. A few minutes later Joske walked out, carrying a red letter jacket on a hanger. On the back, in white letters: Canyon Cougars.

Jeanie's eyes lit up. "Charlie's jacket! It *was* here!" She took it from Joske—"Oh thank you, thank you"—and hugged it to her chest. Then she really did burst into tears.

They followed Joske to the Sheriff's Department and produced their tedious written statements about their whereabouts for the past five days. They confirmed they owned no handguns. Joske said: "You know the drill, Alice. Now we've got to test your hands for gunshot residue." Finally, they escaped.

Jeanie, driving Alice back to the office, said, "Charlie's jacket still smells like him. I am going to keep it in my closet."

Then, after a moment, Jeanie asked, "Who *did* shoot those two men? And when? How long were they just—just sitting there? Dead?"

Alice stared blankly out the windshield, then shook her head.

*****

With Jeanie headed to San Marcos for class, Alice slowly climbed the two steps to the office front door, which Silla pulled open. "Alice! Where've you—hey, what's wrong?"

Alice told her what they'd found in the Apex office. "Shot dead. Both of them, just sitting there, executed, in their big executive chairs. I don't know when, but not this morning. Maybe the medical examiner will say." She wriggled out of her black suit jacket, hung it on the hall coatrack, walked into the kitchen, sank into a chair at the kitchen table, staring at nothing. She felt...empty. Stretched thin. Unable to focus. How did Files and Joske do this, working around dead bodies?

Silla followed her. "Okay, let's hear it." She opened a cabinet and brought down Alice's treasured emergency bottle of Talisker whisky, slightly dusty—a gift from Gran, Jordie's mom in Scotland. She poured one slim finger of Scotch into one of the crystal glasses Alice kept next to the Talisker, added a few drops of water, and placed it in front of Alice.

Then she opened a cold Modelo Especial from the refrigerator and sat down across from Alice. "Tell me."

Alice began with their entry into the hotel, scampering through the lobby and up the stairs. "Didn't want anyone to see us, given that we planned to use Charlie's key, and I was hoping no one would be in the office. I was also hoping to root around and see if any more of Charlie's papers were there."

Alice picked up the glass, sniffed the aroma—salt air, peat—and took a small sip of Talisker. Happier memories flooded back—Gran's farm on the Scottish coast, the town pub, the chilly air, the steep green hills. The churchyard where she and her children had buried Jordie's bones. Life. Death.

"Silla, in case I'm lucky enough to repress all this later, I'll try to tell you exactly what I saw when we unlocked the door and I looked around the corner from the foyer into the office area." So she did. The faces, positions, dried blood on the shirts, O'Leary's hanging jaw, Jerry Weathers' open eyes and mouth. The total silence. "I saw no guns—on the floor, on the desks. It was like they were waiting for someone—both in their big executive chairs, kind of positions of power, you know? And then—bam. And another bam."

"Were they drinking coffee? Eating lunch? Taking notes?"

"Their desks were bare. That is odd, you're right."

"Cell phones?"

"Nope."

"No furniture turned over, no signs of a ruckus?"

"No. Silla, you're bringing out all the stuff that Files and Joske and the crime team probably noticed. Stuff that wasn't there. Hmm." Another sip of Talisker. She began to feel almost human. "I'll tell you one thing I saw."

Silla raised inquiring eyebrows.

"O'Leary's ostrich skin boots."

After a moment, Silla nodded. "Well, that makes sense. Listen, it's past lunch time. The Beer Barn calls. I'll drive. I'm thinking fish tacos."

"Same."

All through lunch they talked only about details of the upcoming wedding.

Thus not until they were driving back did Alice sit up straight and say, "It was someone they weren't worried about."

Silla glanced at Alice, interested. She turned into the office driveway, stopped her truck. "Huh." She looked again at Alice, head to one side. "Hmm."

*****

On a sticky pad back at her desk, Alice penciled a revised to-do list.

Item one, and new, now that she had the test data on the adult water gun—file a wrongful death suit on behalf of Mrs. Boone and Jeanie against the heirs of O'Leary and Weathers.

Thank goodness she could scratch out item two: Bradley Ott would pursue the City's contested case over the concert venue permit. Hopefully Apex would withdraw its Texas application and save the City both money and worry.

Her cell vibrated in her work bag. She'd turned off the sound at the Sheriff's Department. Kinsear: "What are you up to? I couldn't get you this morning!"

"Well—" Should she tell him about the bodies? Yes. "Here's how the day began."

When she got to the recovery of Charlie's Canyon Cougars jacket, and then Joske testing her hands and Jeanie's for gunshot residue, silence fell. "At least they're thorough," Alice said. "And you know that adult water gun you spotted in the dumpster? Lab tests showed it was the roofing mixture. Squirted up on that girder."

"Good God."

"So now I'm tidying up the riverbanks, Ben, as my mama would've said. I'm getting get these lawsuits done and dusted before we escape on our honeymoon. You have any more hints about what I might want to pack?"

A short laugh. "Fear not. Where we're going, clothing can be purchased."

"A sarong? Shorts and t-shirts? Boots and parka?"

"You're gonna love it. I promise."

A Question For Another Day

The rest of the week sped by in a blur. On Monday afternoon Alice learned that Teena Ann's Houston lawyer had helped her post bond on Sunday night and get out of jail. By late Monday Denny had also posted bond with his car as security.

Early Tuesday morning, Alice met Denny at the courthouse with his court-appointed lawyer and found an empty jury room where they could talk.

"Here's the deal," Alice said. "Nothing we can do about the felony fence-cutting charge, that's up to the prosecutor. We'll settle pending litigation on these conditions. *All* of them." Denny must agree to the divorce petition, claiming only his car as his separate property. On the forgery suit, he must sign an affidavit swearing that he conspired with Teena Ann Traynor to facilitate sale of her land to Apex; set fire to Merry's barn; created the fraudulent transfer on death deed that would give him Merry's property on her death; stole Merry's driver's license so notary Olivia Street would notarize the fraudulent deed on which Teena Ann forged Merry's name; and filed that deed in the Coffee County Property Records. Third, he must agree that he was jointly and severally liable for Merry's expenses for security equipment, guards, repairs after the fire and fence-cutting, and legal costs. Alice handed over a draft agreement and the detailed costs Silla had compiled.

"Uh, I'll have to let you know," said Denny's lawyer, glancing at his morose client. Alice knew Denny's lawyer would be hoping to negotiate with Teena Ann's lawyer since Denny had no funds.

"You want more? Listen, Denny stole Merry's letter from TCEQ which explained her right to contest the venue permit, and the deadlines. He *hid* it, mail belonging *to his own wife*! That isn't gonna play well if we go to trial. He can claim it was all Teena Ann's idea. But if he doesn't settle, I guarantee we'll support and push the felony fence-cutting charge. That charge will stick, Merry will still get her divorce, we'll still win our fraud suit, and the State Fire Marshal will be looking hard at Denny and Teena Ann for setting fire to the barn." She glanced at Denny, then back at his lawyer. "If he doesn't take this deal, and we take all our evidence to court, you think he'll ever get another job?"

His lawyer looked at his client, then at Alice. "We'll discuss. I'll get back to you."

"Today," she said.

When she got back to her office that morning, Silla was waiting. "Now do we go after Miss TAT?"

"I'm on it."

Silla had warned Alice that dealing with Teena Ann would be tough. After some thought, Alice sent a letter to Teena Ann's Houston lawyer stating that given the pictures of Teena Ann whipping Merry's dairy goats, Alice felt compelled to take steps to notify the state and national barrel-racing associations of her goat-whipping and cruelty to animals and also of the pending felony charge of cutting a fence holding someone else's livestock.

Alice added that settlement would require Teena Ann to make full payment of all costs incurred by Merry after the fire, for security equipment, personnel costs and repairs, as well as all of Merry's legal costs, including those related to the fraudulent transfer on death deed and the covenants. Teena Ann must also file an affidavit in the lawsuit to enforce covenants admitting that her property was subject to the covenant against commercial use and that, as a condition of any later sale, her property would remain bound by those covenants. She must admit she practiced forging Merry's signature, forged it on the transfer on death deed, and used Merry's driver's license to get it notarized. Alice forwarded the letter to Silla to finalize.

"Whoo-ee! I like this letter! Strong! She won't want you writing the barrel-racing folks! But she richly deserves it!" Silla spun out of Alice's office, then turned back. "Go for it, Alice. Let's get this finished. Almost time to get ready for the wedding!"

Alice was finishing a hurried lunch at her desk—apple and string cheese—when Charlie's bosses at Worth Engineers called to confirm that Charlie had indeed been covered by their group life insurance and that his beneficiaries would promptly receive the full amount of coverage. Hanging up the phone in relief, Alice remembered Charlie's determination to pay Jeanie's tuition through college. But this sure wasn't how he'd planned to do it. Alice called Jeanie and her mother to share the insurance news and to discuss how she planned to proceed against the estates of Jerry Weathers and Conrad O'Leary. They agreed.

That afternoon, she'd placed repeated calls to the lawyer claiming to represent the heirs of Jerry Weathers and Conrad O'Leary. At four, he finally returned her calls. Alice's hackles rose at his pompous tone: "Of course, you realize Apex Partners is an LLC. You will doubtless recall that provides liability protection for its members."

"LLC status for Apex doesn't help either of your clients in the civil suit we're filing. The estates of Jerry Weathers and Conrad O'Leary must still pay the consequences of the appalling criminal behavior of Weathers and O'Leary. We're seeking criminal restitution from them."

More blustering.

Alice rolled her eyes—unfortunately invisible to the caller.

"Do you realize O'Leary and Weathers caused the incredibly vicious death of a young engineer? What they did is absolutely heinous," Alice warned. "Unfortunately for your clients, the publicity will be too. My co-counsel in the criminal restitution suit is Tyler Junkin, a highly experienced lawyer. He'll handle settlement discussions. I suggest you get a move on."

But Alice still wished she had more ammunition against the two men than O'Leary's lies about the timing of his arrival at the ballfield.

Finally, while Alice was driving home on Tuesday, Teena Ann's lawyer called, balking, demanding more time, blaming Denny.

"Nope," Alice said. "This has already gone on too long. I forgot to mention this in my letter, but during litigation I'll also be demanding all veterinary prescriptions issued to your client, specifically including the hordenine we suspect she used on Merry's Jersey bull, resulting in serious injury to Merry."

"Hordenine? What the heck is that?"

"Look it up. That's what our vet found. Not good for your client. I need your 'yes' to our conditions by tomorrow morning, and we want Merry's costs totally reimbursed by close of business Friday. You and Denny's lawyer can work out details."

When she got home, she found carrots for Big Boy, Queenie, and Princess and stood by the barn, watching them munch. She stroked Big Boy's neck, feeling her pulse slow, and watched the sun sink in the west, watched the clouds change from gold to violet. The last horizontal rays lit up a touch of pink in the pasture. Winecups, she thought. So elegant, so tender-petaled, so powerfully pink.

Kinsear called while she lolled in a bubble bath. "Got your targets all lined up?" he asked.

"Making some progress," she said, sinking further into the bubbles. She recounted her dealings with Denny and Teena Ann. "I'm so tired I'm just trying not to drop my phone in the tub."

"Aha. Awash in bubbles?"

She splashed a bit. "Jasmine Delight. When you're not here, I seek consolation in my bath."

"If I were there, I'd scrub your back...."

"Oh yes?"

But she was so tired that she really did almost let the phone slip into the bubbles.

*****

By Wednesday noon, Teena Ann's lawyer had caved in to his client's fears and agreed to Alice's demands. Denny's lawyer delivered the signed agreements and affidavit demanded by Alice and asked if Denny could pick up his belongings at Goat Hill. Silla called Merry, who replied, "Tell him they'll be in the parking lot tomorrow in boxes. He's not stepping into this house ever again."

The same afternoon found Alice in a state of high frustration, trying to draft a petition for criminal restitution. Files called. "Got some news, Alice. You and Kinsear spotted the adult water gun. And you spotted the brass casing at the ballfield. So I think you're entitled to know what we found up in 5-D, in the desk where Conrad O'Leary was sitting."

"Yes?" she breathed.

"A handgun. Preliminary tests look like it matches that casing. Also? A bunch of credit card slips clipped together, with his signature. As if he planned to turn in his expenses. One of them was for purchase of an adult water gun." He paused. "On the same date as the public meeting."

Silence. "So we know," Alice said. "Conrad's gun did the shooting. Conrad bought the water gun. Conrad was there when Rich drove by."

"Yep. We know as much as we can know."

Now her criminal restitution suit looked much stronger.

*****

On Thursday afternoon Alice, at her desk, heard a loud "YES!" She found Silla at her worktable, clutching an open priority mail envelope in one hand, and two checks in the other. "Settlement money with a letter from Teena Ann's lawyer! That disgusting woman has paid all your fees, as required. I'm going straight to the bank. And here's a separate check for Merry's costs—all the security stuff and barn repairs and money for Tonio and Ernesto and Joe. Every penny you asked for. Whoo-hoo!"

She and Silla high-fived and danced around the kitchen.

By mid-morning Friday, Alice's co-counsel, Tyler Junkin, called to say he was well on his way to hefty settlements with the heirs of Weathers and O'Leary. "Told them we need a deal before five today," he added. Nice having Tyler as back-up, Alice thought. Especially a trial lawyer who could explain to those heirs exactly how devastating a jury would find the testimony about the criminal conspiracy of the two men—to cause Charlie's death. After all, if the two men were alive, they'd be facing murder charges.

She and Silla shared an order of tacos for lunch in the office kitchen. "Feels like this roller coaster ride's ending," Silla said. "For Merry, we've got settlements with Denny and Teena Ann. Including Teena Ann's affidavit that the covenants apply to her land, so you win there. For the Boone family, we've got a settlement with Charlie's employer on insurance. And hopefully, with the heirs of Weathers and O'Leary, right?"

Alice nodded. So what was left? She was wondering what the agency would do with the pending Apex application for the venue permit when Bradley Ott called. "Huzzah! TCEQ tells me the Apex permit's kaput. Someone representing Apex called to say the sales agreement's been cancelled, given your lawsuit on the covenants. So there's no venue site. The mayor's thrilled."

"You might call that kid at the *Coffee Creek Caller*. He'd love a story."

"I will. By the way, Walter Bowie sends you his best regards. He's over the moon. That city reservoir's his pet. If you could pat a reservoir, that's what he'd be doing."

So, Alice thought, the reservoir was safe, and so was Coffee Creek—at least for the moment. All the people who wanted their kids to wade in the clear water, to learn to fish, to see the circles on the creek bottom where fish had laid their eggs, to swing from a rope and drop into a swimming hole—all those people could relax— again, for the moment. "Well," she said to Ott, "You know what they say out here—whiskey's for drinking; water's for fighting over."

"No kidding. Again, thanks." Ott hung up.

*****

By five Friday afternoon, when Alice was ready to call it a day, the church's weekly email caught her eye: "Let us keep in our prayers the family of James Surratt, following his death early Thursday morning of pancreatic cancer, and give thanks to the hospice staff who helped ease his last days...may he rest in peace. His memorial service will take place this Saturday afternoon, Laura McDowell presiding."

She had to call Cynthia Surratt. She dreaded calls like this. Finally, she picked up the phone. All she could say was, "I'm so sorry."

Cynthia's voice was shaky. "Oh, Alice, thank you for calling. It went—it went fast. Hospice was wonderful—they were here only a few days, and he was still himself, you know, could still get around a bit. Last thing he did was go to town to buy me flowers, Saturday. But he was so, so tired, and in pain, and having hospice arrive to help was a huge blessing." Then she couldn't speak.

"Let me know if I can help in any way. Please don't hesitate to call. I'll be at the service."

She ended the call and sat for a moment, staring out the office window at the pecan tree, then went to find Silla.

"I just saw the church email. James Surratt died, Thursday morning. Pancreatic cancer, Silla. I called Cynthia and offered to do whatever she needs us to do. Apparently he was at home, with hospice arriving at some point. The service is tomorrow."

"We should send flowers, right?"

Alice nodded. "Cynthia said the last thing he did was go buy her flowers last Saturday, before hospice came."

"Pancreatic cancer." Silla closed her eyes, shook her head. "That can go fast." She looked up, brow furrowed. "You think he already knew, when he came to work on his will?"

"Maybe. Remember his POLST form? He decided against artificial resuscitation...."

They stared at each other for a long moment. Alice said, "He did go up to the Apex office to talk to Charlie the morning of the public meeting, very concerned about what the concert venue might do to the property he loves."

Silla looked thoughtful for a moment, nodded slowly, then said, "May he rest in peace."

Instead of going straight home, Alice found herself walking down Live Oak Street toward the courthouse square. She stood on the sidewalk, gazing across the street at the live oak grove, then crossed the street and walked under the protective spreading limbs of her favorite tree, the massive centuries-old live oak. She leaned against the trunk, touching her hand to the gray ridged bark, thinking of the years and years this live oak had lived on this land. If only trees could talk—an old human desire, but she felt it.

Feeling safe under her favorite tree, she examined the other trees in the grove. Had one tree served, as Coffee Creek legend claimed, as a hanging tree? Had some murderer, some earlier version of O'Leary, or Weathers, been tried and convicted and hanged from a horizontal branch here on the courthouse lawn?

For a moment, she let her mind consider such a fate for the pair.

But that would not bring back Charlie.

That night Alice woke with a start, with the vision of O'Leary and Weathers, quite dead, blood dried on their shirts, awkwardly stiff in their big executive chairs.

Who shot them? A question for another day? But one she herself intended never to answer—at least, not out loud.

What is the greater good?

Ghost justice?

Chapter Thirty-Four

He Was My Bridge

On Saturday Alice and Silla drove to New Braunfels for Charlies Boone's memorial service at the Presbyterian church uphill from Landa Park. They got the last parking spot and hurried inside to the sanctuary. The pews were jammed with young people—Charlie's high school and college friends, Alice assumed. The pastor entered, and Jeanie and Mrs. Boone slipped into the front row.

"That's where they got their red hair," Silla whispered, nodding at Mrs. Boone.

A quiet beginning, as the pastor welcomed those present and read the traditional scriptures. Then, "I've known Charlie Boone most of his life." He praised Charlie's love of family, love of friends, and his excitement over becoming a civil engineer. "He always said he'd like to design a bridge." The pastor glanced at Jeanie, who came forward to the lectern. Her small face scanned the congregation, then she began, voice not quite steady: "My brother was my bridge. He was my bridge across the scary elementary school playground on my first day of school. He was my bridge when I sang my first solo. When our dad died, he was the bridge for Mom and me. He was a connector, he was a bridge to safety."

A young man joined her, holding a twelve-string guitar. His fingers found the frets, and Alice heard the distinctive first chords of a familiar song, then Jeanie's voice: "When you're weary, feeling small....." "Bridge over Troubled Water."

Could Jeanie make it through the song without breaking down? Jeanie managed to do so, but tears streamed down Alice's face.

As the last chord died away, the pastor said, "Charlie, your time has come to shine. May each of us here, as we remember Charlie, become a bridge over troubled waters for those who need our help." Then came final prayers and the benediction.

At the reception Alice and Silla found Mrs. Boone. She hugged them both. "Thank you so much for all you've done. It's such a comfort."

They found Jeanie in a knot of friends, with Griffin Holt firmly at her side. She spied Alice and Silla and excused herself. Hugs, tears, thanks. "My mom is so relieved that she'll be able to pay off the mortgage," Jeanie said. "And that I can stay in school. We can't thank you enough."

"The bridge song," Alice said. "Unforgettable. We'll stay in touch." Another round of hugs followed.

As she walked away from his family, Alice knew she'd never forget her vision of Charlie, in Greece, alive and gazing at the Arkadiko Bridge.

Then she and Silla wheeled out of the parking lot and drove north toward Coffee Creek. Neither spoke for ten miles. Finally Silla said, "Yeah, they can pay off the mortgage, pay Jeanie's tuition, maybe save the rest. But you know they'd give up everything they have to get that boy back."

Chapter Thirty-Five

Fanfare

Wedding week.

On Monday, Alice's best friend, Red Griffin, suddenly appeared at Alice's office door. Silla stood behind her, smirking.

"Ready? Hurry up, Alice! Shut that laptop!"

"Huh?"

"Just grab your bag and come on!"

"What are we—?"

"Massage. Then dinner with your book club."

Silla was grinning as she left.

Alice felt her muscles melt, felt her eyes close, felt herself begin to relax. Limp, happy, smiling, she and Red drove to meet Jane Ann and Miranda at the Tea Garden House, where M.A. stashed them in the small dining room and brought champagne, then cheese souffle, shrimp and rice, and an apricot tart. They laughed, they teased, they toasted.

Hmm. Looks like I really am getting married, Alice thought.

*****

On Wednesday, both Ann and John arrived at the Austin airport, miraculously only twenty minutes apart—Ann from Boston, John from Edinburgh. As always, Alice stood at the top of the stairway, where they'd emerge from the gate corridor, hugging each as they came past security.

What joy to hug these grown children, inhale the beloved smell of their necks, stroke their sleek brown hair, look into their tired brown eyes. Both insisted on immediate Mexican food at their favorite spot. Alice got them there as fast as she could.

Chips, queso, guacamole. Chile relleno for Ann, enchiladas con queso for John. Alice gazed at them...so grown up now. "So how's the semester going? Ann, you're almost finished!"

"I've still got to finish my big paper. It's on Virginia Woolf, Mama, and her friendship with T.S. Eliot. I've found some cool details."

Then she'd be swishing across the stage in her black robe and cap.

John reported that Edinburgh weather had been so cold and rainy he'd spent every day in a pub. "Writing!" He was finishing his graduate thesis on European economic conditions. Would he stay in Europe? Or come home? Alice was afraid to ask. She missed this tall stranger, with the serious face, and his merry sister, with the laughing eyes. She'd been wondering what they thought about the wedding.

"So, Mama, how are you feeling about this event?" John asked. "Are you finally ready?"

"Finally?"

"Well, we've been waiting for many months for you to move forward!"

"Really?"

Alice burst into tears, which brought the waiter hurrying over. John ordered her a Modelo Especial, which made her burst into laughter.

*****

"This dress is spectacular," Ann announced, twirling in front of the mirror in Alice's bedroom.

Her bridesmaid's dress, a deep rose, had spaghetti straps but a skirt that flared like Alice's. "What about boots?"

Alice handed her a new cardboard boot box. "Ivory and blush. What do you think?"

"Perfect! The dresses for Carrie and Isabel—same style?"

"Yes, but Carrie's is light pink, and Isabel's is medium pink. They got the same boots."

"We will be so lovely." Ann twirled again. "May I peek at yours? It's not bad luck if it's me, just if it's the groom."

Alice lifted the hem of the long white protective slip over her wedding dress.

"Oooh! What a delectable color!" Suddenly she grabbed Alice, and hugged tightly, then whispered in her ear. "I miss my daddy every day. I still dream about him. But I am so glad about this wedding. Just want you to know that. So is John. You and Ben deserve happiness."

*****

Thursday flew by in a whirlwind—manicures, pedicures for Alice plus Carrie, Isabel and Ann, followed by wild experiments to decide which flowers each would wear in her hair and how to keep the flowers attached. "Mine keep falling in my eyes!" moaned Ann.

Friday evening, finally. Kinsear insisted on hosting the rehearsal dinner at his ranch in Fredericksburg. As Ann, John, and Alice arrived, followed by Silla and Bender in Bender's old truck, Kinsear appeared on the front porch, wearing his barbecue apron. He kissed Alice, then hugged everyone else.

The rising moon glowed in the east, so bright it was casting shadows as they stood in the driveway. "Full moon tomorrow night," he said softly, taking Alice's hand.

Kinsear had outdone himself. When he invited Eddie LaFarge and Conroy Robison, retired NFL players and Alice's clients, they offered to bring their Mexican-style brisket barbacoa, cooked in a pit at their vineyard for ten hours. The brisket, now uncovered, sat on the kitchen island, emanating such delicious aromas that various hands were snitching bits of the browned crust.

The rehearsal dinner had become a potluck. At the stove, Isabel and her beau, Sam Brody, stole tastes from an iron kettle of barbecue beans. "A little more chipotle?" Sam suggested.

Muddy Mackin, Kinsear's best man, had driven in from his ranch near Big Bend. He was carefully sliding into the oven a big glass pan of blackberry cobbler brought by Alice's friend M.A. Ellison, whom he'd met when he hired Alice years earlier. "Mmm, mmm, look at that biscuit crust," he grunted. M.A. beamed at him.

Also beaming, but nervous, Silla and Bender offered a vast bowl of potato salad. Alice wasn't sure which of them (if either) knew how to cook. Alice's bestie, Red, arrived with Miranda and Jane Ann. Jane Ann brought in a crate of cold Modelo Especial while Red and Miranda unloaded champagne into the refrigerator.

Carrie, Kinsear's younger daughter, finished setting Kinsear's long kitchen table, supplemented by a card table at one end.

"We're almost all here," Kinsear announced. Alice searched the room, puzzled. Weren't they all here?

One more car arrived outside. Alice went to the front door and saw Caroline Herring, her favorite singer-songwriter, emerge. "Surprise!" she called. "I couldn't resist!"

Behind her a green Chevy van rolled in. Painted on the side, above a blue seascape: MACDONALD WIND. Alice gasped. Out climbed her brothers—who built offshore windmills along the Pacific coast—and her sister, a schoolteacher in the Oregon foothills. Alice raced out the door, laughing and crying. Kinsear watched from the doorway, smiling. The MacDonalds hugged in their traditional scrum, all talking at once. "I didn't think you were coming!!" Alice squealed.

"It's all Kinsear," they chorused. "We've been plotting!"

Muddy pronounced a blessing, with special words for the bride and groom, making Kinsear shuffle his feet. Guests lined up at the kitchen island, where Conroy and Eddie sliced the brisket. The air filled with the *pfft* of beer cans, the fizz of champagne, laughter, happy chatter. After dinner, as toasts got more raucous, Kinsear said, "We're adjourning to the big room! Bring your voices! And your instruments!"

Kinsear picked up his guitar. "First, some cowboy songs. 'Oh Bury Me Not,' right?" Everyone knew that one. Then "Red River Valley." Abetted by Alice, Miranda, and Red, Jane Ann led "Ragtime Cowboy Joe." Muddy cleared his throat, picked up his own guitar, and rendered a basso version of "Ghost Riders in the Sky." Caroline borrowed his guitar and sang "Texas Two-Step," one of Alice's favorites.

"Now for Scotland," called John. He produced his violin—Alice didn't know he'd brought it. Ann's sweet soprano began "The Birks of Aberfeldy," with its chorus, "Bonnie lassie, will ye go?", then "Wild Mountain Thyme," with everyone joining to sing the chorus. Then the sweet violin, and Ann's mocking face, began "The Bob o' Dunblane" with its slightly bawdy invitation to a wedding. Alice shook her head, tickled.

Outside the east window she saw the moon rising, almost golden. Standing next to her, Kinsear whispered, "Mañana, full moon for our wedding."

"Okay, big day tomorrow," said John. "Come on, Ann. We've got to get the bride home!"

*****

Alice spent a late and lazy Saturday morning with her children, making lattes, listening to their stories, hearing some post-graduation possibilities. They took old albums off the bookshelves, looked at their baby pictures, their graduation pictures, at plenty of pictures of themselves with their dad, of Alice with Jordie. They talked about their favorite vacations, trips they'd taken, their adventures with their dad. She loved being with the two of them, this last morning before their family changed once more.

What would change be like? Kinsear would have deeper relationships with Ann and John, as she hoped she would with Isabel and Carrie. She knew Kinsear would never presume to treat her children with anything but kindness and respect. She intended to do the same for Isabel and Carrie. All four kids were practically grown. They didn't need another parent. But maybe they wouldn't mind having another reasonable adult they could run their ideas by, occasionally? She vowed to offer no advice, just to be interested in and respectful of what they thought, and to listen to them think matters through.

Time to pack. Packing without guidance! Without even any direction to a specific continent on planet Earth! At least she'd take her own underwear...her favorite travel shirt and travel pants (zippers everywhere)...a fleece jacket...walking shoes, hiking shoes, and bathing suit (she would not want to shop for one in a foreign location). Notebook. Laptop and chargers. And, just in case, passport.

The afternoon weather was perfect. Seventy-five, with no thunderclouds threatening. Alice's pasture, as promised, was covered in bluebonnets, pink bee-balm, and deep violet prairie verbena. Tonio, now returned from Merry's, had mowed a square in the pasture near the treehouse, then rolled out an old carpet from Goodwill and set up chairs Alice had borrowed from the Presbyterian church. He'd run a long electric cable from the house for Laura McDowell's microphone, then gone to change, and, he said, to pick up Merry.

By three Alice was in her apricot dress, swishing back and forth, loving the feel of the silk on her legs. Then she slipped into the new boots. Like satin, inside.... And, as always, boots provided a little height, and more swagger. She smiled at her reflection in the mirror. Her great-grandmother would probably approve.

Ann sauntered in, beautiful in deep rose, with her ivory boots. "What do you think?"

"Stunning." (Of course.)

John appeared, tall and slim in his best jeans (starched to a fare-thee-well) and in Texas tux. He was wearing Jordie's fancy bolo tie, one Alice had found in Santa Fe. "Well?"

"Stunning!"

"Mama, you too. You look so—so—" They both hugged her, trying not to disarrange her hair. Not that the wind wouldn't do that during the ceremony.

Alice looked at the two. "Your dad would be so proud of you both. You are so—so musical, so smart, so funny, so deeply honest and hilarious."

"Mama! Do not cry! You have on mascara!" ordered Ann.

Alice expelled a breath. "Okay." Was it appropriate to thank them for turning out so well, without much help? "Um, thank you both for turning out so well."

That caused eyerolling.

A voice from the entry porch. "Ms. Greer? Where do you want me?"

A young man with a shiny gold trumpet. John took charge. "In the treehouse. I'll show you." He carried the music stand up the ladder and handed it to the young man.

"Never got to play from a treehouse before. Acoustics should be cool."

By four sharp the last car had parked along the drive, and the last guests had been seated and handed programs by Tonio, Ernesto, and Joe Storey, handsome in their blazers. Alice's small suitcase was stashed in Kinsear's car. Laura stood behind the microphone, facing the guests. She nodded to Kinsear, who walked up to stand next to her, followed by Isabel and Carrie, resplendent in rose and pink.

Laura nodded to the treehouse.

Aaron Copland's "Fanfare for the Common Man" rolled out across the pasture.

Alice walked down the aisle, holding a bouquet of bluebonnets, with John holding one elbow, Ann the other.

The trumpet echoed against the hills.

Laura began. "We are gathered here...."

When she asked, "Who gives this man and this woman to be wed?" all four children chorused, "We do!"

Some chuckles, many smiles.

As Laura's last words echoed in the air, pronouncing Kinsear and Alice man and wife, and they kissed, the joyful trumpet began Henry Purcell's "Trumpet Voluntary" and Alice and Kinsear, with huge smiles, walked down the short aisle. They headed straight to Kinsear's car, then to the Beer Barn, followed by a string of cars holding wedding guests. Kinsear grabbed his suitcase and hers from the car and set them behind the bar. M.A. came dashing in the door and headed to the wedding cake, which sat on a table by the bar.

"No one touched it, right?" she called to the bartender.

"Nope. I kept it safe as houses."

Floyd Domino and Bill Kirchen were tuning up on the Beer Barn stage. Below was the dance floor, with round tables behind. On the long counter between the tables and the bar at the Beer Barn entrance stood the buffet area, now covered with dishes of Javier's fish tacos with all the trimmings. Waiters were adding bowls of queso, chips, both flour and corn tortillas, and other taco fillings. M.A. began to cut her magnificent cake, filled with almond custard and iced with apricot meringue, for plate after small plate. The photographer persuaded Alice and Kinsear to feed each other bites.

Wedding guests streamed in. The bartenders got busy. Tables filled, toasts were raised, the noise level rose. Floyd Domino and Bill Kirchen launched into "Unchained Melody" as Alice and Kinsear took the dance floor. After a bit John cut in and danced with his mother, while Isabel danced with Kinsear, and then the floor filled with many dancers.

"Sweet," whispered Silla, dancing with Bender, as Alice passed by.

The air smelled of perfume, chili and cumin, and the effervescence of beer and champagne, and rang with voices, music, laughter.

Alice and Kinsear caught each other's eyes and disappeared into the office shared by the three Beer Barons. They locked the door, hung their wedding togs on a hook, and slipped into airplane gear. They peeked out the door to find the three Barons—Bill Benke, Bill Birnbach, and Jorgé Benavides—waiting outside. Benavides whispered, "The coast is clear." Alice and Kinsear sneaked out the Beer Barn's front door and hurried to Kinsear's car.

"Just checking you have your passport?" he asked.

"I do!"

"Hey. You know what M.A. gave us for a wedding present?"

"What?"

He tugged an envelope from his pocket. "Her pimento cheese recipe. Her note says she wouldn't part with it until we actually tied the knot."

As they pulled out of the Beer Barn parking lot, the beer cans tied under the rear of the car began rattling and continued to do so all the way down Highway 290 to the Austin airport. They left the car in airport parking and entered the airport.

Kinsear reached in his jacket for the tickets. "This way." He walked her to the ticket counter, handed the tickets to the agent, and said, "Paris."

"Paris!" Alice beamed.

"You've been there, right?"

"Right."

"And I've been there. But we've never been there together."

Alice nodded. A new way to think. They'd never been there... together.

THE END

M.A. offers her recipe with the following caveat: "If you don't use grilled piquillo peppers, you can't claim it's my recipe! Use half the peppers in a 12-oz. jar for a small batch, or use them all in a doubled recipe."

INGREDIENTS:

Mix the following in a medium bowl:

Half the grilled piquillo peppers in a 12-oz jar, drained and chopped into ½ inch pieces

1 cup grated Longhorn Cheese (mild cheddar)

½ cup grated sharp white cheddar

Sprinkle with ½ tsp salt, grated fresh black pepper, and ½ tsp cayenne pepper.

Mix again.

Add mayonnaise, starting with ½ cup, and mix to check flavoring and texture. Add more mayo if desired. (M.A. uses Hellmann's but doesn't want to start a fight here.)

Sandwich construction: M.A. says, use brown seedy bread and apply mayonnaise to each slice of bread before adding your pimento cheese.

I live and write north of Dripping Springs, Texas, in the stunning Texas Hill Country, loosely supervised by three burros, with occasional visits from other inhabitants: foxes, jackrabbits, deer, armadillos, skunks, raccoons, owls, hawks, an occasional rock squirrel—and porcupines. The harsh but beautiful landscape, with its limestone-bottomed creeks and springs, won my heart years ago. I left Texas for Wellesley College, then entered graduate school at UT Austin and later the University of Michigan Law School where I grew intrigued by dirt and water law. Current preoccupations: human prehistory, water issues, boogie-woogie piano.

HEARING FROM YOU

Thank you for reading *Ghost Justice*! If you enjoyed meeting Alice and her Coffee Creek companions, please consider rating or reviewing the book. You can stay in touch with Alice and her adventures at www.helencurriefoster.com, and sign up on the email list there for updates and news about upcoming books. Future events as well as pictures of the burros and various aspects of the Hill Country also appear on Facebook at https://www.facebook.com/helencurriefoster.

Check out my blogs at https://austinmysterywriters.com and https://inkstainedwretches.home.blog.

Happy reading!

THANKS AND MORE THANKS

Thanks to family and friends for their generous help—Grace and Bill Bradshaw, Dr. Megan Biesele, and Diana Borden, as well as fellow writers Kathy Waller, Dixie Evatt, and Francine Paino, and, always, Larry, Sydney, and Drew Foster. Any errors are mine. Many thanks to Susan Wittig Albert for her kind comments.

Finally, to Judy Cohen for superb copy-editing, and to Bill Carson for cover, design layout, and sheer professional brio, thanks and more thanks.